Be Mine

Be Mine

LAURA KASISCHKE

HARCOURT, INC.

Orlando   Austin   New York   San Diego   Toronto   London

www.HarcourtBooks.com

Library of Congress Cataloging-in-Publication Data
Kasischke, Laura, 1961–
Be mine/Laura Kasischke.—1st ed.
p.   cm.
1. Wives—Fiction.   I. Title.
PS3561.A6993B4   2007
813'.54—dc22   2006017063
ISBN-13: 978-0-15-101273-2   ISBN-10: 0-15-101273-3

Text set in Garamond MT
Designed by Cathy Riggs

Printed in the United States of America
First edition

A C E G I K J H F D B

for BILL

You shall yourself pluck out your right eye;
yourself cut off your right hand.

— CHARLOTTE BRONTË, *Jane Eyre*

One

I stepped out the door this morning to a scarf of blood in the snowy driveway.

Like a bad omen, or a threat, or a gruesome valentine — a tire track, and the flattened fur of a small brown rabbit.

The florist must have run it over, delivering the roses, running late already by nine o'clock in the morning. When she handed me the long white box at the door she never mentioned having killed anything in my driveway. Maybe she never noticed. "It's our busiest day of the year," she said, breathless, "of course."

I was running late myself when I saw it. What could I do? The damage had already been done — utterly crushed, completely beyond hope — and cleaning it up seemed pointless. It was already snowing again. Soon, the evidence would be buried.

But I also felt such a pang of grief, seeing that bit of brown fur in the blood, that I had to steady myself at the door.

Was it one of the baby bunnies I'd startled from their hole in the garden last spring while planting morning-glory seeds?

I'd screamed when they scurried out of the soft dirt, and didn't go near that edge of the flower bed again all spring, into summer.

The mother rabbit abandons them, doesn't she, if she smells a human on them?

It would have been impossible to know if this dead one was one of those, but I felt sick with it. Guilt. My valentine roses had brought this sad end to something that had only been, moments before, making its way back to its little den under the snow. If I were a better woman, I thought, in less of a hurry, I'd get Jon's shovel out of the garage and dig a grave—a proper burial, maybe a cross made of Popsicle sticks, the kind Chad, when he was seven, made for Trixie's grave.

But it was such a bitter cold morning—a harsh wind out of the east, and so cold that the snow, even in that wind, lingered before it fell, as if the air were heavier than the flakes. And I'd lost my gloves again. (Left them in the supermarket cart on Saturday?) Out there with my car keys and no gloves, I thought it would have been impossible to dig a grave, anyway, in the frozen ground. Already, a couple of crows were sitting in the branches of the oak, waiting for me to leave.

VALENTINES:

From Jon, the dozen roses, delivered half an hour after he'd left for work, timed to surprise me as I walked out the door, and a little card on which the florist had written for him in her girly cursive, "To my dear wife, the only valentine I'll ever need. I love you, and will always love you, Jon."

And from Chad, the first valentine ever to arrive from him by mail. From college. A strange sad moment at the mailbox as I recognized, slowly, the handwriting on the red envelope with a postmark from California:

Ma, you know I love you. Tell Dad I love him too—too weird to send him a valentine. But I miss you both. Am having a great time here. Love, Chad.

I couldn't help but think, then—predictably, sentimentally—of those crude cutout construction-paper hearts. His crayon scrawl. I still have one of them pinned to the bulletin board above my desk at work, although the pink has begun to yellow and the edges have curled: I VEOL YU, CHAD.

And the year he licked away half of a heart-shaped lollipop before wrapping it in a tissue and giving it to me.

This year, even Brenda sent me a card (my nest empty now that Chad's off to college, a way of reminding me about it while pretending to try to make me feel better)—a black-and-white photograph of two little girls in fancy hats and *To my sister-in-law with love.*

Sue brought me some heart-shaped cookies the twins had made, and one of my students, a charming Korean girl, gave me a little box of chocolates, which I left for the secretaries in the English department. And even some secret admirer (or prankster?) left me a piece of paper, torn from a legal pad, folded into fourths, stuffed into a campus envelope, and put in my mailbox at school—red pen in an unfamiliar hand:

Be Mine.

ANOTHER accident on the freeway this morning. I keep telling Jon we need to get out of the suburbs now that Chad's gone, move closer to our jobs, quit this commute. But he just says, "Never."

To him, it's not the suburbs, it's the country, where, as a boy in an apartment in the city, he'd always dreamed of living. To him, it's not ten acres of scrubbrush, it's a farm, the "family farm," and he's never leaving his garage full of gadgets, his shooting range set up out back—target nailed to a pile of sandbags—his bird feeders, his riding mower. It's the little boy's dream left over from the days when he would watch *Lassie* on the black-and-white television in the cramped apartment he shared with two brothers, a sister, and his overworked mother. Someday, he thought then, he'd have an old farmhouse in the country, a .22, a dog.

Well, the dog is dead. And the old farmhouse is surrounded now by subdivisions with names like Willow Creek Estates and Country Meadows—McMansions erected overnight with billboards at the edge of the road proudly stating STARTING AT $499,000. (Are we supposed to be impressed by the expense, or seduced by the bargain?) And so much traffic now that hardly a day goes by that the freeway isn't closed down for an hour or two while the debris of some accident is cleared away. Twice in the last year we've been contacted by developers offering to buy our house, knock it down, and build four nicer, newer houses on our property.

And I'd do it, myself, sell it, pack up, move into a condo—*good-bye to all that*—but Jon's not yet done living his boyhood dream.

"I don't think the neighbors in our condo in the city would appreciate hearing me shooting my .22," he says.

He doesn't care that he puts five hundred miles on his Explorer every week, and that the price of gas is going up every day, and that the earth has nearly been drained of its fossil fuels.

No one seems to care.

We're all driving wildly, blindly, out of our suburbs and into the future without giving it a second thought.

"Fine," I told Jon, "but if they keep building subdivisions, and the traffic gets even worse, I'm going to start staying in a motel in the city on the nights I have to teach."

He shrugged.

Poor, beautiful, blue-eyed Jon. I can still see, in those eyes, the child who never had the tire swing he wanted or the high grass to wade through with a Mason jar for catching crickets—and the true absence he will never get over—a father.

Oh, Jon, I'll live here forever for you if I have to.

But when I passed the flashing lights and the crumpled cars at the side of the road again this morning, I thought, *Jesus Christ.*

When I finally got to the college, I found MayBell in hysterics outside my office. She'd lost her verb-tense transparencies, and could she borrow mine?

Well, I'd been planning to use mine, too, but gave them to her anyway. I am, I believe, a whole lot better at winging it than May-Bell is. And, indeed, my class went well. Habib read a whole paragraph of *As I Lay Dying* out loud in a southern drawl, and we all laughed so hard that a few of us ended up crying.

After work, Jon and I met in the city for our Valentine's dinner. I thanked him for the roses and told him about the anonymous note, the valentine left in my mailbox at school:

Be Mine.

"Wow," he said. He raised his eyebrows and looked at me as if *seeing* me for the first time in a long time.

His wife. A woman with a secret admirer.

He'd ordered his steak rare, and there was a doily of blood all over his white plate.

"Who do you think it is?" he asked.

Truly, I told him, I had no idea.

There's Robert Z, our department's poet, who complimented me this morning on my clothes (a white blouse and olive suede skirt) with what seemed like true exuberance. ("Wow, Sherry. Very sharp!")

He liked another outfit, too, last week—a black skirt and a crocheted black sweater—and even touched the sweater's sleeve, feeling the texture of the wool.

"I like your style," he said. "Like a classy country-western star."

But, surely, Robert Z is gay. He's never *told* anyone he's gay, but we've all assumed it since he first got hired. Thirty-five, no wife, no kids, no ex-wife, no girlfriend—and those green eyes, the great fashion sense, the gym-hard body. We've all—the women in the department, which is nearly all women—examined the poetry for evidence (two books, university presses, *Gray Thoughts* and *The Distance Between Here and There*). But it's so fragmented, elusive—hard little riddlish poems—if there's any reference to romance, or sexual preference, who could tell?

And whether or not he's gay, "Be Mine" seems unlikely, coming from such a poet. Too literal. Too sentimental. Also, I know his handwriting by now. I see it all the time on his corrected papers lying around the Xerox room. It's less fluid than the smooth and looping handwriting of my secret valentine. Robert's writing is stiff. Barbed wire cursive. To disguise his writing, a man might be able to make his *fluid* script appear *less* so, but how could he make such pained lettering *more* fluid? Impossible. It's not Robert Z.

There are students, of course. Community colleges are full of older, lonelier men. More than a few candidates for crushes, I suppose. One man in his early thirties, Gary Mueler, who's been laid off from his job at the auto parts plant and is back in school trying to "diversify my skills," has seemed particularly and pathetically grateful for extra help on his papers. (*There are seven reasons why the automobile industry should be changed in my opinion. I will now tell you the reasons why I think the auto industry should be changed . . .*) On occasion he's seemed to laugh so hard at my lame jokes and little asides that I've wondered if there was something "off" about Gary Mueler. Most likely, he's just nervous.

It could be a prank, of course.

A mistake. Wrong mailbox?

"It could be anyone," I said to Jon.

"Well," Jon said, "you can't blame a guy for trying." His gaze lingered on me. And then, "I have to admit, Sherry, it's a bit exciting to think of some poor schmuck wanting to do it with my wife." He reached under the table and tapped the tips of his fingers on my knee.

I cleared my throat and smiled, and said, "For your information, Jon, I think there have been quite a few such schmucks in the past."

He put down his knife and fork. He passed his napkin over his mouth. "Did you ever grant any favors to these schmucks?"

"No," I said. (It was almost entirely true.) "But there's a first time for everything."

"Stop," he said, holding up the hand with the napkin, leaning across the table, whispering, "You're giving me a hard-on." He nodded toward his lap.

It had been so long since we'd been down this road, I'd almost forgotten it was there. When we were first married, we would talk out this fantasy every few nights:

What would I do if a biker pulled up next to me at a stop sign and asked me to meet him in a sleazy motel and give him a blow job?

(We'd move through the details of what I'd do. . . .)

What would Jon do if a woman in a bikini at the beach lost her top and asked him to help her look for it in the dunes?

(He'd follow her—there would be a towel spread out in the beach grass, naturally.)

We'd point people out in restaurants—him, with the tattoo? Her, in the halter? In a hot tub? In the back of a car? And then we'd spin out the scenarios, and then we'd go home and make love all afternoon or all night.

We'd never acted on those fantasies, of course. And then, like the pair of novelty handcuffs and the bottle of strawberry-flavored massage oil, they had been misplaced somewhere, sometime, between my second trimester and Chad's eighteenth birthday.

But, back at home, in bed, after our Valentine's dinner, Jon continued to talk.

"Do you think," he asked, "this is what your secret friend would want to do?" He slid my nightgown up over my hips.

"This?" He put his mouth to my breasts.

"Maybe this?" He spread my legs, holding one wrist over my head, pushing into me.

TWENTY years of making love to the same man—there may not be any surprises left, but there are no disappointments, either, no frustrations, no humiliations.

It was such a short time of my life, the years of sleeping with those other men and boys, but the wounds still seem somehow fresh—those bad mornings, the hangovers, the regrets, the bladder infections, the pregnancy terrors, the psychic injuries.

So brief, and so long ago, that it should all have faded in my memory, and yet it never has. I can still close my eyes and see myself in the full-length mirror of the apartment I lived in, looking at my body—bony and cold and blemished—as I made my way from the bathroom to the bed where some stranger waited, and wanting desperately to hide myself from him, and knowing it was too late.

And then there was Jon. Some wild friends from the bookstore where I worked introduced me to him, and I never needed to suffer that way again.

I was in my twenties, finishing my master's in English, seeing, among others, a man with a wife and two children, feeling old already. The apartment I lived in didn't have an oven that worked, but it didn't matter. Whatever I ate, I ate raw, or cold. I had a string of Christmas lights above my bed—the only light in my room, but bright enough to read by in the dark—and all my clothes came from the same secondhand store, a place called Second Hand Rosie's run by a transvestite with long, beautiful, braided red hair. I favored black dresses, with wild silk scarves. I was so thin that my shadow looked like the shadow of a broom.

Jon had been, like me, at the periphery of this group of wild friends, which was made up of a thirtyish woman who'd been divorced twice, two gay men, two younger women with crushes on the gay men, and a few others who'd dropped out of the university or come to the city to be near lovers, and then been abandoned by the lovers, and then gotten jobs at the bookstore. A bit of cocaine was involved, and some serious drinking, both of which I wanted to participate in, but would consistently throw up instead, or fall asleep, or have trouble breathing long before the actual party started.

Still, I liked to dance, and there were many long, good nights at a place called the Red Room—a sticky floor beneath flashing red lights.

Jon was a bartender there.

"Sherry, have you met Jon?"

I can still see the ring on the finger of the friend who introduced us as she gestured in Jon's direction—a star sapphire, gleaming like Bethlehem on Christmas Eve, shrunk down to the size of a thumbnail, captured in a stone, set in platinum gold.

My mother had worn a ring just like it.

We admitted to each other right away that we didn't really fit into the crowd that had brought us together. We hadn't, perhaps, come from solid middle-class families, but we'd always fantasized that we had. We'd done well in school. We liked to go to bed sober and read for an hour or two, in total silence, before going to sleep. We wanted to share an old house. Some land around it.

A child or two. Salaries with good benefits and cars that started on the first try.

I ended my relationship with the married man, and the others. Jon broke up with the poet he'd been dating. He bought me a diamond solitaire—the kind of engagement ring we both imagined an ordinary woman would wear. We got married in my hometown at the church where I'd been baptized.

During the ceremony, a sparrow that had gotten somehow trapped in the church ("It's been here for days," Pastor Heine said regretfully) threw itself into a stained glass window and plummeted dead to the floor.

"Let's think of this as a good omen," Jon had said, uneasily, afterward, as we looked together at the soft gray mess of it on the marble floor.

Someone nudged it with the toe of a shoe.

Someone laughed nervously.

"Yeah," his sister, Brenda, said. "Isn't there a saying—you know, if the bird dies on your wedding day, you will be blessed with great happiness?"

(Only years later did she tell me that at the reception, the plastic bride and groom had slid off the cake and onto the floor, the frosting having grown warm under the lights in the hall, but she'd managed to settle them back at the top by pushing their feet way down into the cake before we noticed.)

It was hard to read such a thing, the dead sparrow, as a positive omen, but luckily neither of us had ever been superstitious, and now we've been together for two decades—all these years mostly happy years, productive and meaningful and prosperous years.

The secure jobs. The healthy son. The old farmhouse.

Even the reliable cars—mine a bright and humming small white Honda, easy on gas, four-wheel drive, and his an enormous

barreling white Explorer, moving down the road seriously, mas-
culinely, like the idea of gravity itself on wheels.

Two decades!

A long time, but, all along, there's been passion, and there
still is—although not like those first months, of course, when we
spent all our spare time in bed.

Then, I had a roommate, but Jon had a one-bedroom apartment to himself, so I spent my nights with him there. It was winter, but we slept with the window open because the radiator was
right next to the bed, and all the dry dust that was sent up from
it made sleeping, *breathing,* difficult.

We had sex in the morning, in the afternoon, at night—a layer
of arctic air over us, a burning layer of heat and dust under us.

We made love in the bed, on the floor, in the shower, on the
couch. We made love straight through my periods—blood on
everything. We made love straight through the winter until it was
spring and the green grass was crowded with fat, mechanical
robins.

One morning, on my way out of his apartment to my job at
the bookstore, I crushed a pale blue egg beneath my shoe, accidentally, and had to scrape the mucus mess of it off with a
stick—and even that seemed sexual.

Even the smell of humidity rising from the grass seemed
sexual.

The musk of it. The muck.

Those first weeks of spring I could smell my own body all
the time, and Jon's, while I worked behind the counter at Community Books. And men seemed able to smell it, too. They stuck
around to chat long after our exchanges had taken place—their
books in bags, their cash in the register. Men craned their necks
to watch me walk down the street. A troupe of break-dancers
on the corner stopped what they were doing—their naked

gleaming torsos in the sun—when I walked by. *Ooooh, baby. Look at that.*

The cottonwoods burst, and the fluff attached itself to the two of us as Jon and I walked through the park with our arms around each other.

At home, we had to pick the soft stars of it out of each other's hair.

We got married in July. We bought the farmhouse. Chad was born, and then—and then?

And then the next twenty years happened in the staccato flashing of some colored lights!

Where, I wonder sometimes, have those wild friends gone?

Jon and I stayed in the general area, but it's been fifteen years since I saw any of them around. Several would be older than I am, assuming they're still alive. But it's impossible to imagine any of them like this, like us, so much older, so much time having passed, so fast—and, yet, it seems as if it hasn't actually been so long that it wouldn't be possible to just call up, arrange a time to meet at the Red Room for a drink, to catch up, if the Red Room had not been closed for twelve years now, replaced by a Starbucks.

A few weeks ago, it feels like, since I last saw those friends. Or a couple of seasons. Have I changed? How much?

Sometimes I feel more like that younger woman now than I felt then, back when I felt already so old.

But whether or not those wild friends would recognize me now—maybe I'm better off not knowing. Maybe it's just as well that I didn't keep in touch, can't make that date for a drink to find out.

Besides, I never really was one of them, was I?

Of course they wouldn't recognize me now.

———

Same handwriting, same yellow paper, and, again, in a red pen, today, in my box:

Sherry, I hope you have a great weekend. I'll be thinking of you. I'm always thinking of you . . .

A slate gray February day, Saturday, today. From my study I can see a hawk circling the bird feeder—Mr. Death, waiting for something smaller, and also feathered, to land there. Last night I woke up at least twice to the sound of something in the walls. Mice, or a squirrel, squirreling things away, making itself a nest out of the cold—nuts, pinecones, candy bar wrappers. Jon wants to shoot it, if it's a squirrel. He claims they'll chew the wiring in the walls and burn the whole house down, but I say how likely is that. The house is nearly two hundred years old, and the squirrels have been nesting in it longer than we have, and when the cold weather lifts, they'll find another place to live.

Oh, dear, the hawk just got what it was waiting for. Happened so fast it took me a minute to realize what had happened, looking up from this page to the bird feeder, and seeing something small and gray flustering there, and then the cold swiftness passing over it—a shadow with wings, and then in a heartbeat, both of them were gone.

Be Mine.

Who would send me that first valentine, and then the second, and why?

Have I ever said that to anyone, *Be mine*?

If I ever did, I can only imagine it would have been to Reggie Black, the summer I was seventeen.

But I never really wanted him to be *mine*. I wanted to be *his*.

To be claimed by him. It was the ambition we all had, we girls, back then. Some guy's enormous class ring on a chain around your neck. Some guy's letter jacket. To come to school wearing his T-shirt, his ball cap. To have a bracelet with your name and his name and a + sign engraved on it. To show it to all the other girls, gathered around in the hallway. *Look.*

With Reggie Black, I wanted desperately for him to stake such a claim, but he never did. Reggie was shy. Every day that summer he'd come over while my parents were at work and the house was a small, dark possibility behind us. We'd kiss on the porch. We'd sit on the swinging chair. Eventually we'd go behind the garage, and his hands might find their way to my breasts, but I waited all summer for him to say, *Let's go inside.* He didn't.

Has anyone ever said to me, anonymously or not, "Be mine"?

It took this long to be claimed, finally, and by a complete stranger!

BOUGHT a new dress today at the mall. Silk, with pink flowers, a plunging neckline, very sheer. I'll have to wear, always, a slip under it, and a sweater over it for the next five months. But I love it. At the department store I stood in front of the three-way mirror for a long time and looked at myself in it, and thought, *Well, not bad for her age.*

I owe it all, I suppose, to the elliptical machine at the gym. I swear, it is the fountain of youth. It's restored to me the figure of my girlhood. Or better. Back then, I ate too much. Especially in college, as an undergrad in the dorms. All the pizza, and the popcorn, the cafeteria—the meat and potatoes heaped on my plate. And I can still remember the cheese soufflé, exactly the kind of thing my mother would never have made, so rich that it made the air inside it seem heavy.

And the heft of those white plates, and standing hungrily in a line at the steamed glass windows, and how even the wan green beans, the sliced carrots, pooled and slippery with melted butter in a silver trough, called out to me. These things which, at home, I would have refused to eat—suddenly, now that I had nothing but choices, became what I wanted. Now, when I see myself in photographs from those days, I realize that, although I felt incredibly sexy every minute of every day—braless, in short skirts, no makeup, my dark hair so long it was a hazard around candles and revolving doors—I was, frankly, fat.

Then, graduate school, I learned to smoke, lost it all, and looked no better for it.

And then I got pregnant, and never touched a cigarette again.

Now, I wouldn't touch those green beans if they'd even been *near* butter.

(All this self-control! Where did *that* come from?)

Looking at myself in that three-way mirror this afternoon at the mall, I thought I actually look *chiseled*. All this muscle definition in my arms.

And my waist! The other day I took a tape measure to it, twenty-eight.

And my breasts, 36C—exactly what I always longed for and never managed, even when I was fat. Don't ask me how my breasts got larger as the rest of me slimmed down, but the evidence fills the cups right here on my chest. My diet—no refined flour, no white sugar, no added fats—has done away with even that lip of flesh I carried below my belly button for years after Chad was born—the evidence of my maternity, which I thought would stay with me forever, gone.

Jon says that if he could have my body of twenty years ago again, or my body now, he'd take my body now.

My body, which just keeps getting better, and better, until . . .

A sobering thought:

Once you've entered your forties, how much longer can this go on?

Even the celebrities in *People*, cited as sexier now at fifty than they were at twenty—the photos of those women all look as if they were taken underwater. Something happens to the face. (*The neck, the hands, the knees.*) No amount of surgery can fix that, and no one really wants to see it. Better this blur, the photographers must think—this buttery light, this distant hint at the beauty that was once there—than to look dead-on into what's actually left.

Still, this dress is gorgeous, with or without my body in it. A sensuous memory, a slow song, a beautiful immoral thought turned into something wearable, buyable ($198!). Something you can bring home on a hanger, gather in your arms, accessorize with heels and a handbag—weightless, feminine, eternal, mine.

NOTHING like spring yet, but only one more week until Chad comes home for his spring break. This morning we woke to more snow—a long cold carpet of it on the lawn, curtains of it blowing in fat flakes sideways in a hard wind. While Jon was still sleeping in the bed behind me, I stood at the window for a while, and watched it, and I started to cry.

Why?

The snow?

Or maybe the realization that it was only one more week until Chad would be home, and how excited I've been now, since he went back to California after New Year's, for my boy to come back. And, because I couldn't help but wonder—is this what it will be like from now on?

From now on will I count off the days of my life in black check marks between Chad's vacations?

Season to season. Holiday to holiday.

I could, I suppose, move through them just as I always have — buying the appropriate cards, sending them out at the usual times, putting up the Christmas wreath, taking it down, planting bulbs in the fall, seeds in the spring. But will I do all of it emptily, waiting for Chad?

And, after a few more years off at college, how often will he even come home?

There will be, I suppose, some summer backpacking through Europe. A spring break with his friends in Mexico. Soon, he'll start calling in November to tell me, "Mom, I'll only be staying a few days this year around Christmas, because —"

Then what?

Is *this* the empty nest?

Is that what I was crying about at the window, watching the snow?

At Christmas, Brenda went on and on about it:

So, how is it having Chad off at school? What do you do with yourself? Is it like getting to know yourself and Jon all over again, after eighteen years of motherhood?

She and her partner eyed me smugly from their superior positions on the love seat, childless lesbians with books and Welsh corgis and endowed chairs at a fancy college as I followed Chad around their town house with my eyes. They'd been waiting for years, I thought, to see me crash and burn when my "career" of being Chad's mother came to an end.

Was *this* — the snow and the tears at the window — what they had in mind for me?

Sue predicted it, too. From *her* secure position as the harried mother of nine-year-old twins, she kept making sad eyes at me in the hallways when school started again in August. But I kept saying, believing it to be true, "Of course I'm going to miss him, but all I ever wanted was for my child to be healthy and to grow up, to be a happy young man, so how can I begrudge it now that it's happened by being sad?"

"Because," Sue said. "Because it's so fucking sad."

"Maybe a little," I said. Something like a button or a cotton ball—one of those things you always fear your child will swallow—felt lodged in my throat then, and I wanted to sob it up. But, instead, I smiled.

ICE ON everything this morning. Jon chipped it off my windshield before he left for work. I watched him from the bedroom window as he did it. Beyond him, in the backyard, the neighbor's spaniel (named Kujo by their grandson) was dragging something dead around in the scrubbrush. A raccoon, I think—although he once brought the long slender leg of a deer into the yard and spent hours gnawing it, wild with it, giddy with it, dragging the bloody thing around in the snow as if he were in love before losing interest and leaving it there for Jon to take away.

But this morning Kujo was going about his work, whatever it was, with grim determination, it seemed, rather than joy.

I left about an hour later, and drove slowly. Black ice. I don't even know what black ice *is,* exactly, except that you can't see it, and before you know it you're spinning off the road.

I wore the new dress. Ridiculous in this weather, but I couldn't resist. I wore it with a black sweater, black tights, and boots, and still the wind in the parking lot cut straight through it. I felt silly, but when I stepped into the office, Robert Z looked up from some papers he was grading and shouted, "Now there's a woman knocking hard on the door of spring. Good for you, Sherry Seymour. Brava for you in your beautiful dress!"

I checked and double-checked my mailbox for anonymous notes:

Nothing.

Surprised to find myself so disappointed.

TODAY in the hallway between classes, I ran into Chad's best third-grade friend, Garrett Thompson.

I hadn't seen Garrett except from a distance (graduation) for—how long?

After middle school he was never one of the boys sitting around our kitchen table on summer afternoons eating cereal (Trix, Lucky Charms, Cocoa Puffs—all that starry-dry and empty sweetness) straight out of the box by the handful while the sun turned the air over their heads to dusty halos.

Still, Chad mentioned Garrett now and then. Something he'd said or done in the cafeteria line or on the bus on the way home from school. Garrett, who'd been so much a part of our lives for years, still seemed like family, still seemed like a distant part of our lives.

He recognized me before I recognized him—and when I finally did realize who he was, it was because he looked so much like his father, Bill, who's now been dead for a decade.

Bill Thompson used to change the oil in my car at the Standard station, and we always talked, laughed together, because we had the boys in common. He was handsome—dark, dimpled, the kind of mechanic you'd find on a beefcake calendar: Mr. February. Shirtless, shining with muscle, provocatively holding a wrench in one hand.

And we'd had plenty of time to get to know each other at Cub Scouts, hovering over some project made of marshmallows and pipe cleaners. We'd wound up together at Camp Williwama a couple of times, too, when Jon couldn't get out of work to go with Chad. It fell upon Bill to teach Chad, then, how to shoot a bow and arrow. I was clueless, hopeless, couldn't even string the arrow in the bow. One night around a campfire while the Wolf Pack whooped and howled in the dark, he'd passed a little flask of whiskey to me, and, sipping at it, I felt almost as if we'd shared some kind of illicit kiss—the whiskey tracing a warm sash of Bill Thompson down my throat, spreading across my chest.

But of course it was nothing illicit. We were parents, surrounded by parents, and by ten o'clock our boys were exhausted and we'd all retreated to our separate tents, and then he died.

For a year or two after his death, I'd overhear Garrett say to Chad in the living room, on their knees, moving little men around on the rugs, "My dad's got a motorcycle in heaven now." Or, when Jon came home from work and said hello to the boys before going upstairs to take off his suit, Garrett would say, "You're lucky that your dad is here instead of in heaven." I'd go downstairs and cry a little into a laundered towel, or step outside on the front porch until I'd managed to swallow the sadness down.

"Mrs. Seymour!" Garrett called out.

"Garrett. My goodness. *Garrett.*"

I touched his shoulder. He smiled.

He asked about Chad. About Berkeley. About Mr. Seymour. He said he was taking auto mechanics at the college, and wondered if he could take an English class with me, knock off a requirement, but it wasn't his best subject.

"Of course," I said. "I'd love to have you in class. Sign up for fall."

But then he said he didn't know if he'd still be in school in the fall. He was thinking about the Marines.

I said, "Oh, no, Garrett, you should stay in school. You don't want to —"

"I feel like I owe my country," Garrett said.

"What does your mother say about it?" I asked.

He said, "Mrs. Seymour, my mother's dead."

Dead?

I took a step backward.

We live in a small town. How could his mother have died, and I didn't know it? "Garrett, when?"

"At Christmas," he said. "She'd gone down to Florida with my stepdad for the winter. The trailer they were staying in had some kind of problem. Carbon monoxide. They went to sleep and never woke up."

"Garrett," I said. "Oh my god. I'm so — sorry. Did you — was there a funeral?"

"No," he said. "My aunt went down there and had her cremated. I've got the ashes."

The ashes.

Garrett had his mother's ashes.

He had, I remembered, like Chad, no brothers or sisters. Now, it was just Garrett, I guessed, home alone with his mother's ashes.

Marie?

I couldn't recall her face. We'd only spoken maybe a dozen times, and always in passing, in parking lots, driveways, hallways, maybe once or twice at the grocery store. I suspected she drank. Now, I can't remember why I thought it, but I usually insisted that Garrett come to our house when he and Chad wanted to play. I was afraid she'd drive the boys around in her banged-up car. Maybe I thought I smelled it on her one afternoon waiting for the boys after school. His father drank, we all knew that, because it had caused the accident that killed him.

I put my hand on Garrett's arm. I kept it there until I could find a voice to speak in again, and then I told him that Chad was coming home on Sunday, and would he come to dinner if he wasn't busy?

Garrett smiled and nodded as if he were already planning on it, and I remembered that his mother didn't cook. The few times Chad spent an evening at Garrett's house he'd say they'd had Pop-Tarts for dinner. Sometimes he didn't remember eating anything at all. "I'll tell Chad to call you," I said. "Maybe Thursday?"

"Thursday sounds great," Garrett said.

I watched him walk away down the hallway.

Poor little boy, I'd always thought—even before his father died. There was something so tenderly simple about Garrett—a credulousness about the world that Chad had gotten over early. Chad, ironic, already, at four, watching a fat Uncle Sam dance on stilts at a Fourth of July parade, had said, "That's pathetic." It was, I thought now—this fat Uncle Sam—the kind of thing a four-year-old Garrett would have liked.

Little Garrett.

I was surprised how happy I was to have seen him in the hallway. It had seemed to me since Chad left for college, I realized, that the whole part of my life that had really been *Chad's* life— his high school, his friends, his extracurricular activities—had been scissored out of the world. For the most part, his friends had left, too, in the fall. Pete to the University of Iowa. Joe and Kevin to Michigan State. Mike to Colby. Tyler to Northwestern. And the girls he'd known had scattered all over the country, too. Now, when I drove by the high school it was as if a ghostly fence had been erected around it.

No.

Now it was as if I, myself, had become the ghost—a ghost with eighteen years' worth of skills (Band-Aids, bike helmets, fund-raisers, cookies) passing through a world that had learned to get along quite well without me, which had never even noticed my departure, did not now note my absence in it at all.

But I'd forgotten that there were these others, like Garrett, who would stay behind. Towns like ours have kids like this—kids, who, like their parents, grew up here and will stay here. There are those of us who moved here because we liked the idea of a small town—the cornfields around it, the brick buildings downtown. We moved in from other places, crowded the place, brought our expensive coffee shops with us, pretended we were small-town people ourselves, raised our kids here, and then, having no roots, dispersed when those years were over.

But there was another part of the town that would always be here, and if Jon and I didn't buy that condo in the city, eventually I'd start seeing them at the grocery store, in the checkout lines, pushing their babies in strollers through the drugstore. Eventually they'd be the men changing my oil at the Standard station, the women who'll answer the phone at the dentist's office.

They'll ask about Chad.

They'll remember that I was his mother.

OUTSIDE, a half-frozen rain ticks against the windows. Inside, Mozart on the stereo, a glass of wine, a book about Virginia Woolf I already know I'll never finish reading. The words move around on the page when I try to focus. I've read two chapters already and remember nothing of them. Jon's nearly done with his shower. I can hear him rinse the soap off his back. It's a sound you wouldn't think could be so different from the sound of a man scrubbing his armpits, but after twenty years of listening, you can tell the difference. I can hear, too, the rain outside harden. The minute difference in the ratio of ice to water on the windowpanes changes the music completely if you listen closely.

Have I even spoken to Jon tonight? If I did, what did I say, and how did he respond? Dinner, we ate separately. I made chicken breasts and rice, ate mine at the kitchen table right after cooking it, then put his on a plate with plastic over it so he could microwave it when he got home — late from a meeting after I'd already gone to the gym. Without Chad to organize our days around, there's less to say. *How was your day? Did you like your chicken? Do you suppose this rain will freeze on the roads? Do you remember what it was like before we had a child, when it was only the two of us? What did we say to one another then? Do you recognize me? Yourself? Your life? This house in which we live?*

Is it us?

Is it here?

Is it this?

ANOTHER note:

Sherry, Valentine's Day is over, I know, but I wanted you to know I'm still thinking of you. You are so beautiful that my thoughts of you melt even this frozen month for me . . .

I called Sue at home and read it to her. She said, "Sherry, you sound excited."

I said, "I'm not *excited*."

She wanted to know who I thought it was. Robert Z? A janitor? The dean? A textbook salesman? One of the security guys? A computer tech? A student?

But, I told her, I have no idea. I work with *hundreds* of men — and which one of them has ever paid any more attention to me than any other? Friendly, some of them. Some more than others. A few are a little flirtatious maybe. There was that brief interlude with Patrick, for a while, after Ferris left and we both missed him. We were both young parents then, and we talked about children, had lunch now and then. But they moved his office across campus when they built the new computer lab, and now I only see the back of his head (hair thinning) during all-faculty meetings twice a year. I've taught here for nearly two decades. Who else? Why now?

Am I excited?

Well, if I am it isn't something I wanted Sue to notice. Saying it, *Sherry, you sound excited,* seemed somehow intrusive.

But how could Sue, my best friend for two decades, the person on this earth who knows me best—and knows *everything,* because I've *told* her everything (how many hours on the phone, how many cups of coffee, how many long whispered conversations in the hallway, in the women's room, at the mall, in the car?)—*intrude?* If my secrets had been hoarded somewhere in a vault, I would have long ago handed Sue the key. If there had been some easier way to share all of my longings and desires and shame with her (a computer chip, say, on which I could have stored it all and given it over), I'd have already done it. I'd only parceled it out in words over these two decades because there was no quicker way to do it.

And what a joy, to have someone all these years with whom it could all be shared! What a relief! Sometimes I'm not even sure I've felt what I've felt, or seen what I've seen, until I've described it to Sue.

"It's okay, you know," she said. "You can be excited. I would be excited. I've *never* had a secret admirer."

Still, I refused to tell her I was excited.

If I am, is it something I can even admit to *myself*?

Should I be excited?

Or should I be offended? Annoyed? *Afraid?*

How many stalkings, how many harassments, begin with a series of notes like this?

All day there's been a bright blue sky, and the snow's begun to melt in shiny patches on the lawns, a few luminous rivulets running freely along the shoulders of the roads, the military spangles and insignia of winter starting to wash away. Walking from the car to the Liberal Arts Building, I could smell mud, and there were some crows in a puddle in the parking lot. When I walked by, they flustered and flew off, and a drop of water landed at the center of my forehead—some bit of melted snow falling from the wing of a crow as it flew over, and I felt as if I'd been baptized by a priest of spring.

A CALL at the office this morning from Summerbrook:

Dad's had another "little stroke."

Tomorrow I'll drive to Silver Springs to see him and try to be back Sunday morning in time to pick Chad up from the airport with Jon.

Jon says, "Sherry, we can't drive across the state every time he has some little thing. They only call you for liability purposes, not because there's anything that can be done."

Fine, I said. Easy for you to say. He's not your father. And who asked *you* to go? *I'm* the one going. *I can't bear it,* I should have told him. My *father.* If all I can do is touch his hand here in these last years of his sad life, I will not miss an opportunity to touch his hand.

Jon, who didn't have a father, has no idea. . . .

And without Chad here, I realized suddenly, I don't need *any-one's* permission to go *anywhere* anymore. In the paper last night I saw an ad for cheap tickets to San Antonio, Las Vegas, San Francisco, and I thought, I could buy a ticket. I could just go. After eighteen years spent planning lunches, dinners, rides to soccer practice, who besides Jon would notice if I canceled classes for a few days and disappeared? Why *not* go to Silver Springs, whether or not anything can be done? What do Jon and I do on the weekends that can't be missed anyway?

I go to the gym. He putters around in the basement or naps on the couch, shoots a sandbag with a .22 in the backyard. I pay bills, go to the grocery store. Last Saturday we rented a DVD about a woman who killed her children. All day Sunday I tried to shake the feeling of dread and despair that the movie had settled on me, the aftermath of that horror. All day I felt as if *I'd* killed *my* children, or known someone who had, as if there were blood on my hands—the kind of grief and guilt I used to wake up with, then carry around with me all day, the year after Robbie died. I'd open my eyes after some dream, look at the ceiling and inhale, feeling it somewhere around my solar plexus, the feeling that I had killed my brother, strangled him, suffocated him, injected his veins with air.

Who needs entertainment like that?

So, I'll go to Silver Springs tomorrow morning, stay at the Holiday Inn overnight, just long enough to feed Dad his dinner and lay a cool hand on his, and all I'll miss here is a disturbing DVD, a workout at the gym.

No notes in my mailbox today, but word has gotten around (Beth, our secretary), and everyone's been teasing me about my secret admirer. What if it turns out to be Mr. Connery, they've said, our librarian of the strange small hats? Or the wild-haired grill guy in the cafeteria? Or the new Chippendale security guard—he of the five o'clock shadow and (we're guessing here, no one's seen him with his shirt off) the abs of steel?

Maybe it's a joke, I said.

Maybe someone feels sorry for me. Lonely old English teacher . . .

Robert Z piped up fast.

"Hey, don't sell yourself short, Sherry. There are a lot of us around here who'd be writing you love notes if we thought it would do any good."

(It can't be him, can it? He wouldn't say such a thing in front of everyone if it were.)

Beth said, "What's Jon got to say about this?" and I realized I hadn't told him, yet, about the last note.

"Amused," I said. "Jon's just amused."

"Yeah," Robert Z said with what I thought sounded ever-so-slightly like contempt. "Jon strikes me as a very secure guy."

THE DRIVE to Silver Springs was pure winter again. Gray. Low sky. The hawks must be hungry, with everything frozen solid or hibernating. I saw two of them swoop down at one time on something in the median. I was driving too fast to see what it was they were after, or if a fight over it ensued, but the swooping from opposite ends of the road seemed choreographed—smooth and fast and feathered.

I tried to listen to the radio, but never found a station I could tolerate. Even a few years ago I knew the names of the bands on the rock stations. Chad would tell me about them, his opinions on them, which were usually negative, since he was always one for the rustic poets—Dylan, Neil Young, Tom Petty. Still, he kept me up to date.

Today, it depressed me. The angry din, or the synthetic vapid pop-star stuff. Like a fussy old lady I wanted to complain to someone that it *just isn't music.*

And, at the same time, it seems, truly, like only a year or two ago that I was eighteen in the front row of a Ted Nugent concert, stuffing Kleenex into my ears when the band started up with the sound of a plane landing on my head.

I did not stuff that Kleenex into my ears because I didn't like the music, only because I'd promised my mother that I would— so that I wouldn't weaken my hearing as she insisted my brother had at a Who concert.

Ted was beautiful.

His hair was long and wild and uncombed. He wore leather pants, a belt with a huge silver star for a buckle. Shirtless, glistening with sweat, and insane-seeming, to me he was the perfect man. And the music—serious, industrial, midwestern music. He spit into the audience, and a cool spray of it feathered lightly over my chest. My boyfriend recoiled as I rubbed it into my skin with the palm of my hand, but at the moment, having Ted Nugent's spit on my chest seemed like the most sexual and glorious experience of my life.

But there do not, any longer, seem to be any radio stations that play Ted Nugent. Or Bob Seger. Or the Who.

Or, if they do, those bands have changed so much I don't recognize the music.

After a while, I turned it off and listened to the hum of my tires and the sound of wind blowing around me.

It was, I thought, like the music you'd hear if you were that mouse or vole or sparrow in the median when those hawks swooped down from both sides of the road at once.

At Summerbrook, as always, the smell of sauerkraut and sausage hit me first, and then the antiseptics and bacterial soaps beneath it. Dad was in his chair when I stepped into his room, watching golf on television. Seeing me, he looked sheepish, like a child who was worried he might be in trouble for having had another little stroke. The tears welled up so fast in my eyes when I saw him there, I could barely make my way to his side through the blurred scrim of my love for him.

I kissed his left cheek, and it felt, indeed, a little slacker than it had the last time I'd kissed him.

But he looked the same. Ruddy-faced. Blue eyes a little bloodshot. Like the mailman he'd been, walking twenty miles a day through wind and rain and snow, he looked like something sturdy that had been weathered. He used to step into the back door after work, after I'd just gotten home from school (a mail carrier's day starts at 4:30 A.M. and ends at 2:30 P.M.), and he would smell, I thought, like the *world.* Sky in the stiff blue fabric of his uniform. Grass, car exhaust, breeze on his neck. Birds' nest. Snow. Sun. Leaves.

I would press my face into his chest and breathe it in as he stood at the counter near the stove and poured himself a shot of Jim Beam in a glass, swallowed it in one gulp.

We walked around the halls of Summerbrook for half an hour, and I wondered if I had just not noticed or had forgotten it from my last few visits, or if his shuffle had changed. Now, it was all on the balls of his feet—a kind of graceful tiptoe along the carpeted hallways, holding on to the rail along the wall as the nurses and aides called out to him in their nursery-school voices, "Look at *you,* Mr. Milofski. Going for a walk with your daughter!"

Only ten years before, I know, this would have infuriated him. The tone. The overfriendliness of strangers. He'd have made faces, grumbled under his breath, or, at the very least, ignored them.

But ten years ago he was not yet a child.

Now, he seems flattered by their attention. He smiled back at them and nodded. It reminded me of Chad in his miniature seat behind a miniature table at preschool, having managed to raggedly cut out a construction-paper triangle with his blunt scissors, and the way his fat teacher had lit up, looking at it, praising the triangle — and Chad, clasping his pudgy hands together, looked up at her as if trying to be sure that this praise was really for him, and very much hoping that it was.

We went back, after the walk, to my father's room and sat together with the television off.

After a while, we ran out of small talk, and just sat.

The room was pleasantly overwarm. The sound of a furnace deep under the nursing home somewhere hummed evenly, and eventually it began to feel as if that hum were a part of my body.

We sat as if we were waiting for someone. (Chad?)

Or something. (A bus?)

And it crossed my mind to say to my father, "You know, Dad, now it's just us."

But it isn't, of course. I still have a job, a husband, a home on the other side of the state. And he lives here, in this waiting room, having small strokes in his sleep, waking every day a little changed. I've begged him to let me move him closer to us, so I can see him every day. "You can move me anywhere you please when I'm dead," is all he'll say in response. It's the town he was born in. He'll die in this town. Now, that's perfectly clear. It's just a matter, now, of when.

I watched him in his chair, the slow shutting down of him. The eyes blinking closed, his mouth falling open, and then the regular breathing that meant he was deeply asleep. I remembered being carried up the stairs, like that, in his arms, having completely let go of the world, my head on his shoulder. The swaying of that. The solidity. After an hour or so a nurse came in and said, "Will you be staying for dinner, Miss Milofski?"

It surprised me.

Had I also been asleep?

I looked up.

Miss Milofski? Who? It took me more than a few seconds to understand that this nurse was speaking to me, that *I* was Miss Milofski.

No.

It had been years since I'd been her—that girl who was a combination of her unmarried status and her father's name— but, still, in a brilliant flash I saw her again, *Miss Milofski,* sitting behind the receptionist desk of the dentist's office where I worked in the summers during high school. She was dressed too provocatively for her job, for her office full of matrons, for the conservative town she lived in. Skirts too short, blouses too sheer, sundresses without straps. Eventually some middle-aged dental hygienist would pull her aside and tell her that the dentist had mentioned it, and didn't like it. I looked up at the nurse. I said, "No. I won't be staying for dinner."

I was, I realized, flushed.

Funny, how just remembering that ("You need to dress *less* . . ."—she'd never been able to say it . . .) had made me blush.

I could feel the hot splash of humiliation on my chest—still, or again.

I pulled the sweater closed around my collarbone.

The nurse left as quietly as she'd come.

My father was still deeply asleep. I looked around his room. It was almost entirely empty. He'd never liked any of the framed prints I'd brought, or even the calendars, and had finally said, "Nothing on the walls, please."

There was a radio on his nightstand. A Bible (Gideons—not his, everyone had one). A silver shoehorn on the table next to his chair. And someone had put a fat red rose in a Styrofoam cup on the windowsill.

Who?

Had one of the nurses or aides taken a particular shine to my father? Or the art therapist? Or some old lady from a local church, visiting the shut-ins?

It was the kind of rose you could buy at the grocery store for a couple dollars—mutant, huge, and blindingly red, the kind of flower nature alone could never grow. Science and commerce and nature together had made that rose. It was leaning danger- ously over the edge of the cup it was in, seeming to grow more and more top-heavy, as if burdened with its hyped-up beauty, as I watched.

Its stem was too long, and there was no longer enough water in the cup to anchor it down, I realized.

I stood up and took a step toward it, but it was already too late.

The whole thing was toppled—by what? gravity? my gaze?— onto the floor as I stepped toward it, water splashing over Dad's slippers.

And the petals, which were older and looser than they'd ap- peared, scattered over the linoleum, looking like the remnants of something violent—a shredded valentine, a little red bird torn to pieces by hungry, older birds, a bloody fight between flowers. My father woke up blinking at it, but said nothing. I cleaned it up and put it in the trash before I walked Dad down to dinner.

(4:30. Who eats dinner at 4:30?)

And then I left.

At the airport:

A tall thin young man in a flannel shirt carrying a duffel bag: *Is that my boy?*

It had been less than two months since I'd last seen him, but seeing him there at baggage claim, leather jacket draped over his shoulder, I had the stunned sick feeling that I'd sent a child to California and a stranger had returned without him.

"Ma," he said, stepping toward us. "Dad." I glanced at Jon, who didn't look stunned, not even surprised, just happy to see Chad.

He kissed my cheek. He smelled of airplane—upholstery, ether, other people's laundry. He tossed an arm around Jon's shoulder. He said, kidding, as if I couldn't hear, "So, what's wrong with Mom?"

"She's just happy to see you," Jon said. It was an old joke between them: *Mom cries when she's happy.* Sentimental birthday cards, graduations, baby pictures.

But I wasn't crying. I was staring. I felt unmoved. I felt that I was still waiting for my boy to get off the plane.

As we waited for the shuttle bus to take us back to Jon's car in the parking garage, I saw a woman waiting with a little boy.

Nine? Ten?

Buzz cut, crooked teeth, his pants were an inch or two too short. He was holding on to her sleeve, looking tired and worried, and I had such a stab of longing I almost couldn't stop myself from going over to them, leaning down, smelling that boy's head, burying my face in his neck, saying to his mother—

What?

What could I possibly say to his mother?

You have my son?

Or, the old advice I'd been given so many times, *They grow up so fast, appreciate these days . . . ?*

But how can you appreciate the days, going by, as they do, *so fast?* I'd loved him every second, and still, like a flock of wristwatches and stopwatches and alarm clocks in the wind, they flew right over me, those seconds, while I was packing a lunch, or idling outside his elementary school, or putting a bowl of macaroni and cheese on the table in front of him.

No. If I had spoken to that mother, I would have had nothing at all to say.

MARCH has, indeed, come in like a lion.

A blizzard yesterday.

Jon went off to work in it—his white Explorer a big white space in an enormous white world—but I stayed home with Chad.

For an hour at the kitchen table we played poker. He beat me, as he always did, even as an eight-year-old. I've never learned how to bluff—the impassive way a good poker player looks at her own cards, the nonchalant way she'd toss a blue chip and a red chip on the pile, daring her opponents to bet it all. Jon and Chad always said they could practically read my cards in my eyes. As usual, by the end of the game, Chad had all the chips. "Let's play War," I said, tossing my cards into the center of the table. "That's the only game I ever win."

"No offense, Mom, but that's because it's a game of chance. You need to work on your fake-out skills, woman. You just aren't devious enough."

I baked a lemon custard pie while he did research on the Internet for a paper he's writing on the Second Amendment. Today he's less like a stranger than he was yesterday. More like a fairly new friend, but every once in a while I get a glimpse of the boy he used to be—leaning over my shoulder to get a look at the filling as I spooned it into the shell, exasperated at the computer for taking so long to boot up, looking out the front window at the blizzard as if considering his skates, his sled.

But, mostly, the little boy is gone.

It's as if he's died, but as if his death has been accompanied by no grief.

As if he died and I'd never been given any notice of his death.

As if, even I, myself, his mother, had been an accomplice to his death.

All those years feeding and rocking him, and the birthday parties—the cakes and the candles added one by one until the surface of the whole thing danced with flames—driving him to track meets, band practice, soccer, I was driving him all those years into adulthood. Oblivion. Into my own obsolescence.

Planned obsolescence.

I was in my twenties before I ever heard that term. Another cashier at Community Books, trying to thread a new roll of receipt paper into the cash register, had said it, holding up the old roll, showing me how the last three feet of it were streaked with blue ink. "Planned obsolescence," he said. "They fix it so you have to change it before it's even used up."

For a few days after that I saw *planned obsolescence* everywhere. A conspiracy of it. Pens with cartridges only half full of ink. Bottles of ketchup designed so that the last third of the ketchup in them was impossible to shake out. I imagined everything planned so it wouldn't last, or so that the last gasps of it would be useless, would only serve to remind you that you needed to buy a new one—things ruined intentionally before they had been fully exhausted—and, then, I forgot all about planned obsolescence, it seemed, until today, seeing Chad's razor on the bathroom sink beside his father's.

But that's how it's supposed to be. Isn't that what I told Sue? The whole point of parenthood was guiding him to this, to the end of his need for parents. At the time, it had seemed to be about something else. It had seemed, to me, to be about *me*. About the warmth of his small body beside mine as I read stories to him. The pleasure of wrapping him in a towel after a bath. The feel of his soft baby face nuzzled against the side of my neck.

Well, it hadn't been.

What I'd been there for had to do with *him,* and because I'd done it, here he was, a man gathering all the poker chips across the table from me in the kitchen.

THIS morning Chad said, "Mom, don't you go to work anymore?"

He'd come out of his room in blue boxer shorts and a T-shirt that said UC BERKELEY. In the gray hallway light I could see that his skin was perfect except for the red crease of a pillowcase seam down his cheek. His hair, flecked with blond, was still darker than it had been in the summer, or when he was a baby— all those golden ringlets. It had taken me forever to have the heart to cut that hair. Finally, Jon had said, "Sherry, we can't have people thinking he's a girl when he goes off to kindergarten," and he was right. Chad was always being taken for a girl, a very pretty girl in little boy's clothes. But the first time I cut it, myself, I swore, as I hovered over those curls with a pair of scissors in the kitchen, I thought I heard celestial music—Handel, Bach, Mozart—playing somewhere outside from a passing car.

"I mean, Mom, don't you have to go anywhere again today?"

I said, no, actually, I didn't, that I'd taken a few days off to spend with him. Sue was teaching my classes. I had the leave time. It wasn't a problem.

He said, "That's sweet, Ma, but I was sort of hoping to have a bit of time alone, too. You know, having a roommate at school. It was just so great to think of having a whole house to myself for a bit on this vacation."

"Sure," I said. "I understand. It couldn't hurt for me to go into the office. I always have catching up to do."

And it wouldn't hurt. It *was* understandable. And, still, I couldn't help myself from asking, "What will you do here without me?"

"Crappy TV," Chad said, smiling. "Solitaire."

So, I took a shower. Got dressed. Got behind the wheel of my car. I hadn't really thought I'd go into the office, but once I was in the car I could think of nowhere else to go.

"WHAT are you doing here?" Beth asked when I stepped in. "We thought you were staying home today."

Did she look surprised, or annoyed?

The office was quiet, as it always is midmorning, so why did I feel as if I'd interrupted something by being in it? It was as though I were a ghost, some presence still hanging around after even the grief for me was over, let alone the use, after everyone had gotten ready to get on with their lives. *This is the office when I'm not in it,* I thought.

But there I was.

"I just needed to catch up on some things," I said.

"Well, Sue already left to teach your class."

"I know," I said. "I'm not here to teach the class."

"Oh. Okay," Beth said, and turned back to her computer. I could see, on her screen, a row of cards, mostly aces, before she moved her chair to block my view.

I took the papers and envelopes from my mailbox to my office and opened the one that was on top:

Sherry (Cherie!), You must be wondering by now who is this sad sap so in love with you. But if I told you, would it make any difference? The way I feel about you is all that matters to me, and perhaps I should keep it to my-

self, but for some reason I need for you to know. I know you're a happily married woman, but I also know that I need you to be mine.

I was still standing.

I leaned against the wall of my office.

I need you to be mine.

What does it mean about me that I felt at that moment so overwhelmed with—what? Desire? Longing? Gratitude? Lust?

And how could I feel these things for someone I'd never seen? Why did I find myself (ridiculously: like a woman in a movie) holding this note (torn from a yellow legal pad again, this time a green ballpoint pen) to my heart and sighing?

This time, I decided, I would tell no one about the note.

I slipped it back into the campus envelope it had come in and put it in the back of the bottom drawer of my desk.

CAN THIS be a symptom of impending menopause? The dreaded hot flashes?

I woke up in the night drenched in sweat. Maybe it was the squirrel in the walls that woke me, but when I woke, I was soaking—chilled and burning at the same time—and had to get up and change my nightgown. I went to the bathroom, passing Chad's room, where he looked like a giant in a child's bed, sprawled on top of his bedspread, one arm bent, the other flung over his head—and looked at myself in the medicine chest mirror:

How could I have been so deluded?

Only yesterday, after the note in my mailbox, I'd passed myself in the women's room full-length mirror and thought I looked young enough, not that different than I'd ever looked. I thought I looked like the kind of woman a man might fall in love with from a distance, lie awake at night, thinking of her.

But here was a clear vision of myself in bright light, at night, my face in the medicine chest looking out at me.

An older woman. (An *old* woman?) Lines and gray hairs, despite all the time and money spent at the salon only two weeks ago, and a tired sagging around my mouth and jaw, as if my younger face had begun to melt.

I leaned closer, despite the impulse to pull away. I thought of my mother, in the days before she died, asking me to bring her a mirror and a lipstick. After I'd brought it to her, she looked at herself, handed these things back to me, and rolled over on her side, spoke no more that day.

And, how old was she then? Forty-nine?

I'd thought, back then, being twenty-two myself, that my mother was old—not old enough to die, certainly, but old.

I'd thought, then, that life would sprawl out ahead of me in every direction.

That, by the time of the lump in the breast, even if I was only forty-nine, I would be ready.

Looking at myself in the bathroom mirror—its clean brilliance—I thought of her coffin. White. And my aunt Marilyn weeping and arranging the flowers around it so that the white ones were in front, the brighter colors in a ring around those.

At the center of all that white, in her gray dress, with that bad wig, my mother looked like something that had been accidentally spilled. Or like someone who had been shot and killed in the act of surrendering.

It had been spring.

Riding with my father in the backseat of the funeral parlor limousine, following the hearse from the church to the cemetery, I saw a woman in short shorts and a tight T-shirt walking down a sidewalk with her dog.

The dog was small and black, and the woman's legs looked polished, luminous in the sunlight.

Looking, now, at myself in the medicine chest mirror, I remembered that glimpse of that woman and her dog, and how it seemed like such a short time ago, but how even that sexy oblivious woman with her little black dog must have aged by now.

By now, she might be sixty.

She might be dead.

One moment she was an image glimpsed from a funeral parlor limousine on a spring day, filed away in a stranger's brain, and the next moment she was erased from her own beauty in this world forever.

And I—?

Looking at myself, plain and terrible in the mirror in the middle of the night, I thought, *I have built my house on sand.*

Even my firm body, those gym muscles—all the more ludicrous. I should have let myself grow soft, like my grandmother, I thought. I thought of her pillowy waist, pressing my face into it, feeling her warm flesh behind her apron—my grandmother, who had never seen the inside of a gym, let alone climbed onto an elliptical machine, and who, every morning, sat down at the kitchen table with a sweet roll and a cup of tea with heavy cream, relishing every bite and sip.

Instead, with my hard body, I've become like one of those brides in a horror film—lift the veil on what might appear to be a beautiful girl, and the face of an old hag is revealed.

This, I thought, lifting the veil in the middle of the night at the bathroom mirror, *is who I have become.*

Then, looking more closely, *Where have I gone?*

———

JON WOKE up this morning with a fire in his belly to "shoot the fucking squirrel" that woke us up in the middle of the night. Six o'clock he's out there patrolling the eaves troughs with his rifle. Chad said, coffee cup in his hands, looking out the kitchen window, "Has the old man finally lost it?"

I could see Jon's boot prints, how deep and dark they were in the snow, as if the Grim Reaper on a March morning were out there circling our house. But Jon himself was a blur in a hunter orange parka in the dull gray sunrise over the line of trees between our property and the neighbors'.

"What do you suppose the neighbors think about this?" Chad asked. He was up so early because he was going to drive Jon into work, then take his car to Kalamazoo to visit the girl he took to prom last year.

"I'm not worried about what they think," I told Chad.

The Henslins, whose property borders ours, are an elderly couple. They still slaughter their own sheep, milk their own cows, burn their own garbage in a ditch behind their barn so they don't have to pay twenty dollars a month to have it hauled away. Plenty of times I've seen Mr. Henslin out there himself with a rifle, hunting down the raccoons that got into his sheep feed, or his own aggravation of squirrels. And every October, he puts on his orange vest and hat and drives off with his grandsons and their spaniel, Kujo, returning with a dead deer strapped over the hood of their truck.

But, I suppose, those aren't the neighbors Chad's talking about.

In the last ten years, there are fewer and fewer neighbors like the Henslins. Instead, our neighbors, whom we've never met, zip by our house in their minivans and BMWs on their way to the freeway to work, and back from the freeway to their subdivisions. French Country Estates. Meadowlark Meadows. The subdivisions have all been built in the corn and soybean fields and razed apple orchards that used to belong to people like the Henslins. They feel like strangers, but are, I know, more like us than the Henslins. Jon and I did not, perhaps, raze the old farmhouse and build a McMansion, but our own motives weren't so different from those new residents of French Country Estates. We all had the same fantasies of wildflowers and meadowlarks, of a slower life in the country, and then ruined it with our desire for it.

Our own house was built by a great-great-uncle of the Henslins when he first came here from Prussia, and on some level I think the Henslins still think of our house as theirs. Twice, when we first moved in and the grass got too long for their taste, Mr. Henslin came over here with a riding mower when we weren't home and cut it for us. In August of our first summer, Mrs. Henslin called and told me I needed to pinch the heads off the hollyhocks or they wouldn't bloom the next year. Her great-aunt, she explained, had planted those hollyhocks from seeds that had been given to her by her great-great-grandmother, who'd brought them with her from Prussia.

I would never have thought of it, but I went out immediately and did as she'd said.

Those heads came off like damp, feminine handfuls of a remote past when I pinched them.

Once, I asked her about this great-aunt, but Mrs. Henslin could tell me, it seemed, nothing more than her name. Ettie Schmidt.

Sometimes I tried to imagine this Ettie Schmidt in my house — a small pale woman passing through the halls, rocking a baby by the woodstove. But I could never really see her, never imagine any other wife or mother in this house but me. Beyond the hollyhocks, she'd left no trace of herself when she left.

"Well, it can't look good," Chad said, looking out the kitchen window at his father. Over Chad's shoulder I could see the shadow Jon's rifle cast in the snow. "And won't the school bus be by soon?"

I was about to go to the door, to call out to Jon to forget it, to put the rifle away, come in and drink his coffee and get ready for work, but then he fired—loud, and heart-stopping, and some small animal's final surprise in this world on the roof of our house.

I KISSED them both good-bye after breakfast. "Be careful driving to Kalamazoo," I said to Chad, and he nodded. He knew I'd taken the day off again to be with him, but this girl, this girl in Kalamazoo, had been expecting him, he said.

I don't remember much about this particular prom date except that I didn't think she was beautiful enough to keep Chad's attention very long. Pretty hair, straight and brown, and green eyes—but in her short prom dress standing on our front lawn, wearing her wristband corsage (which I'd paid for and picked up from the florist only an hour before), her legs looked like the trunks of two fruit trees. Thin enough, but shapeless. Her panty hose were too dark for the bridal white she was wearing, and her makeup was of the orangey too-thick variety. Her name was Ophelia. (Ophelia!) And her stepfather was a cop, her mother was a dental hygienist. And Chad had told me they were just friends, which I felt certain was all they'd ever been, and all they were now, despite this trip to Kalamazoo to see her.

"So, what will you do all day with Ophelia?" I asked.

"Lunch," he said. "She's going to show me her campus."

"Drive carefully," I said. "I'll pick Dad up from work."

"Good job, Mom," he said, and winked.

MIDAFTERNOON, I decided to take a nap. A deep exhaustion had begun to settle on my eyelids as I folded Chad's laundry—the T-shirts, the boxer shorts, warm from the dryer, all that soft cotton smelling, now, of powdered flowers and well water, as if, rather than washing and drying my son's laundry in a machine, I'd left it in the rain and sun in a garden for many summers, gone back to find it softened, sweetened. I put what I was folding—a plain gray T-shirt I'd never seen before—back in the basket.

Outside, the sun was straining through the snow clouds, so I pulled the shades. I lay down on the bed and pulled the quilt at the foot of it over me. I closed my eyes, waiting to drift into sleep on the scent of laundry, winter dust, the furnace, the silence of a house with no one but a wife and mother in it, when I thought of it.

The note.

Be Mine.

I opened my eyes.

Sherry (Cherie!).

I rolled onto my side. I rolled onto my stomach, and then, again, onto my back—the thrill of it starting behind my knees, traveling like a man's hands straight up my thighs, between my legs.

How long had it been since I'd masturbated?

Years?

Before Jon and I were married, it was something I did every day. Twice a day! Sometimes in the bath or the shower. Always before I went to sleep. Once on a plane. I'd been on my way to New York to visit a friend. I had three seats to myself. I pulled my down jacket over my lap, and as the plane was hurtling itself down the runway, and then heading nose-first into the sky, rumbling and vibrating and shaking in that disconcerting plastic manner of planes as they leave the earth, I slid my whole hand down the front of my jeans and brought myself to such a fast and shattering climax that I worried, afterward, that I might have moaned and not known it. But I looked around. No one seemed to know.

In those days, everything filled me with longing. The sight of a man loosening his tie. A couple walking down the street with their arms around one another. The tip of my own pinky between my own teeth.

Mostly, then, I think, it was my own body that I wanted. Even the ugly men — the ones I felt afraid of, or repulsed by — when they looked at me, passing me on the street or lingering at the counter when I was ringing up their books and magazines, made my heart race.

Sometimes, even, being looked at, my nipples would stiffen. I would get wet.

I was wild, I think, for *myself*. Sometimes I would take a hand mirror, put it between my legs, watch myself touch myself. I could come in seconds, or I could draw it out for an hour, force my fingers away from my clitoris and lie on my bed with my legs spread — naked, panting, bringing myself so close that I became a girl at the edge of an abyss of pleasure, touching my own breasts, licking my fingers, and then finally allowing myself to plunge into it, torso soaked with sweat, and letting myself thrash myself to orgasm.

This afternoon, it was slower, and my hands between my legs, with some imagination, became the hands of a stranger. But I brought myself to a climax that surprised me. A rocking wildness that brought tears to my eyes, as if, making love to myself, I had been returned to a lover for whom I'd been violently pining for a long time.

When I woke — slowly, languidly, a pleasurable rising from the depths of something to its surface — I went to the bathroom and looked, again, at myself in the mirror.

The horror of the night before had slipped away. In the afternoon light, I looked younger, softer. I could see it, still, my younger face. My hair, still long and dark, was mussed, but shiny. I was, again, a woman you might glimpse in a hallway and remember.

TOMORROW Chad goes back. He couldn't stay the whole week, he said, because he needed to get back to study for a calculus exam he had on Monday. "You can't study here?" I asked. "No," he said. "I can't study here."

We're having Garrett to dinner tonight. When I told Chad I'd seen him up at the college, he just shrugged. When I told him I'd invited Garrett to dinner, he said, "Great," but didn't seem particularly interested. "Aren't you friends anymore with Garrett?" I asked, and he said, "I haven't been friends with Garrett since seventh grade, Mom." I asked him if he wanted to call Garrett, to tell him what time we'd be eating, and Chad said, "Why don't you?"

Garrett answered the phone in the middle of the first ring, as if he'd been there, waiting. It was a local number. Did he still live in his childhood house, now that his parents were dead? Did he live alone? "Garrett," I said, "this is Sherry Seymour. Chad's mother."

"Yeah!" he said. "How's Chad?"

"Chad's fine. He's great. He's here. He's excited to see you. Can you still come to dinner?"

"Sure, yes. I'd love that. What time, Mrs. Seymour?"

"Seven o'clock?"

"Okay. Yeah. Great!"

After we hung up, I listened to the emptiness on the line for a moment. There was another voice, there, in the air—a man's voice. I recognized the word "already," but the rest was just mumbling, the implication of sentence structure, of meaning. When we were in fifth grade, sixth grade, we used to believe these voices that could sometimes be heard on the line between phone calls, or under phone calls, were the voices of the dead. At slumber parties, we'd listen for them through a dead receiver.

And why not? Couldn't there be some remnant of them in the air, still speaking? Couldn't an instrument capable of transporting voices across oceans, across time zones, manage somehow to pick up the voices of the dead?

No.

Of course not.

I hung up.

Tacos.

I'll make tacos. A guy's dinner. Jon will like it, too. Chips and guacamole, and lots of shredded cheese, chopped onion, tomatoes.

GARRETT came to the door in a starched white shirt, carrying a massive red rose wrapped in cellophane with the price, $1.99, still stuck on it with a green tag.

He politely pulled his boots off on the porch and spent the evening in his socks, one of which had a hole at the big toe. His hair was even shorter than it had been when I saw him in the hallway last week—a buzz cut so close to his scalp I could see the pale skin there—and he smelled of Dial soap. As Garrett stood beside Chad with his shaggy hair down over his collar and falling into his eyes and his Berkeley sweatshirt with its ragged sleeves, they looked like boys from entirely different worlds.

I put the rose in a vase and put the vase on the table. I gave both of the boys a beer. It was Jon's idea, but I'd agreed. No reason to pretend that the legal drinking age had anything to do with their drinking beer, which they've certainly been doing for years now. But after each of them had a second one, I didn't offer them any more.

I had, myself, three big cold glasses of white wine—Sue's drink, a bottle of Sauterne she gave me for my birthday last year, trying to convert me from my Merlot—and relaxed.

I put a candle beside the vase, and the flickering light on the rose made it look like a beating heart at the center of the table.

After the second glass of wine, the men around me became beautiful, ravenous strangers. Seconds, thirds, they ate as I sipped and nibbled and passed dishes to them.

Beautiful, ravenous strangers:

Jon in his flannel shirt, telling jokes, "A woman sits down next to a man on an airplane . . ."

And Chad, with his hair grown out like that, the bristly half beard that's grown since he's been here, having not shaved his face once despite that razor beside his father's on the bathroom sink.

And Garrett—whose ten-year-old face I could no longer find in this new one.

Where, I wondered, had he gone, that little boy ramming Matchbox cars against the legs of my coffee table? *Garrett, honey, can you take those toys to Chad's room? I don't want the furniture to get scratched up.* I could still recall the expression of deep apologetic despair on his face when he looked up at me. I remember I took it back when I saw that despair.

Oh, I see now, there aren't any scratches. Just keep doing what you're doing.

But it had, actually, scratched up the legs of the coffee table, and those scratches were still there—a bit of blond etched out of the mahogany, a secret message written by a prisoner, in code, with his fingernails.

It seemed that Chad was purposely refusing to talk about Berkeley with Garrett. Whenever the subject of California, of dorm life, of San Francisco or the ocean came up, Chad changed the subject to tacos. More cheese. Are there any more onions? Please pass the salsa. After a while, Jon drew Garrett out on the subject of hunting, of motorcycles, of cars. Garrett talked about a red Mustang he was fixing up. He kept it in his garage (he does still live in his parents' house, which he now refers to as his). On the weekends and after classes he works on it. Once or twice I thought I saw a look pass over Chad's face—pity, boredom, contempt?

Or was it simply the curiosity, and the lack of comprehension, a college boy from California would naturally have for the life of a hometown boy studying auto mechanics at the community college? A path not taken. Never even a path. For only a split second I wondered if it would have been, somehow, better, to have raised Garrett, rather than Chad. A boy with a keen understanding of motors. One who stuck close to home, whose work was physical and dirty and crucial.

I never would have thought so when I was reading Greek myths at bedtime to Chad, or driving him to piano lessons, begging him to practice (then letting him quit when he didn't).

I never would have thought so those summers when I told him, no, he shouldn't get a job. He should enjoy himself. He would only be fifteen, sixteen, for a whole leisurely summer once in his life.

Early on, I could see how competitive he was, but I never once said, "Chad, you don't always have to be the best at everything, you know," although there were times I should have said it. Even in second grade, he had to be the best reader, the boy to finish his math sheets first. Later, he had to win the essay contests, have the highest scores on the standardized tests.

Was it only an illusion, or did he always have them, too? It always *seemed* that he did, but, surely, that couldn't have been the case.

Still, I never once let go of the idea that everything had to be *just so,* did I? He had to have all of it—the lessons, the software, the whole Scholastic encyclopedia, sent to us one by one for six months in the mail, although he almost never used them. Occasionally, I took one off the shelf and paged through it myself. *Apples, Arizona.* I wanted his life to be ordered like that. I'd read about it in a child development book. The importance of order. His homework supervised. His self-esteem promoted. I never buckled him into his baby seat without double-checking that it was correctly installed. I never let him ride even his tricycle around in the driveway without his helmet on.

Would it have been better, or any different, if I'd provided, instead, the kind of house the Millers, who'd lived down the block from me when I was growing up, had provided for their children? The garbage spilling out of their garage into their yard? The older children watching the younger children while the parents worked? Unspayed cats living and procreating in their backyard—some with little cat bites taken out of their ears, rolling in the dirt of their front yard, interchangeable, yowling all night, sneaking down the block to shit in my sandbox.

Once, one of their cats came up on our front steps carrying something dark and bloody and writhing in its mouth while my mother and I were sitting on the porch, drinking lemonade and waiting for my father to get home from work.

"Oh my god," my mother said, leaping to her feet. "It's got a rat."

But in high school I got to know one of the Miller boys. Not well—just chatting in the cafeteria, and we had one class together—but well enough to find that he was a warm, funny boy. He laughed mostly at himself. It was easy to tell him the story about his cat bringing a rat to our house. ("Hey," he said, "we always wondered where that rat went!") His hair was red and tangled and he always smelled, I thought, like dandelions, and it was clear that what I had imagined taking place in his house because of the disorder—violence, neglect—had been something else, something I couldn't imagine.

I poured myself another glass of wine and pushed my plate away. Jon reached across the table and stroked my hand. He said, looking at me, but speaking to Chad, "You know, your beautiful mother here has a secret admirer."

I opened my mouth to protest, but nothing came out.

"Yeah?" Chad asked, and put his taco down. "What's that all about?"

"She's been getting secret love notes in her mailbox at school."

"From who?" Chad asked.

"Someone who's in love with her, naturally," Jon said.

"A crackpot," I said, and sipped from my glass. I could taste the grapes in it. Melted, oversweet—a sweetness like something rotting. Something green, left too long in the sun, withered on the vine. "Or someone making fun of an old lady."

"Or somebody sucking up for a grade," Chad said.

Jon gave him a cold look. "How would you suck up for a grade by leaving anonymous notes?"

"Well, maybe he'll come around later and reveal his true identity after he flunks a test or something," Chad said. "It's brilliant, really." He picked up his taco and bit into it, as if he were satisfied with his explanation, as if the conversation were now over.

I couldn't help defending myself. "I don't give tests," I said.

"Oh, yeah, I forgot," Chad said with his mouth full. "You don't flunk anybody either, do you?"

I shrugged, a little sheepishly. I am, I admit it, an easy teacher. So many of my students have had hard enough lives—been in jail, been pregnant teenagers, had parents abandon them, failed miserably all through school—that I hate to make their lives any harder. With some exceptions, these are older people and inner-city kids who've found their way to the community college despite the odds, despite themselves. But Chad had never liked the whole idea of it, even when he was eleven years old. "It's not a college," he'd said, "if you can get a degree in auto mechanics or air-conditioner maintenance. That's not *college.*" I never tried to explain.

"No," Garrett said. I looked over at him. "I know who it is," Garrett said.

"Who?" Chad said. "Do tell, bro." He put his taco down again.

"It's Bram Smith. My Auto II teacher. He was joking one day about this gorgeous teacher in the English department, that we should all go over and sign up for a lit class. I knew right then that he was talking about you." Garrett looked over at me.

Was I drunk?

Was I imagining that Garrett was looking at me appreciatively, that his eyes softened on my face as if he truly thought I might be the teacher his Auto II instructor had described as gorgeous?

I shook my head. "Bram Smith," I said. "But I don't know him."

"He's part-time," Garrett said. "He's great." Garrett smiled. "Apparently he thinks you are, too."

Chad sighed and leaned back in his chair. His eyes were narrowed in Garrett's direction. "How old's this redneck?"

"Chad," Jon said, drumming his fingers on the table, annoyed. "Are you jealous or something?"

"No," Chad said. "But if some greaser is stalking my mother I think I ought to—"

"*Chad,*" I said—in that tone, and immediately regretted it. *Saying* it made it obvious that I was *thinking* it: *Garrett is a "greaser."* I softened, and said, "I don't think anyone's going to bother to *stalk* me."

"He's about thirty, I think," Garrett said.

"Well he better stay away from my mother." Chad was still looking at Garrett as he said this. Was I mistaken, or did Garrett, looking down at his plate, suppress a smile?

The discussion was over, and dinner was over, and in the bright overhead light of the kitchen, scraping plates, I felt such an emptiness—too much wine, and I'd barely eaten anything— that I was surprised I didn't simply float away with it. From the living room, I could hear Jon and the boys laugh about something. The television. I could feel the white wine in my chest, rising out of me, burning and fragrant, as if I had been sipping perfume all night, as if I had eaten a cheap bouquet of grocery store roses and now could only wait for them to pass through me, to be shat out, flushed away.

Bram Smith.

Maybe, once, I'd glimpsed someone who might have been Bram Smith, Auto II instructor, at an all-faculty meeting.

But could that have been him—a tall man in an olive green T-shirt, muscled, with dark hair and one of those mustache and beard combinations that went only as far as his upper lip and chin, neatly trimmed, both elegant and masculine, the kind of man I'd quit looking at ten years ago at least, and who, I thought, had also quit looking at me?

A HEADACHE this morning, and that dull sense of dread and insatiable appetite that is a hangover. Still, I got Chad's laundry done, packed his suitcase, made breakfast by 6:00 A.M., and Jon and Chad left for the airport. When I said I wouldn't be going with them they seemed—relieved?

Fine, let them go alone together. No one has to worry that I'll cry at the curb, that I'll mope on the way home.

"Bye, Ma," Chad said so casually that it was as if he were off to soccer practice, and he'd be home by lunch. "I'll call you when I get there," he said, and kissed my cheek.

I saw, watching them from the back porch as they were backing down the driveway, that they were laughing.

At me?

Another slate gray day, but a little warmer, and the breeze seems to have something in it—a dampness, or a spray, it seems, of spit, something living, bacterial even, an impulse, a compulsion toward life, no longer simply a frozen denial of it.

After they left, I went back to bed and had a dream:

I took an apple out of the crisper and bit into it. It was soft, like a sponge. Salty, warm, it made me gag. It tasted the way I imagined an animal's heart, or a man's testicle, would taste if you ate it, but I couldn't help it, I kept eating.

Why?

A sense of duty? A longing for adventure?

A hunger? A repulsion?

The whole time I was eating it (and I ate the whole thing—seeds and core and stem and all) I was gagging, and wondering.

THIS afternoon in my mailbox (I checked one last time before I left to go home) a piece of white Xerox paper, a heart drawn in the center of it, and, written in tiny block letters:

DO YOU EVER THINK   OF ME? WHEN I
THINK OF YOU, I THINK OF YOUR SOFT
BROWN HAIR AND WHAT IT WOULD
BE LIKE TO PRESS MY FACE
INTO IT, KISS YOUR
NECK, AND FINALLY
BE ABLE TO TELL
YOU ALL MY
DESIRES.

Stupidly, I'd unfolded it in the hallway. I should have folded it back up right away when I saw what it was and taken it into my office to read it, but, seeing it—the heart, the careful tiny lettering—I was frozen before it, I was turned to stone there at my mailbox in the main office with Beth only four feet away from me at her desk, and half a dozen people either coming or going, and Sue reaching around me to get her own mail. "Sherry," she said.

When I could finally glance away from it, I saw that Sue was reading the piece of paper in my hand. "Jesus," she said. "This guy's serious. Sherry?"

"What?" I asked, and she burst out laughing.

"Good lord, Sherry, you siren. You man magnet!"

Finally I was able to fold it back up. She followed me back to my office door where, twice, I dropped my keys trying to unlock it. She laughed, loudly, again, then said, "Your hands are shaking! Come on, do you know who this is? Are you holding out some vital piece of information from your best friend?"

I whispered back to her, "I don't want to talk about this in the hall."

"Oooh," she whispered back. "You *do* know something."

When I'd finally managed to get the door open, I cleared some books from a chair so she could sit down, and told her, "I do think I know who it is."

"Well, do tell!"

Sue:

I have loved Sue for twenty years, as long as I've loved Jon. We first met at a part-time English instructors' meeting, where she made a joke about the department chair's taste in clothes. "It's like she's trying to spontaneously combust. Everything she wears is made from petrochemicals."

Sue herself was wearing a crinkled tie-dyed skirt, sandals. It was late August. Her hair was a solid golden mass down her back, all the way to her waist. Her teeth were so white they looked like paper, and this was before everyone had those teeth, before tooth-whitening systems were sold in drugstores. Hers were simply brilliant because she was pure, and young, and didn't drink coffee or red wine or smoke cigarettes. She did, already, carry the bit of extra weight around her hips, which would turn into this middle-aged softness, and which would be exacerbated by driving everywhere she went and being too busy with the twins to exercise.

Back then, she was a runner and a cross-country skier. A smell always wafted off of her of evergreen, as if she'd brought northern California with her to the Midwest in her hair when she'd moved here.

Today, she looked tired.

In the unflattering overhead light of my office, I could see that the little pouches she'd always had under her eyes had turned, now, to real bags with deep creases beneath them and a bluish fluid filling them. Since fall, it seemed, she'd gained another ten pounds, which she didn't have room for, and hadn't bought new clothes to go with them. The buttons of the white blouse she was wearing were straining against her flesh, and even the sleeves of it were pulled tight across her arms. Her hair, which she'd cut short long ago, looked badly dyed—hennaed— and dry and gray beneath the reddish brown, making her look as if something—rust, blood?—had been sprayed on her from a low-flying plane as she was walking under it.

When, I thought, looking at her in my office, did we get old?

Certainly, it seemed a long time ago that we stood together in one corner of the Writing Center laughing about the department chair's polyester dress (all geometric designs, tied up with a patent-leather belt) but not *that* long ago. That afternoon in the Writing Center, the late-summer sun had been pouring in through the plate glass windows. There was a gentle dust settling in long angular streams on the tables and chairs and on the hair and arms of the part-time English instructors. The smell of autumn—its textbooks, its ditto fluid, its calendars and red ink—was in that dust, all implication, suggestion, that the future was on its way, but, outside, the sky had been entirely empty and blue. Not a cloud anywhere. The carpet, then, was orange, institutional. In a few years it would be replaced with mauve carpeting, which would not seem, at first, to us, as institutional as the orange, but then would become the color with which every institution replaced its orange carpet. Twenty years ago — and it felt, perhaps, like a few years.

Or even less than that.

But, I thought, looking at Sue's arms, those years were a part of us now.

They had settled in our bodies.

We had not, of course, felt them passing, because they *hadn't*. They had instead *accumulated*. We were *wearing* that passed time.

And, still, through the mystery of love and friendship, Sue also hadn't changed for me at all. She'd remained the young woman who'd sat in the backseat of my car with me when I got the news (through campus security, coming for me to the door of my first-year writing course) that my brother was dead, and who, the next year, wore a chain of daisies in her long blond hair as maid of honor at my wedding.

Before Sue, I had never particularly wanted or needed to have female friends. The girlfriends I'd had in high school and college — I let them go without much interest, just a slow loosening, a gradual forgetting. But here Sue still was, my best friend. I'd never even *chosen* her as a friend. There was simply a bond formed between us that first day in the Writing Center, and here we still were, serving out the comfortable terms of it.

"Well," Sue said, leaning forward. "Tell me. Who is it?"

"Bram Smith," I told her. "He's a part-time auto-mechanics instructor."

Sue lifted her eyebrows. I couldn't tell if she was skeptical or simply surprised.

"Bram Smith?" she asked. "That unbelievable stud?"

"I don't even know who he is," I told her. "Is he the one with the dark hair, the —?"

"Yeah," Sue said, as if humoring me, as if she knew I perfectly well knew who Bram Smith was. "The one with the muscles, Sherry. The one with the dimple. The sexiest man who has ever set foot in this godforsaken place. The one every woman here with any estrogen left in her system at all has been fantasizing about for three years. The one who looks like every sexy cartoon ever drawn of the devil. Don't play dumb with me, Sherry. You know perfectly well who Bram Smith is."

"No," I said. "I mean, I've seen him, I guess. Now that you . . . describe him."

Sue snorted. "Right." A half smile. She looked away from me.

"Honestly, Sue," I said. "It was Chad's friend Garrett who told me it was him, that he'd been talking about me in his class."

"Well," Sue said, standing up, smoothing down the wrinkled front of her linen skirt, no longer smiling. The sun from my window was gray but mottled with a bit of yellow, as if it were shining through clouds that had been washed into thin patches. It fell on Sue's chest where it was exposed by the too-tight blouse, and the skin there looked, I thought, damaged. (When, I thought, had *that* happened?) Thin. Spackled with brown. I remembered a low-cut black dress she'd worn to a New Year's Eve party, how all the men seemed to gravitate toward the hors d'oeuvres table near which Sue stood, flirting with the one she was going to marry and with whom she would have twins. It had looked painful for those men when they had to tear their eyes from that slit of white flesh revealed by her dress.

I looked from that damaged skin back to her face.

Could I be reading her expression correctly?

Was she *jealous*?

"I've got to go," Sue said. "I'll be late to get the boys." She opened the door and stepped out into the hallway. "Good luck with all this, Sherry," she said. "Keep me posted."

"Any word from your lover today?" Jon asked when I walked in the door.

I said, "Yes. As a matter of fact there was."

He put his newspaper down on the ottoman and looked at me.

The sunset in our picture window lit him up, made him glow—robustly, handsomely. Jon, I thought, at least, has not changed much. There's some gray in his hair now, and a few lines around his eyes, but, if anything, these things have made him more attractive. Women have always looked at Jon when we walked into a restaurant together. The demeanor of the mothers of Chad's friends always changed when we joined their semi-circles at an event—posture improved, stomachs sucked in, a lighter laughter, more batting of the eyes. And, if I showed you a picture of him twenty years ago and a picture today, you would know instantly that this was the same man, and that the decades that had passed had been fairly kind ones, that life had been mostly good to him, that he was a physically vital man and would remain so for many years.

"Tell me," he said.

I took it out of my purse, the note, and handed it to him.

Jon looked at it for what seemed like much longer than he needed to read it, and then looked up. "Holy shit," he said. "We aren't just talking some kid with a crush here. This is serious stuff."

"Are you upset?" I asked. I thought of those months, so many years ago, of my infatuation with Ferris Robinson, how, when I confided in Jon, he had been titillated at first, then angry, and then sad, and then desperate, and then giddily attentive, and then had grown so cold I thought our marriage was over. "Are you angry?"

"Frankly," Jon said, standing up, walking toward me, stopping in front of me, putting his arms around my lower back, "I'm a little embarrassed to say that I'm almost unbearably turned on."

He pressed his body against me. He had an erection.

LAST night, after we made love (or was that *making love?*—Jon, pushing me onto my side, then onto my stomach, putting himself in me from behind, saying, *You think this is what your mechanic wants to do?* grabbing my breast, cupping it, pinching the nipple hard enough that I gasped, then orgasmed so quickly it shamed me) he fell asleep, but I lay awake a long time.

Too long.

I woke up exhausted.

In the morning light, the kitchen looked hazy—everything haloed with that glow that comes from exhaustion, and a kind of dull ringing deep in my ears. I thought, briefly, about calling in sick, but I'd missed my classes last week, having taken the time off to spend with Chad. If I missed again today, they'd be confused, my students. The ones who were doing poorly might throw in the towel altogether. The ones who were doing well would feel betrayed. *Another crappy absentee teacher.* I had to go.

I drank a cup of coffee black, standing in my bare feet, wearing my bathrobe, at the kitchen window. Before Jon left for work, he bit my neck and said, "You be good today."

In his dark suit, he'd looked so handsome, smirking at me as he stepped through the back door into the driveway, that I had a sudden recollection of the thrill of seeing him for the first time, at that bar, and how I thought (maybe because he was friends with the wild bunch who'd introduced us) that he looked a little dangerous. *Too* handsome. The kind of man you'd have to worry about losing to some other girl, some flashier girl. He'd be, I thought then, the kind of guy who would be constantly pursued. Or, he would, himself, be the pursuer. Surely, I thought, he knew how beautiful he was, and the power it gave him. What man *wouldn't* abuse such power? Those blue-green eyes. The solid build.

Tail chaser, my mother used to say about certain kinds of men. It was derogatory and appreciative at the same time, coming from her. She liked a man with spunk. *Milquetoast* was the kind of man with whom you didn't want to waste your time.

But, as it turned out, Jon wasn't dangerous.

As it turned out, Jon was the safest man in the world.

When we walked down the sidewalk together, he always insisted on placing me on the inside so I wouldn't be splattered with mud, or hit by a car. After Chad was born, Jon installed smoke detectors. Not just a few, but a smoke detector in every room. Even the .22 in the garage, even the shooting of the squirrels off our roof, was his attempt to keep his family safe. Never once in twenty years had it ever crossed my mind that my husband had lied to me, or had anything to hide, or had even had a thought he'd chosen not to share with me.

No, if he ever looked at other women, it must have been when I wasn't in the vicinity.

Surely, he did look. *All* men looked at other women. Joggers, bikers, college girls waiting at the bus stop in short skirts.

But I couldn't imagine it.

Jon's loyalty seemed so fierce that it was impossible to picture him, like every other man on the planet, following with his eyes, from behind the anonymity of his steering wheel in a passing car, the line of spine and hip and leg exposed by shorts and a halter top on a summer day crossing the street.

Did he look at other women?

Does he?

And if he doesn't—does such loyalty come at a cost?

Or, is it the loyal one, anyway, who pays the price for such loyalty?

Maybe the *object* of that loyalty—me—would be the one who paid. Maybe the price was finding yourself married for twenty years to a handsome man, a perfectly lovely man, in a marriage without tension, in a life without apprehension, or mystery, or surprise. I always knew, after all, what Jon would say when I asked him if he loved me. I always knew that he would walk in the door every night at 5:45, after an oddly stimulating day designing computer software ("I love my job," was the only thing he ever really said about his job, and the only thing I really knew about it) and say, "Hi. Sherry? Are you home?" Or, if I came home later than he did, that he would be waiting for me in the love seat with his newspaper.

But, last night, for a moment, entering me from behind, grabbing my breast too hard in his hand, he *was* the stranger he was pretending to be.

And, maybe, that was what he was trying to achieve—the status of a stranger. (*You think this is what it would feel like to get fucked by your mechanic?*) Have I, perhaps, become as little of a mystery to him over these years as he has become to me? Is that why it turns him on to imagine me through a stranger's eyes, or a stranger inside of me?

Do I seem as safe (and dull) to him as he does to me?

Should I be flattered that he's so excited by another man's attention, or insulted?

I WORE the silk dress again—although by late morning there was an east wind, and I could feel it streaming through the cracks in the windows as I got dressed for work. It rattled them in their frames.

Yesterday, with the sunlight and the warmer temperature, a fly, dead between the glass and the screen all winter, came back to life. (Or *seemed* to come back to life: Is that possible, do flies hibernate, or die and resurrect?) This morning it was buzzing when I woke up, tossing itself frantically against the storm window, making a fuss. But by the time I was out of my shower, that wind had started up, and the cold front could be felt coming in, and that fly was fading, and then by the time I'd bothered to open the curtains, its bumping into the glass had stopped, and it was crawling slowly, despondently, through the dirt at the bottom of the sill—and then, by the time I was dressed, it appeared to be dead again.

Well, spring crept out for a moment and retreated, but I was determined to wear a spring dress. I shivered in it as I started the car, which was so cold that the engine sounded, grinding to life, as if it were deciding whether or not to start, whether or not it was interested in pulling out of the driveway in this cold. But it did start, and the heater began to work quickly, blowing sashes of heat hard into my face through the vents with the smell of the dust gathered there a little at a time over the many miles traveled—72,735 of them on the speedometer this morning—and being spewed back at me in the form of warmth.

I turned the radio to the classical station, but it wasn't classical music. It was, instead, some kind of half-modern symphony, the soulless straining of violins and synthesizers in disharmony.

A gray frost on the dead grass.

The trees were bare and black against it.

The snow had melted just enough to expose the shoulders of the road, littered with fast-food bags and cigarette packs.

April may be the cruel month, but March is the dirty month. The garbage month. The white had turned to the color of ashes, receded enough to reveal the litter that was there all along, but there were no leaves or flowers yet to distract the eye from the trash piling up around us on every side—our own trash, of course, but seeming to be nature's trash, the trash of the gods, so much of it.

I merged onto the freeway, feeling, as I always did, the rush of it—the smooth tar of it under my wheels and the way the traffic parted and shifted to let me in.

I was an object among other objects. A particle in motion. I didn't need to think about driving, I was so accustomed to it— so I thought about *him*.

Bram Smith.

Had I ever, really, even seen him?

I wasn't sure.

I had been over and over that scrap of memory from— when? A year ago, two years ago? That man in the corner of my eye, in the olive T-shirt, with the chiseled features—could that really have been him? Was I really even remembering anyone at all?

It didn't matter.

I had already burned the image of that man into my brain within a few hours of Garrett's having mentioned him at dinner—an image built out of what I thought I recalled and what I had been told, until the fantasy had a smell (oak, engine) and hands, and a voice. And then I had gone over it and over it, that burned image, during the making of dinner, and the cleaning up afterward—the dishes wiped with a paper towel before stacking them in the washer, the crumbs wiped off the table with a sponge—and the shower, turned so hot I could feel it in my bones, and while Jon and I made love, and as I lay awake afterward—hearing the fantasy's voice in my head, speaking my name—and making the bed this morning, pulling the floral sheets up, and putting on my makeup, eating a bowl of oatmeal at the kitchen sink. And all the time I was thinking of him, I was also feeling sheepish for thinking of him. I scolded myself for thinking of him. *You don't even know it's him.*

Even if it is, you don't know who he *is.*

In truth, by the time I was traveling down the freeway this morning at eighty miles an hour in my silk dress, whoever Bram Smith really was didn't matter.

He was, already, a fully developed character in my imagination:

He would have a deep laugh, I thought. His hands would be large, but skillful, a little dirty because he worked with them. His knuckles would be battered, the palms calloused. Younger than I, but a grown man. His body would be solid. He would smell like earth, and soap. Making love with him would be exhilarating, terrifying. A man who left love notes for complete strangers was a man of passion, a womanizer. I would never be able to trust him.

But did I want to trust him?

No.

What *did* I want from him?

What I wanted, I thought, really, was to ask him if it was true.

Did he mean it when he'd written *Be Mine?*

Was I really the kind of woman who could inspire such interest?

From a younger man?

A man like you?

I was imagining asking him, and his answer (*yes*), and his hand tracing a path from my neck to my shoulder, and then from my shoulder to my breast, and then leaning into me, telling me *yes,* breathing my name (*Cherie*) into my ear with the smell of the

dust of the car's heater, a hot breath of it entering me, whispering *yes,* when it happened—when it leaped out of the sky and
into my path:

Shit.

I slammed on the brakes, but it was too late, as if I'd been
struck by lightning, but the lightning was solid, had a body, with
mass, with weight—a body that was tossed onto the hood of my
car, where it erupted in a fountain of blood. Somehow I came to
a stop at the side of the freeway, the radio still on, my windshield
wipers rhythmically sloshing the blood off my window with
them. And then I was standing in my silk dress at the side of the
road with the wind cutting straight through to my skin, and a
man in a white lab coat was running from his car to mine along
the shoulder, shouting, "Ma'am, are you all right?"

I shook my head as if to let him know I had no idea. I asked
him, "What happened?"

"You hit a deer," he said, and then turned to point to the median, where a tawny mangled thing, lying on its side, lifted its
head, then let it drop.

Cars and trucks whirred by us with incredible speed. My
dress snapped around me in the wind of them. Here and there I
glimpsed the face of a driver—repulsed, or concerned, or surprised. The man in the white lab coat looked at me, and, seeing
that I wasn't hurt, said, "You're lucky. Really lucky. You could
have been killed."

"Honestly?" I asked him.

"Honestly," he said.

We looked at one another for a few seconds, but his features
were a blur to me. He was no one I had ever seen before.

"Really," he said. "I saw the whole thing. I pulled over because I thought you might actually be dead."

"I'm not," I said. "I'm fine."

From the corner of my eye I saw it again in the median, raising its head, and lowering it, either to die, or to rest.

The man in the white lab coat stepped around the front of my car to inspect the damage, then called over the wind of the traffic to me to say he thought it was fine to drive, but that I'd want to have someone straighten out the bumper. It was a mess.

Neither of us said anything about the deer. Helping it. Or killing it. It wasn't until much later in the day that I thought about that—the inevitable sin of that, because what could we have done? Had either of us tried to cross the freeway to it, we would have suffered its fate.

"How can I thank you?" I asked him as we parted.

"Drive carefully," he said, and shook his head.

At the office there was much, much drama about my accident. Beth told me to sit down after I told her why I was late, and she brought me a cup of coffee with so much sugar and cream that it tasted like syrup, or medicine—thick and sickening, I couldn't drink it—and then she proceeded to inform everyone. "Sherry hit a deer on the freeway!"

Condolences, commiseration, and, all the time, I was in my silk dress, shivering—not from cold, it was warm enough in the office, but still from the surprise of it. The solidity of it, that animal, and then the blood cascading over my white Honda, a ghastly rain of it on the windshield. When I parked my car in the college parking lot, it was still bloody, the windshield, and I couldn't stand to go around to the front of it, to see if there were any remains of that deer on my bumper, on the hood.

So many people, it turned out, had hit a deer—so many stories swapped in the office—that it began to seem surprising there were any left for me to have killed. Robert Z hit *two* a year ago, a doe and her fawn. (They'd leaped out of nowhere in a snowstorm as he was driving home to visit his parents in Wisconsin for Christmas. Only the fawn had been killed. The doe had glanced off of him, and she'd kept going.) Beth's uncle had careened into a whole herd of them up north in a fog, totaled his car but been given permission by the state police to take one home for the meat.

And there were worse stories. Someone's neighbor had been killed, swerved to avoid a deer on a country road, hit a tree instead, and died instantly. Someone's cousin had been killed when the deer he hit crashed through his windshield, landing in the car with him, crushing him—landing, it had seemed to the paramedics on the scene, into the cousin's *arms*.

"Your commute is too long," Amanda Stefanski said. "Have you thought about moving into the city?"

Amanda is the newest teacher in the department—a short, plain woman in her twenties. She has a warm heart, is always ready with solutions to problems, considered advice. Every Christmas she puts in our mailboxes homemade cards signed with x's and o's, telling us to love Jesus, to celebrate His birthday. Once, Sue suggested we try to fix her up with Robert Z "if we can find out he's not gay." No, I said, she was too homely. She wouldn't be Robert Z's type, even if he wasn't gay. Amanda's hair was dishwater blond, the bangs trimmed raggedly and too short across her forehead. Her jaw was large, strong as a man's, although her eyes were large and blue and her shoulders were delicate.

Sue had narrowed her eyes at me when I said she was too homely, and I said, "I mean, she's lovely, truly lovely, but—"

"Okay," Sue said. "Not lovely enough for *your* Robert."

"He's not *mine*," I said. "This has nothing to do with me. I just wouldn't want to see Amanda get hurt. I mean, Robert's—"

"Maybe Robert's not as picky as you are."

"Fine," I said. "I'm sure you're right. Set them up, Sue."

But eventually Sue must have begun to see the fact of this herself because she never brought the subject up again with me, and as far as I know she never tried to arrange anything between the two of them.

Amanda leaned down and embraced me. She smelled like Windsong, or Charlie, some kind of inexpensive but pleasant drugstore perfume. "Really, Sherry," she said, "you need to move. It was one thing to live out there when it was the country. There's too much traffic now."

"Thank you, Amanda," I said. "But, really, the deer had nothing to do with the traffic. It—" But Amanda had her eyes closed tightly, as if she were praying or trying to block out what I was saying. I said, "Well, maybe we will. I mean, Jon won't move, not yet, but I might rent a place for Monday and Wednesday nights. We'd already talked about it, before this."

Jon.

I hadn't thought, yet, to call him.

He would be hurt, I supposed, if he knew that he was the last to know—although it was over now, and what could he do? And I hadn't been injured. The car was drivable. When I got off the freeway I'd stopped at a gas station and called the police to report it. A deep-voiced woman had taken my statement—the location, my license plate number over the phone—and she said she was sorry but that these things happened all the time, as if she thought I had called to complain.

Anyway, there was nothing Jon could do, and I had to teach. I was already late. When I stood up to go, Robert Z said, "Now be careful in the hallway, sweetheart." He came over to me and squeezed my elbow. "Walk slowly."

I saw it, again, on the drive home:

A tan twisted body, looking half human, half animal, in the median, sprawled.

The knees were bent as if it were running, still, in its sleep. In its death.

I slowed down. I felt I should. Out of respect, or to really *see* it.

I looked closely and saw that it was a doe, no antlers.

It was dusk, but I could see her clearly, even her face, and that the eyes were wide open—and the awfulness of it struck me then, that here was a thing I'd killed. Some escaped, transfigured daughter of a goddess—the ghost of a younger woman trying to escape from something or someone just behind her, giving chase.

Where had she thought she was going? Was she trying to get back to the dark of the woods on the other side of the free-way, wondering how she'd come to this wrong road, and where to go—but blindly, led by scent and a dull drumming in her ears?

Jesus, I said under my breath. *Oh my god, forgive me.*

But would the gods blame me for this? Or forgive me for this? Or would there be some special punishment in hell for the woman who'd killed this beautiful animal, this divine creature, whether it had been an accident or not?

Maybe an elliptical machine in hell.

An endless aerobic dance in bare feet on a burning floor.

I was holding the steering wheel so tightly that I couldn't feel my fingers anymore, and then I was home, in my own driveway, and Jon came to the door and said, "Hey. I hear through the grapevine that we're going to be having venison for dinner tonight."

————

I'D FORGOTTEN to call him long enough that it had begun to seem pointless to call him. I'd see him soon enough when I got home, I thought, and show him the mangled bumper, tell him I was getting it fixed tomorrow, that Garrett had set it up.

In the hallway after class, I'd run into Garrett and told him what had happened.

"Wow, Mrs. Seymour. That could've been bad. You're really lucky. What happened to your car?"

I told him about the bumper, and he looked concerned—an expert, calculating the trouble—and offered to take a look. So I got my coat and led him out to the car, which was, despite the snow falling steadily all day, still a gruesome sight. The blood on the windshield had gotten sticky, thickened, but it still looked like blood, and there were dark streaks of it down the white side of the car, down the hood.

Garrett hadn't worn his coat, and as he knelt at my bumper in his thin shirt I remembered watching him in his Cub Scout uniform outside in the winter during a pack meeting, shivering but refusing to come in, to put on his jacket.

Kneeling at my bumper, Garrett didn't shiver, although his shirt was rippled by the cold wind around his shoulders in a way that made *me* shiver.

"This can be straightened without much trouble," Garrett said, looking up at me. "We need some tools. Do you have time to bring it over to the garage?" He nodded in the direction of the auto-mechanics building.

"Not today," I said. "Tomorrow?"

"Sure," Garrett said. "It's not going to hurt to drive it. But you'll want to get a car wash."

We laughed together at that—the blood on the hood of my car, what would that look like to someone driving by me on the freeway?

While we stood outside, snowflakes accumulated in Garrett's short, dark hair. I remembered snowflakes like that in Chad's hair, bending over him, brushing them off his head with my glove— the starry hundreds of them, scattered, and that first winter of his life, zipping him into his insulated snowsuit. All one piece. How blunt he was in my arms as I carried him from the car to the house, the house to the car. A bundle. A package. Looking at Garrett's hair full of snow, I felt a stab of such deep longing for Chad—a physical ache—that I had to look away. Where was Chad now?

Somewhere else.

Somewhere no snow fell.

Garrett went back to work on my bumper, and I watched him, and it felt to me, standing bereft and useless in the snow as he picked blond fur out of my grille and tossed it to the curb, as if Chad had been erased from the earth. As if there was nothing left to him but the memories of him. Imagining him in Berkeley was no easier or less fanciful than imagining him in heaven. "Garrett," I finally said, snapping myself out of my imaginary grief. "You'll catch pneumonia. Let's go in, and I'll buy you a cup of cocoa."

"I'm not cold," Garrett said. (They always said that, these boys. *I'm not cold, I'm not tired, my hands aren't dirty, I don't need a hat.*) "But, well, okay."

The cafeteria seemed stiflingly hot when we came in from the cold and sat down at a table together. Garrett got a cup of coffee, not cocoa, and I got a bottle of water, because I was thirsty, sweating in my coat, even in my silk dress.

We chatted about the cold, about classes, about deer and freeways and traffic. I felt lighter than I had for days, maybe even weeks. Such pleasant company. Such a polite, easy young man. We conversed effortlessly—not like mother and son, or student and teacher, but like friends. Old friends. He seemed genuinely relieved and astonished by my good luck, hitting a deer on the freeway and only having a bent bumper to show for it. He leaned back in his chair and said, "That must have been something, hitting an animal that big, that fast, in all that traffic." He slammed his fists together. "Lord, Mrs. Seymour, that could've caused a chain reaction. You were lucky you didn't see it coming, or you might have hit the brakes, the guy behind you would have hit you. Wow."

"I did hit the brakes," I said. "I think."

"Maybe not," Garrett said. "I think you didn't."

In only half an hour, Garrett had become the expert, the arbiter, of my accident. He shook his head as if to clear it, then talked about Hondas, the newer models, the steel frames, that I was lucky there, too. He compared my car to other makes and models. He sipped his coffee (black) from the Styrofoam cup, and I couldn't help but think to myself that what he was doing was a perfect impression of a man. Garrett (hands full of LEGOs and Matchbox cars, or standing on the back porch waiting for me to unzip Chad's coat so I could unzip his, too) pretending, so convincingly, that he was a man.

"Okay, Mrs. Seymour," he said, looking at his watch. "You'll bring the car by tomorrow?"

"Yes," I said. "In the afternoon?"

"Great," he said. "Just over to the automotive entrance. I'll tell Bram."

"Oh," I said. "Bram."

I put the top back on my bottled water and looked at it. AQUA-PURA. On the label, a little stream poured whitely down the side of a lush green mountain.

"We can't do any work on anybody's cars without our instructor's permission."

"Will he be there?"

Garrett smiled and put his empty Styrofoam cup down too hard on the table. It tipped over, but nothing spilled. "He might be," Garrett said. "Maybe I'll get extra points for bringing you over. Have you gotten any more notes?" he asked.

"I did," I told him, "get another note."

I looked down at the table and saw a smudged reflection of myself in the Formica—a younger woman, a college girl, without lines or details, talking about love notes and crushes with a friend—and then I looked back up at Garrett, and saw that he'd lifted his eyebrows, and suddenly we were both laughing. He was teasing me, the way Sue would have teased me, or Jon, or Chad. "Garrett," I asked, "do you have any real reason to think that Bram Smith is writing these notes?"

"Well, yeah. He talked about you again the other day," Garrett said, nodding. "This English department babe, and on and on," he said and made a hand gesture that indicated wheels turning, rolling into infinity. "I don't want to embarrass you, Mrs. Seymour, by saying much more."

"Isn't this Bram Smith married? Is something wrong with him? Why is he so interested in old English teachers?" I looked again at the label on my Aqua-Pura, projecting myself into the mountain scene. I was meandering along the stream. I was stopping to dip my hand into the chill waters.

"Mrs. Seymour, you're not old!" Garrett said it with such sincerity that I looked up. And there it was in his blue eyes—the little boy I'd asked not to smash his toy trucks into the legs of my furniture. Wide-eyed. Worried. A newcomer to this world.

"Thank you, Garrett," I said. "But I'm a lot older than your automotive instructor."

"Well, what can I say? He's got great taste in women?"

I blushed. I could feel it, mottled on my neck, and the heat of it in my cheeks. I felt like a little girl again, turning scarlet in the back of the school bus when a boy I liked said I was pretty. Garrett was standing up, pushing his chair into the table, smiling down at me, humoring me sweetly, sincerely, with tremendous kindness, and I thought of my father then, the way the nurses called out to him in the hallway, and how grateful and content he seemed—the child, among the children who had somehow become the adults.

"Who told you?" I asked Jon as he took my coat from me—graciously, gently, like a solicitor, or a parent.

"Chad did. He called."

"What?"

I could smell meat burning in the kitchen. Was Jon making dinner? How long since *that* had happened?

"How in the world did *Chad* know I hit a deer?"

"Garrett e-mailed him."

"Oh," I said. E-mail. I'd forgotten about it, forgotten that Chad spent hours every day now checking messages, sending messages. I'd forgotten that the world had shrunk to this, that he and Garrett didn't need pens or phones to talk to one another anymore.

"And, Sherry, neither Chad or I is too thrilled to be getting this vital information about our wife and mother from an outsider."

I said, "I'm sorry. I had to teach, and then I forgot, and—"

"It's okay," Jon said. "I'm just glad you're all right."

He pulled me to him. I put my face into his chest, into his T-shirt, then pressed my ear just above his heart and listened to the steady humid thump of it.

"I guess you need to get a place in the city after all, to cut down on the commuting, Sherry. That's fine with me, a couple nights a week, if that's what you want to do, honey. I'm sorry I didn't insist on it before."

He pulled back and looked into my face.

"Besides, it'll be a good place for you to rendezvous with your lover."

He was smiling. He moved his hand up to my neck, then down to my chest, unbuttoned the top button of my dress, and slid his hand to my breast.

BY THE time we were done making love, the roast Jon had tossed in the oven to surprise me with—at a hundred degrees higher than it ought to have been because he hadn't bothered to put on his glasses when he turned the temperature dial—had blackened and shrunk down to the size of a fist.

We'd been lying on the bed, Jon still on top of me, when the smoke detector went off, and we had run down together, naked, laughing, to turn the oven off, open the windows, waving our arms around in front of our faces to clear the air. Then, when he'd pulled the roast out and thrown the ruined thing into the garbage, we realized we were hungry and the only thing there'd been in the refrigerator to eat was wrecked.

"Let's go out," Jon said.

"But it's so late," I said.

Jon looked at his watch, the only thing he was wearing. "Since when," he asked, "is 9:30 too late to go out?"

He was right, of course. Since when *was* 9:30 too late to go out?

But I knew since when—since eighteen years ago, when Chad had to be nursed and put to bed by eight o'clock.

How was it, I thought, that such a brief period of time—that year of his infancy—had caused us to form habits that had lasted this long? I remembered Jon joking on the phone with his sister, leaving a message on her machine the day we brought Chad home from the hospital:

"Hey, Brenda, we had that baby we were talking about. If you want more details, give us a call. We'll be home now for about the next eighteen years."

It had been a joke that had taken on a life.

"Get dressed," Jon said. "We're going to Stiver's."

Stiver's, a truckers' bar down the road. Hamburgers. Beer. Karaoke. I'd never been there, but it sounded to me like the right thing to do. I said, "I'll take a shower first."

Jon said, "To hell with that. Just put on your sexy new dress."

WAS STIVER'S like anything I'd imagined it would be, all those years passing it on the way to the freeway?

By the time Jon and I had stepped inside, I'd forgotten whatever those years of accumulated impressions had been. Driving by it, I'd always marveled that there were people in a bar at six o'clock on a Tuesday night, at two o'clock on a Wednesday afternoon. Driving by it with my child strapped into his car seat behind me, or on my way to pick him up from school—hurrying, *flying,* off the freeway, I'd glance at it and marvel:

People with nothing to do on a Thursday afternoon but drink beer in a dumpy bar.

No children waiting for them. No dinner to be made. No homework to help with.

Did I feel sorry for them, or did I envy them?

Stepping into Stiver's with Jon for the first time, I could no longer remember what I'd felt about the place and its patrons then—only the vague impression of a kind of vast expanse of exemption from motherly duties going on in there. Deserts, prairies, contained inside its badly sided exterior. KAREOKE NIGHT misspelled on the rollaway board at the door.

It must have been someone's house at one time — a double-wide trailer. There was a window box under the one big, blacked-out window that faced the road (nothing in it but cigarette butts) and a screen door with no screen in it. I'd known it would be crowded inside because there were so many cars in the parking lot (Jon had to circle it several times before deciding just to park at the edge of the lot, in the dirt) but still I was surprised by the crowd, the closeness, and it seemed to me that every person in that room turned to look at us as we walked in, emerging from the cold outside into the smoke and dimness of the bar, and continued to watch us as we made our way to a table crammed into a corner.

The music was deafening, all-encompassing. I couldn't see where it was coming from, but a wildly out-of-tune voice, a woman's, was wailing a country song. Jon shouted over it, "I'll go to the bar and order," after pulling out my chair for me to sit.

While he was gone, I looked around. Over at the bar, two men (in their fifties?) — one in a cowboy hat and one in a cap — had turned all the way around in their chairs, beer bottles in their fists, to look at me. They smiled and nodded. I smiled back, then looked away. When I glanced back at them, they were simply staring. They turned around when Jon came back to the table with two beers.

"All they had was Old Milwaukee," he shouted over the music. "I ordered us two burgers." He shrugged. "We'll see."

The singer had changed. Now, a man was bellowing "Blue Eyes Crying in the Rain." Over Jon's shoulder I could see the heads and shoulders of dancers on the little dance floor, moving in time to the man's bellowing. Jon reached over and squeezed my hand. "Having fun yet?" he shouted.

Was I?

Yes, I was.

The beer tasted metallic on my teeth. It reminded me of high school, drinking cheap beer in my boyfriend's basement while his parents slept upstairs, directly over our heads. There was always a swirl of steam that rose when one of those cans or bottles was opened, and it always made me think of genies, spirits, smelling of skunk, yeast—a spirit that never rose from a bottle of good wine or when the seal was broken on a bottle of expensive cognac.

How long had it been since I'd drunk a bottle of cheap beer?

Jon laughed when he saw I'd finished it already, and got up to get me another.

I watched the dancers.

One woman, in a silvery tank top, was moving so sensually—grinding, slinking, against her dance partner—that it was impossible not to watch. Another couple danced stiffly, not looking at each other, as if they were having an argument while dancing. Two women in their twenties danced together as their boyfriends watched from the bar.

"Excuse me, miss?"

It startled me to look up and find the man in the cowboy hat standing over me.

"If your date wouldn't mind," he shouted down, "would you like to dance?"

I looked from the man back to the dance floor. I looked over my shoulder and saw Jon's back at the bar, then turned to the man again and said, "Sure. He wouldn't mind."

An icy rain had fallen outside while we were inside Stiver's.

They never brought us our hamburgers.

Instead, we drank four beers each, and by the time we left I'd danced with the trucker and his friend through seven or eight songs — several slow ones, in their arms.

The one in the cowboy hat, whose name was Nathan, was a huge, lumbering dancer. I felt like a child in his embrace. He smelled like my father — smoke and aftershave — but under his khaki jacket, he had on a tight T-shirt, and his muscles were surprisingly solid. He was a strong man. And I was right, he was a trucker. He was from Iowa, on his way to Maine with a load of something. He had no idea what it was, and didn't particularly want to know, he said.

But the other one danced as if he, like I, had taken lessons all through childhood. It was studied dancing — although, unlike me, he had a natural affinity for it.

He was graceful. He could hear the music, it seemed, in his limbs. I felt awkward at first, dancing with him. He rocked on his heels and watched me for a while, waiting for me to begin a rhythm, or a style, and at first I wanted to turn, go back to the table, ask Jon to take me home.

But then I saw the appreciative look he had on his face, watching me dance (was I good at this?) and at my body, and I couldn't help it, I slipped out of my self-consciousness like a sheath, and then, as if we were having a conversation, he began to dance in response, his body close to mine, brushing up against me. At one point I felt the back of his hand brush against my breasts. Surely, I thought, it was an accident, but my whole body responded to it — and then a slow dance started up, and without asking me, he took me by the waist, his hands pressing into the small of my back, and my face pressed into his shoulder.

The man singing the lyrics to the country song was belting them out with such passion I felt the intensity of it move down my neck, down my spine, to the place where this trucker, whose name I never learned, had his hands.

His face was next to my ear, and I could hear him breathing.

It was like making love in public, with a stranger, and every once in a while we turned so I could see Jon over his shoulder — and Jon was staring, sipping his beer, leaning back in his chair, watching me in the arms of another man in front of him with a look on his face I'd never quite seen before — as if he were a stranger, watching strangers, but also as if he were a part of it, as if he could feel that trucker's hands on my hips, his body hot and moving against mine.

This one smelled plainly of sweat.

He was younger than Nathan.

He didn't want to talk about where he was going, where he was from. When the song ended he moved his hands up and down my back, looked into my face as if he were considering kissing me, then thought better of it and said, "Thanks, beautiful," before leaving me standing on the dance floor, trying to regain my bearings, to find my way back to Jon.

In the parking lot, Jon said nothing.

He unlocked the passenger side of the car for me, and when I got in, he reached down and pushed the hem of my dress up over my knee, leaned over, caressed my calf, looking into my eyes in the vapor light attached to the eaves trough of Stiver's. He slid his hand up, then, to my thigh, and said, "You've been naughty," in a mock-serious tone — then put his hand fully between my legs, and for the first time I realized, myself, how warm and wet I was, and he said, "When we get home, I'm going to fuck you hard for this."

I could hardly catch my breath. When we got home, my knees were so weak he had to help me out of the car.

———

"WHAT the hell is going on? Where the hell are you?"

"What's going *on*? I've been waiting by the phone all night. When you get this message call me *right away*."

"Jesus Christ, I have to get news about my own mother now from *Garrett Thompson*? Should I call *Garrett* to find out where the hell my mother is?"

"You can call me, you know. It's three hours earlier here. I haven't gone to beddy-bye yet. I'm waiting to find out what the hell is going on there."

It wasn't until we were done in bed (Jon hadn't pulled out of me before he started again) that I saw the message light on the answering machine blinking with seven messages from Chad.

I was, I guess, too drunk to remember his phone number. I had to look for it on the caller ID, and then I misdialed and a groggy-sounding woman answered, then hung up on me when I said I thought I had the wrong number.

Chad answered the phone on the first ring, sounding wide awake and furious. I thought his voice was shaking—a tremor he'd always had, even as a two-year-old, when he was angry or upset, and which made him sound as if he were speaking from the caboose of a train rattling across uneven tracks. "Gee, thanks for calling, Mom," he said.

"I'm sorry, Chad. Your dad and I went out—"

"Until two o'clock in the morning? On a school night?"

I couldn't help it. I laughed.

"So, it's funny, Mom? That I've been sitting around my dorm room all night, worried sick?"

"No, I guess. It's just . . ." I was afraid to go on. I was afraid he'd be able to tell that I was drunk.

"So why don't you tell me what happened."

"What do you mean?" For a crazy second I thought he meant at Stiver's, with the truckers.

"What do I mean? I mean Garrett says you hit a deer on the freeway, Mom. Are you *okay*?"

"Yes, Chad, of course I'm okay. Just the bumper's bent. Everything else is fine." I paused. "Except the deer."

"Jesus," Chad said. "People *die* that way. You guys need to move into the city. This commute is dangerous. Let me talk to Dad."

Jon was in the shower. I could hear the water running. He was singing, too, something operatic and ridiculous. Soon, he'd fall into a deep sleep.

"He's already in bed," I told Chad. "I'll tell him to call you tomorrow."

"Good," Chad said. "Now you'd better go to bed yourself. Did you go to the doctor? Did you make sure—"

"Nothing's wrong," I said.

"You don't know that, Mom. Sometimes people have skeletal or internal injuries without any immediate symptoms. Did you hit your head?"

"No, Chad," I said. "I hit a deer." I couldn't help it. I started to laugh again. I *was* drunk.

"Real funny, Mom," Chad said. "This is all real funny. Just go to bed, and tell Dad to call me in the morning. And thanks for getting back to me in such a timely manner."

He hung up.

A HANGOVER this morning. And, from sex, the exertion of it, my stomach muscles ache. I'm sore between my legs. A stinging burn just under the skin of my inner thighs. All these familiar, nearly forgotten, vague pains of passion.

"I want you to find out who this secret admirer is," Jon said last night, turning me over, looking into my face as he entered me, "and fuck him."

"Okay," I whispered.

"I want you to let him do anything he wants to you," he said.

"Okay."

"I want you to fuck another man."

Jon's eyes were narrowed, and the look on his face was more intense than any expression I'd seen there for years. My heart sped up, seeing it, as if I'd caught a glimpse of an animal at the zoo, outside its cage, or a man sauntering into the bank with a gun. *Anything could happen here, now,* I thought, and I was as excited as I was afraid to find myself in this ordinary place suddenly lit up with so much extraordinary potential.

"Do you understand?" he asked, putting his hands on my shoulders, his face on my neck, slamming into me.

Yes, I said, arching my back to meet him.

It wasn't until after we were done, after I'd gone downstairs, called Chad, hung up the phone, and gone back upstairs to find Jon out of the shower and already asleep, naked, on his back in our bed, that I wondered how serious he had been—or, if he was serious at all.

That expression on his face—it had *seemed* serious.

But that was sex.

That was the moment, that was the fantasy. Surely, he wasn't serious. We'd never even come close, in the past, to acting out any of our fantasies—even when we were young, and childless, and only marginally employed, with so much less to lose, and so much more time on our hands. And that one time—with Ferris— when it had seemed that I might stray, Jon had reacted, in the end, with anything but pleasure. Those many years ago, when I'd told him about Ferris's profession of love, and the kiss (how innocent now, it seemed, that furtive parking lot kiss) and my own confusion, before Jon's tearful pleading (*You can't ruin our family, Sherry. You can't do it, to me, to Chad. Please, tell me you won't do it, that you'll just turn around now and come back*), he'd been furious. He'd picked up a bedside lamp and, holding it by the neck, had shaken it at me.

I'd been in bed, in a nightgown, holding a book (*Mrs. Dalloway*) so tightly in my hands that the pages held the indentations of my fingers forever. He was standing over me, and I suddenly realized how vulnerable I was—how easily my bones would break, my skull, if he wanted them to, or even (maybe especially) if he *didn't* want them to, but lost all control of himself, all notion of what it was he wanted.

What was my body made of, anyway, after all, I thought then, but so much tissue, and blood? I would rip open, like a pillow. I would crack to pieces, like an egg—and, still, stubbornly, absurdly, I was thinking about Ferris, the pencil behind his ear, pushing an overhead projector through the hallway, looking tired and intelligent and overwarm in his button-down shirt, telling me he was in love, for the first time in his life, and too late (two kids, a pregnant wife) with me.

Go ahead and kill me, I'd thought, looking at Jon with the lamp in his hand over me, raging.

But he put it back down on the nightstand and walked away.

No, I thought.

My husband did not really want me to fuck another man.

Even if he thought he did, holding my shoulders as he said it—*I want you to fuck another man*—he was wrong.

Surely, if my secret admirer revealed himself, Jon would feel jealous, threatened. The titillation was in the possibility, not the act itself, I felt sure.

And what about me?

Had I ever really wanted a lover?

Until now, no. I was sure of that. Not even Ferris. I could still remember the relief that washed over me along with the fluorescent light when he told me in a corner of my classroom after the students were gone that he'd taken a job in Missouri, the way my whole life seemed opened up to the possibility then of being the woman I'd wanted to be — the farmhouse, the child, the car that started on the first try — forever.

But Chad had been a toddler then. I was so much younger. Now, I'd already been that woman. Now, I was free to be someone else if I wanted to be. Now, did I want a lover?

In the dark, beside Jon, in our bed, I thought about that for a long time, without any idea of what the answer would be. Trying to look for the answer to that question in my own mind was like finding myself suddenly inside an echoing tunnel:

Do I want a lover? Do I want a lover to want me? Do I want Jon to want me to have a lover? Do I want Jon to want me to want a lover?

I couldn't even decide on a question long enough to decide on an answer.

Finally, I fell asleep.

And woke up like this — blinking in the wan morning light, too hungover to go to work. All these dull aches — the stomach, the thighs, the skin. My lips, parched. My eyes, stinging. Thirsty. A warm throbbing just behind my cheekbones.

Cheap beer.

I called in to cancel my office hours.

I showered, drank three glasses of orange juice, made a grocery list:

Milk, linguine, bread, cereal, orange juice — and a hundred other little things written out shakily on the back of an empty envelope (spring dress, department store credit card bill opened and paid several days ago) addressed to a Ms. Sherry Seymour—a woman I could not imagine would have woken up on a Wednesday morning with a hangover after dancing all night at Stiver's with two truckers, but a woman who, I realized after staring at that name long enough, I also was.

AFTER the shopping, I put the groceries away and lay down for a cool, dry, but delicious nap.

It was a gray morning again—a misty rain on the way to the supermarket, but the sun had been attempting, at least, to burn its way through the clouds.

This, I thought, opening the car window just an inch to smell the air, *will be the last real winter day.*

Spring—I could feel it there, at the edges of the world, or waiting, impatiently now, beneath all the layers and layers of winter that had been so painstakingly laid down. I thought of the bulbs in the garden—how they'd be stretching, pushing, triggered by the change. Soon, they'd writhe to the surface and stab into the world again. And the birds would be back with their songs. The baby bunnies. The frogs trilling in the Henslins' pond.

On the bed, there was a pool of that cool, new, white light.

When I lay down for my nap, I didn't bother to close the curtains.

I lay at the center of that light and fell asleep.

Dreamless.

During that brief nap, a century might have ended and begun. Many winters passed, bookended by mild and rainless seasons. I slept through them all. I doubt I even rolled over once. I imagine my eyelids never even fluttered. In that envelope of unconsciousness and time, I was no one. I was nowhere. I was completely free of everything I'd ever been, or done, or thought, or said—and when the phone rang, and I woke up quickly, blinking, I felt completely renewed. Born again. Fresh out of the nest, or out of the ground. Ready for the world. I knew exactly who I was, and what I wanted. I stretched. The pains were gone. I yawned. I let the machine—with its hours and hours of empty memory waiting to be filled, and all its little wheels and pulleys sucking the sounds of the world into it bloodlessly and without judgment—get the phone.

It was Garrett.

I sat up in bed so I could hear his message better.

"Hey, Mrs. Seymour, this is Garrett. We were kind of expecting you to bring the car in today, but you're not here. Are you still planning on it? Can you give us a call? Bram says any time this afternoon is fine. There are plenty of guys here to look her over."

Did I imagine it, or was there a bit of low, dark laughter in the background as Garrett hung up the phone?

It could have been just the sound of an engine starting up.

Or a crow flying over.

Or, it could have been Bram Smith laughing in the background.

Bram Smith—still an imaginary character with muscular arms, wearing a T-shirt, jeans, maybe even smoking a cigarette like a man straight out of my adolescent summer dreams—which, until that moment I'd almost forgotten completely but now came rushing back to me with all the sexual intensity of a summer afternoon—lying on my back on my bed in my childhood home, a cacophony of birdsong outside the open window, and my whole life ahead of me, made, still, of fantasy, of television light, silk, as if millions of worms somewhere were busily at work spinning that future for me.

I WORE sheer gray hose, my taupe suede skirt, a pink blouse, a strand of pearls, and a fingerprint of Chanel No. 5 on each wrist, and drove my car straight to him.

Two

Suddenly, spring.

I knew it had come the morning I drove past that doe, as I always did, on the freeway, and a shining black turkey vulture was hunched over her.

At first, driving by, seeing that vulture on top of her, it appeared to me, horribly, as if she'd somehow grown huge dark wings and was trying to fly. But then I saw its red face and knew it for a buzzard, and that spring had finally come. They're the first, surest sign of spring, those buzzards. Their return means that the roadkill has thawed, that there's enough soft death around, again, to keep them alive.

First, the buzzards, then the other birds came back, all of them at once. Robins hopping across the muddy grass like windup birds, toy birds. Then, wide *V*s of geese honking across the sky every evening at dusk. Then sandhill cranes, looking prehistoric and awkward in the fields, nodding slowly, seeming to be searching the ground for something they'd lost. And the others—I had no idea what they were called, where they'd gone, only that they had traveled thousands of miles to leave us here all winter, and now they were back.

And there were shadows again!

The telephone poles had them—long crosses laid down on the road. Then, trees, still leafless, cast gnarled shadows against the sides of the house. Even *I* cast a shadow—a long gray dress before me in the morning, and then a darkness dragged behind me at twilight—as if my body had been ironed down to this featureless impression, this afterthought.

For a hundred and twenty dollars a week, I found an efficiency apartment in a complex called the Rose Gardens, right across from the college, where I could sleep on Monday and Wednesday nights. I brought a coffeemaker and two cups, two dishes, two bowls, two spoons, two forks, two knives, and a couple of towels. It was already furnished with a small, round kitchen table and two chairs. Jon hauled a futon in for me—just a mattress, I didn't need a platform, it was firm enough on the floor—and struggled to get it into place.

It was as comfortable, really, as the two-thousand-dollar state-of-the-art Posturepedic Jon and I slept on at home.

BRAM Smith looked only vaguely as I'd imagined him. He was a fantasy, certainly, but a slightly altered version of the one I'd had. When I pulled my car into the garage at the Automotive Instructional Building, I knew right away which of the men (milling around with tools in their hands, bright pieces of painted metal, crowbars, chrome) was Bram. I'd seen him *hundreds* of times, as it happened—at faculty meetings, in the cafeteria, in the library, in the bookstore.

He *was* dark-eyed and muscular, with black hair, but he was smaller and smarter-looking than I'd imagined, a kind of studious version of my adolescent fantasy. Instead of six feet tall, he was only a couple of inches taller than I was, and despite being solid with muscle, he was too slender—elegant, even—to be physically imposing.

When I'd glimpsed him, before, around campus, I'd mistaken him for a mechanical-drawing instructor, or a computer programmer. Handsome, certainly, but not the kind of man I'd imagined with his hands deep at work inside an engine all day, or writing passionate secret love notes to English teachers.

Still, when I saw him there—then, I knew:

Of course.

You are my lover.

And as if he'd been expecting me, he smiled when I drove in. "You're here," he said when I unrolled my window. "Our deer slayer."

I parted my lips to speak, but said nothing. All I could do was stare.

He had perfectly straight, white teeth, and eyes so deep that it was startling, almost too much, to look into them. You could slip, looking into those eyes. The strong jaw, the neatly trimmed beard and mustache—that was what I'd invented for him in my imagination—but the graceful hands, long-fingered and clean, were entirely his own.

He was wearing a gold watch. At the collar of his black T-shirt I thought I saw a glint of gold chain. There was one insistent dimple to the right of his smile.

"Pull it up, Mrs. Seymour. Let's straighten 'er out."

Later that afternoon—after the fender had been removed, remolded, replaced, and the last blond bristles cleaned from it, after there'd been jokes from the guys about venison sausage and whether I'd had to speed up to hit it, or slow down, and about waiting until the season started before I went out hunting again—I went to my mailbox and found what I'd fully expected there, this time from someone whose reality I believed in, could have reached out and touched, whose arms I could have found myself in simply by turning around, by walking directly into them.

You are so beautiful I'd do anything to make you mine.

I had to lean against the mailbox, a weakness beginning in my ankles, traveling up my spine.

I slipped the note in my bag.

I went to my office, picked up the phone, asked the college operator to connect me with Bram Smith's voice mail, on which I left a message of my own:

"Thank you—" I had to inhale, out of breath, and my voice was shaking. "I'd like to buy you a cup of coffee. Whenever you're available. To thank you."

A desperate afterthought, I left my office phone number for him to call.

THEN, it was the weekend. Sue came over with the twins on Saturday. I hadn't seen her since the afternoon in my office when I'd told her that Bram Smith was the author of those notes. She hadn't even called, and I'd been too preoccupied to remember to call her. But, over our years of friendship, we'd passed many weeks like that, even a few months. Our lives got busy, or there was some vague conflict neither of us wanted to confront, some unspoken disagreement that only a little time apart could resolve. A few calls, a couple of cups of coffee later, everything was back to the way it had been.

The twins seemed taller and wilder than they had when I'd last seen them two months before at Chuck E. Cheese's for their ninth birthday. "Hi, Aunt Sherry," they said in unison, and then went straight from Sue's car to the scrubbrush out back. One of them picked up a stick and charged after the other one, hooting.

Sue was wearing sweatpants and a T-shirt that said MICHIGAN STATE UNIVERSITY on it, a college with which Sue had no affiliation. Like Chad, she'd gone to Berkeley. The entirety of the Midwest had been completely unknown to her when she'd been in college. ("I couldn't have found this place on the map when I was twenty years old," she said whenever the subject of her origins came up, "and now I've been here longer than I've ever been anywhere. Life is strange.")

Jon came to the door to say hello, patting Sue lightly on the back in greeting, and then he said he was going to the hardware store. "I'll get out so you ladies can bitch about your husbands."

"Thank you," I said, joking.

Sue smiled vaguely and headed toward the kitchen.

"Good lord," he said when we were out of Sue's hearing range. "She looks terrible. I mean, *terrible.*"

"The kids are tiring," I said. We could hear genuine screaming out back now—a high jarring war whoop. Kujo had wandered over from the Henslins', and one of the twins had his face buried in the mangy dog's neck.

"See," I said, pointing at the other one, who was whacking his long stick against the trunk of a tree. He was the one doing the screaming. "You'd look tired, too."

But, cruelly, and shallowly, I was happy he'd noticed. Another woman, my age, falling apart physically was like a bitter little compliment to me for having managed to keep myself from doing the same. When we were younger, I had always considered Sue to be the beautiful one. California blond. Those high cheekbones. When we were out in the world together, men seemed equally drawn to both of us, but she was always the one who got their attention in the first place. That long blond hair.

"Well, how does having rambunctious twins pack on sixty pounds?" Jon asked. "Jesus."

"I don't know, Jon. It's hard to stay thin. And it's not sixty pounds."

"Okay, *fifty* pounds. Well thank god my woman stayed slim," he said, and stepped out the door, patting my butt as he went.

I cleared my throat and said, loudly enough for Sue to hear so she wouldn't know we'd been whispering about her, "Get some C batteries for the flashlight, will you? I'll need it for the efficiency, okay?"

"Scared of the dark without me?"

"Well, that, and something's stuck in the garbage disposal, and I wanted to get a closer look."

We kissed over the threshold. Jon put his hand affectionately on my neck and looked into my eyes.

"I love you," I said.

He said, "I love you, too."

AT THE kitchen table, Sue had spread out something olive green and in many pieces on the place mat. "LEGO tank," she said when I looked over her shoulder. "I promised them I'd get it put together if they'd play outside without arguing for an hour."

But it looked impossible — like something so far from being, from *ever having been,* a tank that no amount of time could put it together. And Sue's hands — the fingernails vaguely blue, the fingers looking swollen — did not appear up to the job at all. Looking at the pieces on my table, it seemed long ago, another lifetime, that I'd last assembled anything made of plastic, or stepped on those fragments in my bare feet in the middle of the night in Chad's room — sneaking in to pull a blanket over his shoulders or to turn off the tape recorder in his room, playing lullabies or Mozart. What came to me, thinking of that, was the sad physical sense of something having been removed from my body, a whiff in the air of Chad's little-boy hair, and also—and this was new—a sense of relief, as if a cool breeze had come through a window and blown the clutter neatly into the drawers and closets where it belonged.

I poured tea for Sue, put a plate of cookies between us— Pepperidge Farm, chocolate chip. She took one right away, held it in front of her, but didn't bring it to her lips until she'd rolled her eyes and said, "I wasn't going to eat cookies this year. Thanks, Sherry." And then she bit into it.

For just a second, I considered putting the cookies away.

Would a better friend have done that? Would a better friend have acknowledged that, yes, there had been some weight gain, that it wasn't healthy, that the cookies, anyway, had just been placed there for the twins, or out of politeness? Should I have offered her an apple, instead? Or was it right to say, as I did, "Oh, you deserve it, Sue. You look great." What would Sue have done?

She would have been, I thought, honest with me.

When I got my first real adult haircut—when the long wild layers had begun to look outdated, and ill-suited, or so I thought, to a thirty-two-year-old mother from the suburbs—Sue had taken a step back, in shock (and horror?), when she saw me step into Starbucks.

"Oh my god," she'd said. "Sherry, that's so awful."

"Great. Thanks," I'd said, my eyes filling with tears so that Sue looked, to me, as if she were on the other side of a shower door rather than only a few feet away from me, holding a huge cup of cappuccino in her hand.

"Oh," she said, "I'm so sorry I said that."

But she never took it back. She never told me that it was flattering, my new haircut, or that her first impression of it had been wrong. That was never Sue's style. When she said a thing, she meant it.

And, it had been a favor, really, hadn't it? Even Jon had admitted, finally, after I badgered him about it for two solid weeks, that, yes, the hairstyle aged me a bit. It was more conservative, maybe, than it needed to be. That, yes, if he had his choice, I'd grow it out. And when I finally did, and passed myself in a plate glass window one afternoon and admired the hair of the woman in that glass, I realized that the new style had been a terrible mistake, that Sue had been telling the truth, and I felt thankful that she'd been willing to do it.

I knew, watching her eat the cookie and reach out for another, that if I had gained as much weight as she had, she would pull the plate away from me and tell me I was fat—something I could never have done.

We talked about the usual stuff. School. Robert Z. The weather. Jon. (Sue has never taken a stance on Jon. When I complain, she listens. When I praise him, she does the same.) We talked about Mack, her husband, on whom my stance has always been amused defense. They'd come within a few heartbeats of divorcing over and over, and when Sue had been the most serious (rented an apartment, consulted a lawyer), I couldn't bear the idea. "No, Sue," I'd said. "You just can't let this happen. You'll be lonely. You'll miss him more than you can imagine. And the boys. And *Mack*—"

In truth, *Mack* was always the one whose loneliness I couldn't bear to consider.

Big, dumb Mack—the world's most peaceful and passive man.

Once, I saw him shed actual tears when he had to chop down a tree, the roots of which had worked their way under the foundation of their house and were cracking it to pieces down there, in the dark. He was already forty years old when he married Sue, who was six months pregnant with the twins. At their wedding, he'd sung, himself, in the echoing baritone of a former high school musical theater star (a little too loudly, and slightly off-key—"Sunrise, Sunset") and his mother had set to wailing in the front row of the church.

It was impossible to imagine Mack, the manager of a vegetarian restaurant specializing in raw-food vegan entrées ("What would *that* be?" Jon always joked. *"Water? Leaves?"*), weathering a divorce. Sue had told me that he'd been discharged from the Peace Corps after only a month in Africa because he had chronic problems with blisters on the bottoms of his feet. After only two weeks, he couldn't walk at all, and then they got infected, and briefly there was some scare that he would have to have his feet amputated, and he'd never walk again. To this day, even in the dead of winter, Mack wears only Birkenstock sandals, often with thick black socks.

Today, there wasn't much to say about Mack. The boys had been getting in trouble in school, but just for boy stuff and mostly because they refused to sit still during free-reading time. We ended up talking for a long time about whether it was a good or bad thing for Sue and Mack to insist that the boys keep taking tae kwon do, although they seemed to hate it. "Don't they need to learn discipline?" she asked me. "They're not going to learn it from me or Mack."

I smiled. I shrugged. I had no opinion. When Chad was that age, if they were teaching tae kwon do in the area yet, I hadn't heard of it.

While we talked, the boys came and went from the house, and they ate cookies, too. Crumbs on the table and on the floor. Occasionally we'd hear a piercing scream coming from the back-yard while they were out there, but Sue didn't even bother to get up to look out the window. We both yawned a lot. At one point I felt the need to stand up and stretch, and Sue said, "Have I become a burdensome bore to you, Sherry?"

I sat back down right away, and said, "No!"

"Admit it. I'm boring you to death, Sherry. Why do you always have to be so nice?"

"I'm not being nice," I said. I laughed. I said, "I'm sorry."

Sue laughed, too. "See," she said, "you're so nice you're apologizing for my being boring." She picked up a cookie. She said, more seriously, "It's okay. Someday you'll crack, Sherry Seymour, and we'll all get to see your true self."

I rolled my eyes. I said, "If anyone has seen my true self, Sue, it's you."

"Sure," Sue said, finishing the cookie, changing the subject to her mother, and then to my father, and then for a long time we talked about the difficulties of having elderly parents, while the boys screamed outside, and, occasionally, Kujo barked loudly, once, then stopped. From far away—some fenced-in yard, or from a chain tied to a tree?—a dog barked back. After a half hour or so Sue looked at her watch and said, "Oh my god! I have to go to the store and get some dinner!"—and I was, frankly, happy to think of getting on with the day.

A shower. A magazine.

I was surprised to find myself thinking, too, of heading to bed, to *sex*, with Jon when he got back from the hardware store. How long had it been since I'd anticipated *that* on a Saturday afternoon? I started sweeping the cookie crumbs off the table before she'd even stood up, but I thought she gave me a cold look when I did, and I shook my hand out over the sink and turned to her with the warmest smile I could manage. "Please," I said. "Don't hurry. It's so great to have you here."

"No," she said, standing up, brushing crumbs off her legs onto the floor as she did. "We've got to get home."

"You're sure?" I asked, twice.

"Yes," she said, each time. She went to the hallway to get her purse, and I couldn't help noticing as she walked away that her shirt wasn't tucked in behind her, and a loose roll of flesh was exposed around her waist.

"Don't let me forget my LEGOs," she called from the hallway.

"Right," I said.

I swept the pieces, like the crumbs, into my hand. She'd never gotten the tank put together, so I put it all in a Ziploc bag. When I handed it to her, she handed it back. "Here," she said. "If you could get this put together and drop it off later . . ."

"Sorry," I said. "I never could do those. But I could send it to Chad in California if you want me to. He could FedEx it back."

"Oh, forget it," Sue said. "This isn't your problem." She stuffed the bag into her coat pocket, and we stood facing one another in the hallway for a moment.

"It was so nice of you to come over," I said, and immediately regretted it. It sounded fake, and formal—the kind of thing you'd say to a new neighbor, not the woman whose hand you'd been squeezing in a death grip when you pushed your baby into this world. (Jon had passed out, so Sue, who'd been in the hallway as our "second string," had to be called in.) And Sue seemed to bristle at my tone, too. She said nothing in reply, but told the boys—who were watching something loud on the television in the living room by then—that it was time to go. They reflexively whined, but they were past us and outside slamming the car doors before we'd even made it to the porch.

Outside, it was truly a new season. The leaves hadn't quite come out on the trees, and the grass wasn't yet green, but everything was damp and brilliant and getting ready. Down the road, I heard the Henslins' cows lowing—a sound of contentment, I thought. The sound of warmth, of mud, of sun, of a life being lived, at the moment, anyway, without enough information for worry.

We moved from the porch to the porch steps. I could hear one of the twins shouting angrily from the backseat of Sue's car. But there was also birdsong, and the wind chimes I'd tied to the garage eaves ringing sweetly.

"Gosh, we talked all afternoon," Sue said, "and I never even asked you how *you* are."

It wasn't true, and she knew it. She'd asked me, and I'd said I was fine. It was her way of asking again, and it crossed my mind that there was something suspicious about the way she was looking into my eyes, as if she'd been waiting all afternoon for the information she might be able to extract from me now in these last seconds of it.

But I just shrugged. "Nothing new here," I said.

"Well, what about your secret admirer?"

"Nothing to report on that subject," I lied.

BRAM had said, "It's your neck I can't get over."

He put his lips on the little pulse point at the base of it, and then moved his tongue in circles there for a few long minutes, before moving up, under my ear, pushing the hair away, sinking in his teeth. "I told you," he whispered, "didn't I, that I'm a vampire?"

I tried to laugh, but what came out was a breathy sigh. He was undoing the top buttons on my blouse with one hand, smoothing the hair away from my neck with the other, pushing

me backward onto the futon, tongue and teeth just under my ear
until my whole body—the entire length of the skin that held me
together from my forehead to my feet—rippled with it.

Goose bumps.

A rabbit stepped on your grave, my grandmother used to say.

Chills, but so warm that a trickle of sweat ran cold at my rib
cage down to my stomach.

He put his face between my breasts, and I could feel his
breath, hot on the damp flesh there. He reached behind me, un-
fastened my bra, then slid his hand around to my chest, and
cupped one breast in his hand, looked at it, put his mouth to it.

He *had* said he was a vampire.

Over coffee in the cafeteria a few days before, I'd asked him
how he'd come to be named Bram, and he'd said, "I'm a vampire." I smiled. I could barely look at him—those deep dark eyes
in the cafeteria glare. The sound of trays clattering, college girls
squealing. Someone, back in the kitchen maybe, was pounding,
it seemed, with a spoon, on a pan. The cash register was ringing
up coffee and hamburgers, tinnily, hysterically. The whole place
seemed so chaotic and alive, it was like a kind of hellish festi-
val—a carnival just beginning to get out of hand. Soon, it
seemed, the food fights would start, and then the screaming, and
then the orgy, and then the bullets would start ricocheting
around the room.

"Really," I said. "It's unusual. Did they name you after Bram
Stoker?"

"Yeah," he said. "Believe it or not. My mother was an odd
bird, as you can imagine, naming her son after the *Dracula* guy."

"Why did she?"

He was drumming the fingers of one hand on the tabletop.
There was a silver band on his right hand. With his other hand,

he squeezed the Styrofoam coffee cup he was holding just hard enough to make it buckle, but not to crush it.

"She was an English teacher," he said, nodding in my direction. "Like you. But high school. She liked *Dracula*. In her spare time she wrote vampire novels."

"Really?"

"Really."

"Did she publish them?"

"One. It was a kind of trashy paperback. Out of print now."

"Did you read it?"

"No," he said. "By the time I was old enough to be interested, she died. And after that, I couldn't stand it. I'd pick it up, but it was too weird. My dead mother, the vampire lover. You know, it's the kind of thing that could make a teenager crazy. And now I don't even have the damned thing."

"What was it called?"

"*Bloodlover*. One word."

"Wow."

"Wow is right. I'm sure it's full of sex. That's another thing you don't really want to read about, written by your mother, when you're seventeen."

"No," I said. "You don't."

He leaned back in his chair.

I could see that, although he wasn't tall, his body was long. His stomach muscles beneath the T-shirt he was wearing looked solid. He was built like a runner, I thought. There was a line of sweat in the gray cotton, which split his torso exactly in half.

It was warm in the building. Only the first week of March, but the rise in the temperature outside had not yet inspired the college custodians to turn the furnace down—and here, in the cafeteria, the steam had built up so thickly on the windows that rivulets of it were running in jagged lines down the glass. Those of us who had to spend the whole day in our hot offices and classrooms had stripped off whatever we could. Sweaters, of course. Panty hose. Overshirts. I'd even taken off my strand of pearls because it was growing slippery and oppressive around my neck.

"So, tell me about you," he said.

I could think of nothing to say. My mind was suddenly a photograph of nothing. I'd bought him the cup of coffee, ostensibly in return for the work he'd done on my car, but I could tell by the way he looked at me, and he could tell by the way I *couldn't* look at him, I supposed, why I'd called and asked him to meet me.

"It's okay," he said when it became obvious that I wouldn't be able to speak. "You can tell me another time."

SUNDAY, late morning, I took to the garden with a rake.

I always did this in March, when there was a break in the weather long enough to clear away some of the winter debris. There would be more winter, I knew—icy rain, another snowstorm—but today it was sixty degrees, and all the brittle branches of the honeysuckle, the dried-up mums, the dead vines, even a few husks of hollyhock blooms I'd failed to pinch off the summer before, and which had clung brown and withered to the stalks through winter, yielded easily to the rake, as if they'd given in to death so long ago there wasn't even the vaguest connection to this earth any longer. The roots were so withered that they came out of the dirt in a quick dusty cough when I yanked only lightly with my garden gloves, and they emerged covered with dust. In only a few hours, I'd managed to cart seven wheelbarrows full of last year's garden to the scrubbrush at the edge of the yard. Tomorrow, Jon will burn it, and it'll go up fast and smolder down to a very light gray ash, nothing left over at all from last summer's wild blooming—no evidence that it was ever there. Gone without a trace, like a thought.

Once the garden was clear of the detritus, I could see the little green shoots of tulips stabbing up into the spring warmth, and the few snowdrops, already blooming, nodding demurely in the sun. Every few minutes, I thought of Bram, his hands on my breasts, his body on top of mine, and I had to lean on my rake to steady myself. Jon came around the side of the house from the backyard, where he'd been putting golf balls into mole holes, and I smiled at him, distantly. "What are *you* thinking about?" he asked.

I told him nothing.

"Is THIS skirt too short?" I asked.

Monday morning. We'd replaced the storm windows with the screens over the weekend, and propped one of the bedroom windows open about an inch that night. A breeze that was cool but that carried, too, an implication of spring—a scent of foliage, or freshly washed hair—was whispering through that inch of openness.

It was a silvery skirt I'd bought a few years ago but had worn only once, and then only to a tea party thrown for women faculty at the house of a ceramics instructor. Even there, even then, I'd been self-conscious—although, in truth, the skirt is only an inch or so above my knees, which would have been a *long* skirt to me fifteen years ago, when I regularly wore skirts so short that sitting down in them was dangerous.

"Are you kidding?" Jon said.

He looked away from the mirror, in which he was watching a reflection of himself secure the knot of his tie, to me in my skirt. "There's no such thing as a skirt too short if you've got gams like that."

I smoothed it down over my thighs. "Thank you," I said.

"Your boyfriend's going to like that one," he said, turning back to the mirror. "Is that why you're wearing such a short skirt to work today?" His tone was playful, but I could feel my pulse quicken a bit at my wrists.

Friday, when I'd come home after the night before, in my efficiency, on my futon, with Bram, I'd felt numb, like someone who'd been left in a hot bath too long—a bath full of rose petals, steeping and silky and reeking with sweetness. I remembered that when we first moved into our house, Mrs. Henslin had brought us a bag of homegrown strawberries as a welcome present. After taking them from her, thanking her for them, I forgot about them. I left them on the back porch. It was August, and by the time I realized what I'd done and opened that paper bag again, they'd turned into something that made me recoil in horror, and that bag of fruit smelled the way I thought I smelled that night, walking into my own house, seeing Jon there, waiting for me on the love seat with his newspaper. I wasn't sure if it was shame I felt, exactly, or if it was fear. I felt like a woman who'd been sent out of the village in which she'd lived her whole life and was returning to it after a long absence, seeing it again. What would she find?

"Hi," Jon had said. "Long time no see."

"Hi," I said, and tossed my purse on the table by the back door.

He stood up.

"You look tired," he said. He kissed my cheek. When I felt the familiar lips there, and smelled him, I had to take a step back. "Have a wild night last night?" he asked.

"No," I said—too quickly?

He put his arms around my waist and whispered, "You can tell me. You've been fucking some other man, haven't you? You can tell me."

He was joking, I was sure—this fantasy, half teasing and half serious, which had taken on a life of its own. But, when I looked closely at his face I thought *no. He knows. And he doesn't care.* Still, I said, "I haven't, Jon."

BRAM met me in the cafeteria. He was pouring coffee into his Styrofoam cup when I got there. "Hey," he said, looking up.

He was wearing a lavender-colored shirt, and the sight of him in it—that delicate spring color, and the masculine body in it, even the sight of his hands, one of them holding a coffee cup, the other reaching into his jeans for change to pay for it with—it crossed my mind that I might faint, that if I didn't steady myself by holding tightly to the strap of my purse I might leave this world, suddenly, something hot and all-embracing swooping down on me in a dark funnel of feathers and sweat, taking my consciousness with it.

"Hi," I said.

He looked at my legs, then at my face.

Those eyes.

He said nothing, needed to say nothing. After a second or two I said, "Let me buy that for you," nodding at his cup.

Bram looked at the cup himself, as if he hadn't realized he still had it, and shrugged, and said, "Okay." He leaned toward me as I reached over to take the coffeepot from him. I could feel his breath on my neck when he said, "So. Tonight?"

"Yes," I said, in a whisper, before I even knew I'd opened my mouth to speak.

He took a step back. I poured the coffee into my cup, but only halfway because my hand was shaking and I was afraid I would spill it.

Bram waited at the end of the line as I paid for the coffee, and when I joined him there he said, "I can't sit down this morning, I'm afraid. I'm meeting a student in my office. See you later?"

"Okay," I said.

This time, my tone was businesslike, although I'd felt disappointed. The word *jilted* flew quickly through my mind—a dragonfly on fire—before he smiled at me. That dimple. And he looked, again, at my legs, and my blood seemed to surge at my wrists, behind my ears. When he looked back into my eyes, I had to look away, over his shoulder, where I glimpsed Garrett standing in a crowd of students, talking to a boy who looked like Chad, but wasn't Chad—just the jawline, the hair, had reminded me of Chad, who would never have worn that boy's nylon Red Sox jacket.

Bram turned. As he walked away, I stood still with my coffee shivering blackly in the Styrofoam cup in my hand—a bit of light sparking in ribbons across it, like the sun over a very deep but narrow lake.

Saunter, I thought, looking up from the coffee to Bram's back. The man *sauntered.*

His walk was so casually sexy (such a long gait—even slowly, it could get him quickly to wherever he needed to go) that it made him look like a man who'd never once in his life been in a hurry. As he passed Garrett, he must have said something to him, because Garrett turned, and they high-fived, and the boy who looked like Chad gave Bram a thumbs-up, and for a horrible moment I imagined that thumbs-up had something to do with me, and the bad moment caused the coffee in my cup—even half full—to spill over, and one burning drop landed on my ankle.

Was it possible?

Could Bram have told anyone?

Could this all somehow be some kind of—plot? Joke? Game?

No.

I took a sip of the coffee. It burned my lips.

No.

This was just a bit of terror left over from high school, where such games had been invented, perpetrated, and then abandoned. It was just the cold bad memory of a January morning in homeroom after a weekend during which I'd let Tony Houseman touch my breasts, under my shirt, inside my bra, in the backseat of his brother's car.

Up front, his brother was driving.

He'd dropped us off at the movie we'd gone to see (*The Way We Were*), then picked us up afterward.

All along, it had been that brother I'd been in love with. Bobby. A senior, when I was a freshman. Bobby was quiet and brooding, while Tony, his little brother, was a class clown—a boy who never shut up, who cracked so many jokes that, by default, a few of them were unforgettably funny, but mostly were lame, tiresome, crude.

Bobby, to my knowledge, had never had a serious girlfriend, and he ran with a group of boys who seemed to be the same— indifferent to girls, but radiantly handsome, athletic boys who occasionally shook one another's hands in the hallway, a gesture so adult and masculine it made everyone else passing in the hallway appear moronic and childlike, as if we were cartoon characters who'd stumbled into the real world.

Tony and I made out through most of the movie in the back of the theater, which was mostly empty anyway. He'd invited me to the movie, then paid for the movie, bought me popcorn and

an enormous 7 UP. I felt obligated—and he was attractive
enough. I let him run his hands up and down my side, put his
tongue so deeply into my mouth I felt I might gag, and then he'd
pulled away with his hand an inch or so from my breast and said,
"Can I touch it?"

"No," I said, moving my arm into my torso to trap his hand.
"Not now."

"When?"

I didn't want, I suppose, to appear stingy. I said, "Not in the
theater. Later, in the car."

We hadn't been in the backseat of Bobby Houseman's car
two seconds before Tony began the tongue explorations again. It
was dark in the car, eleven o'clock at night, and we were on the
freeway when he pulled away and whispered, *"Now?"*

"Okay," I whispered back.

Up front, Bobby Houseman seemed to be nodding to the
music on the radio, watching the road ahead of him, but as soon
as Tony started to push my shirt and bra up, exposing my breast
in a way I hadn't anticipated at all, Bobby Houseman glanced in
the rearview mirror—and I could see him looking directly into
it, then directly into my eyes, and then to my naked breast.
"Squeeze it, Tony," he said. "Bite it, buddy."

My whole body flushed with shame, but it was too late. I was
here, I'd allowed this, I'd agreed to this, it would do no good now
to struggle away, to pull my shirt down fast. I let Tony do it. I let
him squeeze my breast, and then put his face down to my chest
and feel around there with his mouth until he found my nipple,
which he clamped down on hard, while his brother watched, and
then said, when Tony resurfaced and looked toward Bobby for
approval, "Good work, Tone. Good job, little brother. Next time
get into her panties. Stick your finger up her." We'd finally pulled

up in front of my house by then and, heart pounding, I pulled my shirt down and hurried from the car, straight to my room, and got in bed with my clothes on.

The next day, Sunday, I spent convincing myself that it had never happened. Bobby Houseman couldn't have seen into the backseat. He didn't see my breast. He didn't watch as Tony bit my nipple. He wasn't really talking about me. He was talking to Tony about something else. It was some brotherly conversation they'd had that had nothing to do with me. Because it was impossible that Bobby Houseman had watched his brother feel and bite my breasts. Or if he'd watched, he hadn't *seen*.

But, after homeroom, during which one of Tony Houseman's pals licked his lips at my chest when I walked in, and then in the hallway—those boys, passing me in a masculine wall, starting to laugh—when one of Bobby Houseman's friends turned around and said to Bobby, "So you say they're nice little tits? Little brown nipples?" and Bobby Houseman answered loudly, "Yeah, but you have to ask my brother what they taste like," it was as if veil after veil were being ripped off of me in quick succession, exposing me to myself so quickly I could hardly keep walking.

No.

That was high school. I'm a grown woman now. And Bram Smith is no high school boy—although he isn't thirty, as I'd thought he was, but twenty-eight. (Perhaps I was on that date, or one like it, the day he was born.) But, when I'd said to him, "I know you know that nobody can know—" he'd looked at me with grave sincerity, the wisdom of a man who'd had many secret lovers, who'd been one, and said, "Discretion? You bet. Of course. You have nothing to fear from me, sweetheart. I'm the soul of discretion."

Still, when Garrett looked from Bram to me, then caught my eye and waved, I flinched. I wanted to turn, walk away as if I hadn't seen him, but then he called out, "Mrs. Seymour!" and nodded good-bye to his friend in the red nylon jacket, sprinting over to me.

"Garrett," I said when he was at my side.

"Just wondered how Chad's doing," he said. "I e-mailed him a couple times, and got nothing."

"Chad's fine," I said, trying to smile more naturally than I was smiling. "Chad's probably just busy with school."

"Yeah, well, if you talk to him, tell him I said hi. Are you walking over to your office? If you are, I'll go with you."

"Yes," I said. "But I'm stopping in the women's room first. I'm sorry."

"It's okay," Garrett said. "I'm just glad to see you."

This puppylike joy. Where, I wondered, did it come from? Both of Garrett's parents had struck me as somber, if not morose, back when they were alive. And the tragedies of their deaths—how had Garrett come out of that nest with this personality?

This optimism?

I thought of Chad. Jon, at least, if not I, was *made* of optimism—and yet Chad, *our* son, would never have stood in a cafeteria speaking so happily and without pretense to the mother of one of his friends. He would never have worn this simple plaid shirt. A pocket with two pencils in it. The buzz cut. All this unabashed plainness, this pure spirit of it. If, somehow, Chad had found himself here instead of Berkeley, he would have been like some of the students I'd had in my classes, scowling in the back, too bright to bother shining. He would have nodded politely to the mother of his friend, certainly, but he would not have waved to her, smiling. He would not have jogged across the cafeteria on a Monday morning to ask her a question about her son.

But, I couldn't walk to my office with Garrett. My hands were trembling. If I had to speak to him, more than a few words, I wasn't sure I could keep the sound of it, of *Bram,* out of my voice.

We parted at the ladies' room.

"I'll see you around, Mrs. Seymour," Garrett said. "You have a great day."

IN MY Introduction to Literature class I was strangely nervous, seized by the kind of stage fright I used to have as a very new teacher.

We were discussing the first act of *Hamlet,* and the students seemed to be both bored and made anxious by it—a kind of confusion that manifested itself in yawning, fidgeting, defensiveness. Derek Heng's arm shot up and he said, "What's the point of reading *Hamlet* if we don't understand it?" to which every other head in the room nodded. Earlier, Bethany Stout had suggested that we find a better translation, because the one we were reading was so old-fashioned—a statement that had struck me as both sadly ignorant and somehow very savvy. I was so surprised by her suggestion that I was only able to stammer out the obvious, that this wasn't a translation, that it was old-fashioned because it was old.

"The point," I said, answering Derek Heng, "of reading *Hamlet* is to *learn* how to understand it."

But, because it seemed obvious, then, that the problem was that I wasn't *teaching* them how to understand it, I felt something like the moat around a sand castle cave in somewhere near my sternum, and I could go no farther, found myself completely unable even, flipping the thin pages of the text on my lap, to find some passage that they might see the beauty and relevance of.

(*Alas, poor Yorick, I knew him, Horatio, a fellow of infinite jest.*)

My body felt cold. I was wearing a skirt that was too short, I was sure of that now. I let them go early and went back to my office.

There, I listened to the messages on my voice mail:

Two messages from students with excuses for missing class. A car wouldn't start. A baby had an ear infection. A message from a textbook saleswoman, a wrong number, and Amanda Stefanski asking if I would have time for a cup of coffee tomorrow or the next day, that we had a problem student in common and she wanted to ask me for some advice. And then, Jon, asking if I'd seen my "boyfriend."

You be a good girl, he said. *But not too good.*

And there was such a lighthearted obliviousness to the statement that it made me, briefly, angry, before I thought, *No.* It wasn't Jon. It was the bad class. I was cold, and tired, and even if I *didn't* yet, I *should* have been feeling guilty.

Still, for the first time, I thought to myself that this fantasy of Jon's was insulting, that it was like the kind of market testing his software firm did when they came up with an idea—shopping it around to see if anyone but themselves would find any value in this particular piece of intellectual property before any more time or energy was invested in it—and I held the phone away from my ear until the end of the message.

Last, the physician's assistant from Summerbrook Nursing Home calling to tell me that my father was being put on a low dose of Zoloft.

He's been so depressed these last few weeks, she said. *He's completely lost his appetite, and he never wants to leave his room. Give us a call?*

I dialed the number to Summerbrook as quickly as I could— my fingers fumbling on the numbers as I punched them. Already, however, the physician's assistant had left for the day, and the nurse's aide I spoke to didn't seem to know who my father was.

I sighed, exasperated. "Can you transfer me to room twenty-seven?" I asked her.

She wasn't sure, she said, but she would try.

There were a long few minutes of dead space in which I could hear what sounded like Lake Michigan roaring in the distance—a fluid undulating rhythm that might have been coming from the phone, or from inside my own ear—and then there was a click. She'd managed it, the transfer.

The phone rang eleven times before an old man (my father?) answered it.

"Dad?" I asked.

"Yes?" he said.

"Dad, it's me. Sherry."

"Yes."

"Are you okay, Dad? I had a message that you've lost your appetite."

"Huh?"

"Dad, are you feeling okay? Are you fine?"

"I'm fine," he said.

"I'm going to come to visit," I said.

"I don't need anything," he said.

"I know, Dad," I said. "But I need to see you. I miss you."

"Do what you need to do," he said.

I said, "I love you, Dad"—although I still didn't feel certain the man on the other end of the line was my father.

How could I know?

What did my father's voice sound like now, and how could I recognize it?

The voice of that younger father was the one I would have known him by, and that voice was gone, and now his voice was interchangeable with the voices of all elderly men—a scratchy, distant voice, like something rising from beneath a boulder, like the voice of a small bird being held too tightly in a child's hands.

He said nothing more. There was a knocking on the other end of the line, as if he had dropped the receiver and it had bounced or rolled across the floor.

And then a click. Someone had hung up the phone.

I STOPPED by the grocery store on the way to my efficiency, bought a bottle of Merlot and two glasses, two steaks, two potatoes, and a bunch of asparagus that looked so green and robust it was impossible to imagine that it had been picked and bundled in California then shipped across the country in a crate. This seemed like local produce. The stems had about them all the lushness of spring, and the tips were such sharp arrows they seemed dangerous. Weapons disguised as vegetation. I stood for a moment in the produce aisle, drew them to my face like a bouquet, and inhaled.

An old woman passed me then, both pushing and leaning on her grocery cart, which was empty except for a few brown-spotted bananas.

She looked at me, and I looked at her.

The skin on her face was powdery and thin, and I felt sure that if I touched it something white and sparkling would come off on my fingertips.

I'd seen her before, I felt certain—once, in a room at a lab in the basement of the hospital where I'd been waiting for some routine blood work. Cholesterol. Hormone levels. Iron. White blood cells. A count of those things circulating in the blood that could be quantified, interpreted. She'd been there knitting, wearing a gray dress, and the quiet sound of her needles clicking against one another had felt, that afternoon, like a quiet affirmation of time passing. Seconds adding up to something. Eternity being parceled into baby blankets, being turned into winter scarves.

But the old woman didn't seem to recognize me, or to like me, in the produce aisle. Her eyes on me were small and watery, watching skeptically as I inhaled the greenness that had stabbed out of the ground two thousand miles from here, as if I were still trying to get the sun and water and earth out, after it was gone, as if she knew how futile that was.

She looked at me as she passed, pushing those bananas in her cart, as if she had some notion of who I was, what I was up to, and she did not approve.

At EXACTLY eight o'clock, Bram arrived in a bleached white shirt. Outside the door to my efficiency, through the peephole, he looked like the kind of dark and mysterious stranger you might think twice about letting in—but the kind of stranger you would, eventually, let in.

I opened the door.

For a moment we stood awkwardly in the one room. Then, I nodded to the bottle of wine on the counter next to the kitchen sink, the two new glasses I'd rinsed and dried and set next to it, and I said, in a voice that seemed to come from behind me, from some other woman, one I'd never met, "Would you like a glass of wine?"

He smiled and glanced down at his own shoes, as if he were willing himself not to laugh, and then looked back up at me with his eyebrows raised, directly into my eyes, and said, "Sure. But I had something else in mind first."

He reached over, took my hand, drew me closer to him, and brought the hand to his mouth. He put his lips to it first, moving them softly across the knuckles, and then his tongue.

The solicitous warmth of it, and watching him do it, seeing his head bowed over my hand—and my hand, as if it were detached from my body, the focus of this intense concentration, by this gorgeous younger man—made me feel, briefly, as if I might actually swoon. I had to take a step toward him, lean my shoulder against his, to steady myself.

He turned the wrist over then and kissed the thin skin there. Delicately. He looked up at me. I was breathing deeply. He turned back to the wrist, brought it to his mouth, making small circles on it, and then his teeth, lightly, biting at the cool white flesh, the veins and nerves so close to the surface I could feel it shoot through my whole body.

I leaned over and put my face to his neck, moaning as I did it, smelling him, smelling what must have been exhaust fumes on him, machine, and oil, and masculinity.

And then we were on the floor, on the matted gray carpet of the efficiency.

He kissed me deeply, and I kissed back hard, my mouth wide open, my hands on his shoulders.

He pulled back to take his shirt off, and after he tossed it in the direction of the kitchen table, he leaned over with the expression of a serious physician, or a mechanic—an expert about to take a look at some part of me that concerned us both, and began to undo the buttons on my blouse.

The first button, undone, and I began to tremble, and he said, "*Shhh*. Everything's okay, baby. Baby."

And then the second and third, and he opened it and pushed the blouse away from my body, and reached behind my back, unhooked my bra, pushed it up over my breasts.

For a moment he just leaned back on his heels and looked at me, my body spread out under him. I was still trembling. He was breathing steadily, but my breath was ragged.

I felt cold on the floor—an object, an anesthetized patient, or even a corpse, being observed in a laboratory, except that my nipples were stiff, and I couldn't help but arch my back toward him, involuntarily.

I was pushing myself toward his touch, aching toward it, dying for it, and finally gasping and groaning when he did touch me, one hand lightly brushing a nipple, and then the other, and then two fingers on a nipple, squeezing, and then the other, hard enough this time that the shock of it shot straight through me, and I made a loud animal sound I'd never made before, and then he reached with his other hand under my skirt, inside the crotch of my panties, pushing a finger into me, and I knew I was so wet there it shamed me, and then he pressed his palm against my clitoris, rubbing it as he pinched my nipples with his other hand, knowing exactly what he was doing, what it was doing to me, watching me from what seemed an amused but excited distance as I came in shattering waves beneath him on the floor.

Afterward, Bram just sat back and looked at me for a minute, and the silence and his appraisal of me grew so uncomfortable I tried to pull the blouse over my naked breasts.

But he laughed and said, "Oh no you don't," and opened it again, pushed my skirt over my hips all the way and pulled the panties down over my ankles, spreading my legs, and said, "Now I'm going to fuck you, sweetheart."

IN THE middle of the night I woke up on the futon to find Bram standing over me. Moonlight shone through the window that faced the alley, and a garage, and, beyond it, the parking lot where I'd parked my car.

He was putting on his boxer shorts, and the shadow he cast over me was cool, blue, long.

Seeing the length of him over me—the dark line of hair from his crotch to his breastbone, the flesh of him made tangible by moonlight—I thought it was the most sensual, earthly thing I'd ever seen.

The pure masculine beauty of it.

The *forbidden* beauty of it.

I was a married woman sleeping on a weeknight with a man many years younger than I was. We had fucked on the floor of the apartment, and then again on the futon, and then taken a shower together that had ended with me on my knees, the hot water shattering across my back, his erection sliding in and out of my mouth until he came in warm and salty pulsing intervals in my throat.

In the dark, his shadow over me and the sight of him in the moonlight, the thrilling terror of it, made me catch my breath, and then he looked down, and saw that I was awake. I thought I saw a flash of sympathy cross his face. He was sorry. He hadn't wanted to scare me. He said, "It's just me, gorgeous."

"You're not leaving, are you?" I asked. I couldn't help the note of longing in my voice.

He said, "I was thinking I should go. So I can change clothes in the morning. At home. Not go into work smelling like pussy."

The crudeness of it made me catch my breath again. It had been high school since I'd heard someone use that word, or any word like it, meaning me. I said, "Oh."

"But now I'm not so sure," he said. He was smiling, the flash of it reflected in the light from the window. "It looks awfully inviting to just get back in that nest and cuddle up with you."

I reached up, and he knelt down into my arms and crawled back under the sheets with me. We woke again together in the morning to the sound of a garbage truck—*beep, beep, beep*—backing up beneath the window.

———

Driving home that night, between thoughts of Bram, I thought guiltily of my father, picturing him in his chair, in his room—that enormous rose in the Styrofoam cup on his windowsill, and the way it had sunk low over the ledge until it had fallen onto the floor.

In my imagination, this time, there was no one there to pick it up, just a puddle of water and shredded petals on the linoleum at my father's feet, the cold and damp of it soaking into his slippers. Who knew how long it would lie there on the floor before a nurse's aide found it and cleaned up the mess?

I'd go to see him as soon as I could arrange it, I thought.

Maybe, I thought, the Zoloft would help.

I liked the name of it, anyway. *Zoloft.* As if joy could be made into some kind of airship, a ship my father could board, and be lifted, *lofted,* from the despair of age and physical decay into— what?

He'd been a good man, but he'd always been morose, I thought. My friends had always said, "Your father's so easygoing," but they only knew him from a brief and occasional conversation in the driveway, a moment or two passing in the kitchen on a weekend. My father had been anything but easygoing. I could still picture him at the kitchen table on a morning he didn't need to go to work—cigarette dangling at the edge of an ashtray, his fingers drumming dully on the surface of the table, staring at some point ahead of him, on the beige wallpaper. If I didn't clear my throat before walking into the room, he would start, and gasp, and swear.

"Shit, Sherry. Why are you sneaking up behind me?"

I was thinking of this when I saw *her.* If I'd been looking for her, I didn't register it consciously—but then she was everything out the windshield, in the median, that dead doe, looking as if she had fallen from the sky, had landed softly, but that the fall had killed her nonetheless.

The grass around her had begun to grow. Not yet emerald, but a color of green that held the promise of more greenness in it. Her fur had begun to bleach out. Now, she looked a little like a pure, white deer—the kind that might wander out of the forest, in a fairy tale, nuzzling the hand of a virgin.

But, other than that, she was unchanged. She hadn't moved an inch.

Wasn't there supposed to be, I thought, some county service that came out and hauled the roadkill away? And, if not, what other changes would I see in her over the spring as I passed her on the freeway? Coming. Going. How long, I thought, until she'd melt completely back into the earth? Would her shadow last all summer there? The impression of her lingering in the grass? Or would the grass finally grow up around her, fertilized by her, and cover the whole bad memory over?

"You look worn out," Jon said from the love seat when I walked in. "Rough night?"

The front and back doors were open. The kitchen window was open, too. From the Henslins' farm, the smell of manure wafted in. But it wasn't a bad smell. It was sweet, and only if someone told you what it was would you have known that the smell was waste, was shit, spread all over their fields.

"I'm tired," I said.

Jon was wearing khaki shorts and a T-shirt I'd bought for him during a trip we'd taken with Chad to Mackinac Island. The long expanse of that suspension bridge was stenciled onto the T-shirt, each end of the bridge aborted, as if it connected nothing to nothing.

The summer we'd gone there, Chad was four years old and didn't want to drive across the bridge—the longest of its kind in the world—but we'd taken him anyway, although we had nothing to do on the other side of it but turn around and drive back. We just wanted him to be able to say he'd been across it, and to show him that there was nothing to fear.

It was August, a windy day, and fall seemed to be blustering down from the Upper Peninsula already—a dark purple sky over the bridge, portending rain—and each time a gust of it rocked Jon's sedan, Chad whimpered.

I kept saying, "It's fine, Chad. It's fine"—turning around to smile at him in the backseat. "It's fine. Mommy and Daddy wouldn't take you across a bridge if it wasn't safe."

This seemed to comfort him. He progressed from covering his eyes with his hands to looking fearfully out the window. At one point he was distracted enough from his fear to notice a boat in the water below. "Look," he said—but then the wind blew the car again, and it rocked hard to the left, and Jon said, "Whoa," and Chad began to cry. My hands were wet with sweat. I'd read newspaper stories, plenty of them, about cars being blown off the Mackinac Bridge in high winds. It *wasn't* safe.

I knew that, but Chad didn't.

Maybe, by now, he did.

And, if he's learned that by now—that cars do blow off that bridge—and he remembers what I said (*Mommy and Daddy wouldn't take you across a bridge if it wasn't safe . . .*) would he think it was amusing, that false comfort, or that his mother had simply been ignorant, deluded, or a liar?

When Jon stepped toward me with his arms open, wearing that T-shirt, I started to cry. *Chad. Bram. The dead doe. My father. Jon.* All the losses and betrayals, and even the love, the dreams, the fantasies—burdens made of memory, burdens made of air, so easily blown off a bridge.

No. I was, I thought, just tired.

"Oh," Jon said, kissing the top of my head. "Sherry, what's wrong?"

I looked up at him.

Jon. Jon, just as he'd always been Jon, looking down at me. He took a step backward. He brushed a tear off my eyelashes. He said, "Tell me what's wrong," and the expression on his face was so kind, wise, so bright with love that, I knew, if I told him the truth, he would say, *Of course. I know. Didn't you know? I always knew.*

And, if he didn't already know—fully, really—when I told him, he would understand. We were adults. He would take the responsibility on himself. He would say that his fantasy had been a kind of permission. That he'd participated, of course, in his way.

"Tell me," he said.

There was a bright and watery sheen in his eyes which turned them entirely into my own reflection, fed me back to me—myself, miniaturized, drowning. Outside, the sun was setting, and the frogs that had thawed in the ponds near our house had begun to chirr—rhythmically, like some kind of engine, like the generator at the center of all of it: the world, sex, spring, a gentle machine made of amphibious flesh, but the source of *everything,* nonetheless. Unending. Freezing, thawing, chirring, vibrating, damp and green out there. There were pink and red streaks of light coming in through the windows, pouring baptismally over his forehead.

"What have you been up to, Sherry?" he asked.

I backed away from him and sat down at the edge of the love seat.

He knelt down beside me.

He said, "Were you up all night fucking your boyfriend, Sherry?"

I inhaled. I could feel my lips quiver. I said, "Yes."

Jon inhaled, too, then. He said, "Tell me all about it."

I said, "What do you want to know?" I could see that his hands, folded in front of him as if he were praying, were trembling.

He said, "How many times did you do it?"

"I don't know," I said.

"Come on, Sherry. You know. Tell me. I'm not mad." There were a few brilliant beads of sweat on his forehead. Where had they come from? How had they sprung to the surface so quickly?

I shrugged. I said, in a voice that sounded to me as if it were rising out of a deep, empty well, "Twice, I think, on the floor, and once on the futon."

Jon pushed the skirt up over my knees, and then he looked up at me. One of those beads of sweat was traveling, swiftly, toward the bridge of his nose. "Are you sure it wasn't four times?" he asked. "It couldn't have been four?"

In truth, I *wasn't* sure. I said, "It might have been four times."

Jon smiled again. He licked his lips. "Did you like it?" he asked.

"I liked it," I said.

Jon's eyes were wide, expectant, and he was breathing heavily.

"Did he like it?"—and, again, for just an instant, that same flash of anger passed through me: *market testing*.

"He loved it," I said, and looked as deeply, as openly, into his eyes as I could as I said it.

Jon put his fingers on my knee then, and for a few more seconds he just stared at it, as if it were the first knee, the only knee, he'd ever seen, and then he was between my knees, parting them, pushing the dress all the way up, over my thighs, and his face was pressed into the crotch of my panties, and he was biting me there, pushing the panties aside with his fingers, clawing and biting, and moving around with his tongue, with his teeth, a finger inside me, and then two fingers, and then he was unbuckling his pants—breathing raggedly, pushing into me, looking down at himself inside me as he did it, and then back up into my face from the great distance of his sexual pleasure before he came.

I WOKE up with the alarm. Jon was already awake, propped up on an elbow, smiling (impishly?) down into my face. I had told him the truth, I remembered, and it was all still fine. I had told him the truth about what I was doing, and he hadn't asked me to stop. He kissed my eyes. He kissed my neck. He said, "I liked that a lot."

I said, "I did, too," but I didn't look at him. I looked at a tiny black spot just over his shoulder.

It was an ant.

It was crawling so slowly across the ceiling that I had to squint to see that it was moving at all.

To that ant, I thought, our ceiling must have been like the arctic, like the Sahara, but also like death, being, as it was, without weather.

Jon said, "And it's all true—about your lover? Four times, Sherry? On the floor, on the futon, on—"

I put a finger to his lips. I said, *"Shhh."*

The sound of his voice—too eager, too loud—would ruin everything, I realized, if he kept talking. The morning, the moment, the last twenty years. I would move, I feared, from a vague dissatisfaction to something else entirely. I would shift from disliking the sound of his voice so close to my face in the morning to hating it. The ant, lost in its ant dream above us, would hear him, too, if ants could hear. It would realize suddenly where it was, and also where it wasn't.

THE DRIVE into work seemed strangely brief. I never even had a chance to glance in the direction of that dead deer. For the first time I noticed that the trees had leaves, and seeing that sudden, new green, I thought that whatever had been done to them, whatever life had been stirred in the dirt around those trees and had made its way into their sap, into their veins, and resulted in this furious blooming, I could feel it in my veins, too.

Something erotic. Something warm, stirring. Something that had been there for a long time, waiting to be summoned up by warmth, and to spill over into this upheaval of green.

But, even thinking it, on the freeway, passing a truck of cows (one of which had its nose and mouth pressed out of the slats of the trailer, smelling the wind, or was it trying to cry for help?) I felt ashamed for thinking it:

I was nothing like those trees.

I was a middle-aged English teacher carrying on with a younger man—an auto mechanic—making love on the floor of a student efficiency, spending a fortune on new dresses and shoes, planning my day around a cup of coffee with a stranger in the cafeteria, a rendezvous with him again at night.

Still, the shame of it didn't lessen the excitement of it. I put in a CD. *The Well-Tempered Clavier,* but then, at the first brilliant notes, I thought *no,* and fished around under the seat for something of Chad's, something he'd left behind, and came up with Nick Cave and the Bad Seeds, and put it in.

I turned it up, the bass rattling the windows of my car, and the voice of the singer (Nick Cave?) low and melodic, reminding me hopelessly of Bram—and, although I was behind the wheel of my car, driving eighty miles an hour down the interstate, inwardly, I swooned.

That swooning, I realized—these years of being a mother and a wife, that girlish swooning was what I'd missed.

The sensation of dangerous longing for something just beyond my reach.

The terrible implosion of desire. The warm flood of it. The rushing blood of it. It was what the trees (I thought of them again) must have felt just before that final push toward leafing.

GARRETT was waiting for me outside my office when I got there in the morning. He was reading a poem I kept tacked to my door—a poem about a dead lamb, by Richard Eberhart:

I saw on the slant hill a putrid lamb, / Propped with daisies.

I'd tacked it there so many years ago I'd forgotten why except that it had made me cry when I first read it in an anthology. Robert Z had professed it to be doggerel. ("Sherry, sweetheart, what the hell is this, Hallmark Training Camp? Good god. 'Putrid' is *right*.") But now I couldn't bear to take it down. It had been with me through years of teaching, greeted me every morning outside my office. Ferris, before he'd moved away with his family, used to stop outside my door to read it, or pretend to read it, every day between his classes, coming to and from his own office a few doors down from mine. I would find him there, touch his shoulder, and he would turn and look at me, meaningfully, painfully.

It was yellowed now, but still stuck there with a bright silver tack. The last lines were, *Say he's in the wind somewhere, / Say, there's a lamb in the daisies.*

It never failed to make my eyes sting, that sentiment—the idea that the dead lamb was not dead, but had, in dying, become a part of *everything*.

Garrett was startled when I came up behind him and touched him on the shoulder.

"Mrs. Seymour!" he said, turning around. "I just wanted to come by and tell you about something. Do you have a minute?"

I did. I was early. I had a half hour to kill before I was to meet Bram in the cafeteria, and then Amanda Stefanski, back at my office. "Come on in," I said, opening the door to my office with a key.

Garrett followed. I motioned for him to move a book off the chair and sit down, and he did. He put a foot up on his knee and then, maybe thinking it was too casual, or somehow disrespectful, he took it off and placed both feet on the floor in front of him, straightened up, looking uncomfortable in the vinyl chair.

I sat down at my desk across from him and smiled.

Garrett was wearing a blue T-shirt under his white dress shirt, and I imagined he would take off that white dress shirt when he went to Auto II, that they would all be there in their T-shirts, bent over their machines, shouting to one another over the gunning of engines, the steady roar of that big garage where I'd first seen Bram—or seen him for what felt like the first time.

I could tell that Garrett was too hot in my office. His cheeks were flushed, and his neck. They never got the temperature right in the buildings when the weather changed, and the institutional windows, of course, wouldn't open. I said, "Garrett. Are you okay?"

"I'm great, Mrs. Seymour," he said. "I just wanted to come down here and tell you the news."

"What is it, Garrett? I'm all ears."

"I joined the Marines, Mrs. Seymour," he said. "The Delayed Entry Program. I leave for boot camp in August."

I looked at him.

The sunlight through the window had made a halo on the wall behind him, where, tacked to the wall, I had a print of Dalí's *The Rose*—a spectacular surreal red blossom floating in a blue sky over a vast desert. I'd bought it and put it there years ago, while I was still trying to grow roses in the garden, before small black worms ate them all one summer, destroying hundreds of dollars' worth of bushes and turning the gorgeous blossoms into velvet rags.

When it first started happening, that destruction, I'd gone to the library, but found nothing about small black worms and roses, so I called Mrs. Henslin, who had a rose garden of her own that seemed to thrive wildly every summer without my ever seeing her, even once, tending to it.

She came down one morning in an apron and thick hose and stood over my roses, then bent to look at the leaves, those worms. She said, "You need poison if you're going to grow roses."

She shook her head, as if my ignorance were astonishing. She said she'd have one of her grandsons come down with a hose and spray them.

"Oh," I told her. "I'm not sure. I'm afraid, really, of those kinds of poisons."

Mrs. Henslin laughed. In the bright summer sunlight I could see that her cheeks were shot through with little blue lines, that they looked like streams, thin estuaries, on a map, or seen from the sky. She was wearing pink lipstick, but I could see there was a brown spot on her lower lip. An age spot, or a scar, or a malignancy.

"Well," she said, shaking her head, "you can't grow *anything* without poisons."

I wondered, then, what they were using down there, on their farm—on the soybeans, on the corn—and was that what I sometimes smelled, chemically sweet, on the breeze through the bedroom windows when the wind was blowing out of the east?

Well, the roses all died.

I had, I supposed, *let* the roses die.

I replaced them with simple annuals—mostly marigolds, which spread like a cancer through the bed, where, occasionally, some leftover branch of a rosebush would bud inexplicably in the summer, although the buds always dropped off into the marigolds before they bloomed.

"Oh, Garrett," I said. His eyes were so blue they seemed nearly colorless in all that spring light. He was smiling so widely I could see the place where the flesh pulled tightly across his cheek-bones, revealing a beautiful skull beneath the flesh—the per-fectly formed bone behind the face he'd inherited from his father.

"Why, Garrett?" I asked.

Garrett looked down at his knees, at his jeans, where the denim had turned pale as it began to wear away. He said, "Well, my recruiter says it's a great way to finish school for auto me-chanics without having to take, say, a lot of English classes—no offense. And I have time to finish up this semester, and finish the work on my Mustang. I can rent out the house, get my stuff to-gether. Chad and I can hang out for a while when he gets back from school for the summer."

Chad.

Chad?

I suddenly wondered if it was possible that Chad was Gar-rett's only friend—Chad, who seemed to have so little interest in

Garrett, and who, I felt sure, was not planning to spend his summer hanging around with him.

"Have you heard from Chad?" I asked, and for just a moment, irrationally, I imagined that Chad had talked Garrett into this, into joining the Marines.

"No," Garrett said.

"Garrett," I said. "I'm happy for you. But, I'm also worried. There's a war, Garrett. You—"

Only the night before there'd been a photograph in the newspaper of a marine from the town next to ours. He'd been killed in a car bombing, and the stiff portrait of him in the paper—staring straight ahead as if staring down the barrel of a gun—had been impossible not to stare back at. That dead marine had looked, in that photograph, nothing like Garrett, of course, sitting across from me in all that radiant spring sun, lathered up with boyish hope for the future. But that boy's mother hadn't seen death on her boy, either, had she?

"I know, Mrs. Seymour," Garrett said. "I know that. That's why I want to go. The country needs me. I owe it."

Garrett went on then as I listened, about the country and its need, and his own role in the greater scheme of threats and desires that made up the world—his little bit of history in it. He said, "I wouldn't mind traveling, either. I've never even been out of the state, except for Florida."

And, as Garrett described it, the world he was going off into, I didn't imagine death in it, or even men. I thought, instead, of those trucks ramming up against the legs of the coffee table on my living room floor, little Garrett making truck noises, lost in fantasy, having fun. As he talked about it, the world grew smaller and smaller in my office, until I could have tucked it into my purse, or slipped it into a pocket, or swallowed it in pill form with my morning orange juice. I pictured tiny planes taking off and landing in a sandbox. LEGO tanks dismantled on the kitchen table. Snowballs. Dirt clods. Boyish conflicts.

Still, when he stopped to take a breath, I asked, "Is it too late, Garrett? Did you already sign up, or can you think about this?"

He'd signed. They'd given him a T-shirt. He undid the buttons of his white shirt and showed it to me:

SEMPER FI.

"Do you know what that means, Mrs. Seymour?"

I did. I'd had three years of Latin in high school, two in college, but I shook my head.

"Always faithful," Garrett said.

There was a knock at my office door.

I glanced at my watch.

As soon as I saw how late it was, I knew it was Bram.

"OKAY," Bram said. "So, I can't come to your office. What else can't I do? Can I do this?"

He reached across the table in the cafeteria and stroked one finger down my neck.

"Bram," I said, and moved away from his caress, almost spilling coffee out of my Styrofoam cup as I did—although every nerve in my body had come to life, suddenly, flowering in the direction of Bram's finger on my neck.

"Sorry," Bram said. "I lost my mind."

He was smiling that half smile. That insistent dimple on the right side of his face. He ran his hand through his own dark hair. He said, "I really can't get over your neck, Mrs. Seymour. I'm sure you've been told this a million times, but it's like a swan's."

Calling me Mrs. Seymour—he was making fun of Garrett,

who'd seemed surprised and nervous when Bram came to my office and found him there.

"Okay, Mrs. Seymour," Garrett had said several times, standing up fast, heading down the hallway. "I'll see you, Mrs. Seymour. Thanks for listening, Mrs. Seymour."

Bram had stared after him.

"What's this all about?" he asked, nodding in the direction of Garrett's back.

I told him that Garrett had joined the Marines.

Bram's eyes continued to follow Garrett down the hallway. "Good," he'd said.

"Your neck," Bram said, leaning toward me, "was the first thing I noticed when you brought your fucked-up car into the garage. I knew right away that I wanted to sink my teeth into it and make you squirm."

My lips parted, but I could say nothing. I looked away, around the cafeteria. It was full of people I knew. Colleagues. Students. Secretaries. The film of perspiration, which may have been invisible but which had spread across my flesh, was evaporating now, cooling me. My flesh rippled with it—my chest, my arms. Could they see it? Could they guess what Bram Smith was saying to Sherry Seymour?

I said, "Bram," and moved my chair back a little from the table. "Don't."

He leaned back then, too, and crossed his arms. Over his shoulder I could see Amanda Stefanski talking to a student, a boy in baggy pants. She was laughing, clasping her hands over her stomach as if she were leading a prayer. I looked at my watch. I was supposed to have met her in my office ten minutes ago. Had she come to the cafeteria to look for me? Had Beth told her where I was?

I inhaled, cleared my throat, and looked back at Bram, who was staring at me, unblinking, with that half smile.

I tried to smile back, but also tried to lean away from him, tried to play the part of a woman having a casual conversation with a colleague in the cafeteria. Still, every time my heart beat, it nudged my body in his direction.

We were, together, I knew, a secret sitting out in the open. Surely, anyone looking in our direction could have seen it on us. And, although a sober voice inside me said, *You don't want to broadcast this business, Mrs. Seymour,* it thrilled me nonetheless at every inch of my body to be the woman with the secret in the cafeteria, the one sitting across from Bram Smith, who was still looking appreciatively at her neck. I could feel the illicit thrill of it in the very cells of my body, and, despite myself, I leaned across the table toward him again, even closer, and he took it as the invitation it was and leaned toward me, too. We were close enough that I could hear the breath going in and out of his lungs. He reached over, again, and touched my neck with the tips of his fingers. This time, I let them linger a moment before I moved away. Then, I took a sip of my coffee, and swallowed, and looked around the cafeteria.

No one had seen.

No one was even looking in our direction.

Amanda was still babbling with the boy. Beyond her, I could see Robert Z, with his back to us, standing with two cups of coffee at the unopened doors of the elevator. A few tables over, my student Habib was studying an enormous textbook laid out on the table in front of him, his face so deep into the book that it looked as if he were counting specks of dust on its pages. I thought I caught a glimpse of Sue rounding the corner near the vending machines. Beth was just slipping, with an armful of copies, into the Xerox room. All the people from my former life,

I thought, were busy doing ordinary things, the things I also used to do. . . . I looked back at Bram and let my hand wander toward his on the table between us, and he put the hand with which he'd stroked my neck on top of my hand—and, again, I let it stay there for a moment before I pulled it back to my lap. When I did, he leaned back in his chair, looking as if he'd just won a card game, or a game of wits, and his half smile was erotic, so intimate I had to look away. I looked down at the table between us—flat and dull, like a pond that had been drained of water centuries before, and my reflection on it was also flat and dull, like the body of a woman who would be found at the bottom of such a pond.

Bram cleared his throat, and I looked up at him again.

He asked, "What are you thinking about over there, beautiful?"

I inhaled, and even the air entering my lungs felt sexual, felt like a caress. I couldn't look at him, but I had to ask it. I said, "I'm wondering what it was about me, in the first place, Bram. Why me, what made you decide to write those notes?"

It was what I'd wanted to know all along, but hadn't dared to ask him until now:

Why me?

How had *I* attracted the attentions of a man like this? When had he first seen me, and what had made him think he wanted me, made him think to himself, *Be mine?*

Bram took a sip of his own coffee.

When he put the cup back down on the table between us, he was still smiling.

"What notes?" he asked.

"The valentine," I said.

"The valentine?"

"Be mine," I said.

He shook his head. The smile had faded a little. He looked at his watch, a gold Rolex, or what appeared to be a gold Rolex, and then he checked the time there against the clock on the wall over his shoulder. He said to the clock, "Sorry, babe, I didn't write any valentines."

I said, "The other ones? The yellow legal paper?"

Bram's expression, when he looked back from the clock to me, was, I thought, a little sheepish, and also genuinely confused. He shrugged. He said, "I'm not really a Hallmark kind of guy, hon. It's a good idea, though. Wish I'd thought of it."

I could only stare at him.

He looked down at his watch again.

That deep, brilliant gold.

It had been a present, he'd said. His mother had given it to him before she died.

I shook my head. I blinked. I said, "You didn't write the notes?"

My voice sounded hoarse to me. I cleared my throat again, but there was something in it—dust, pollen, something that was invisible in the air, but had settled inside me.

He shrugged again, and said, "So someone's been writing you love notes?" And something crossed his face. Annoyance? Jealousy?

I touched my own neck then. I said, "I thought it was you. It's why I—"

"Well," Bram said, leaning back in his chair. "I guess you've got the wrong guy, Mrs. Seymour. Maybe you better keep looking. I'm just a mechanic. I don't write poetry."

"Sherry!"

I turned.

Amanda Stefanski was on her way over to the table. She was wearing an orange dress—too frilly, too sheer. It made her look like an enormous lampshade, I thought, but I saw Bram's eyes move from her waist, to her breasts, to her neck. That half smile again. I couldn't help but watch his expression, although I knew I should be looking up at Amanda. I said, "Bram. Do you know Amanda?"

Bram stood up then, and offered his hand. He said, "No, but I've certainly seen you around. Nice to finally be introduced."

The look on her face, I thought, was overeager. A puppy, trying to please. But she also looked a little confused, and she glanced from Bram back down to me. I stood up then, too, and said to Bram, "Amanda and I have a meeting now. It was nice talking to you, Bram."

"Oh," Amanda said, "don't let me interrupt you guys. I'll just meet you over at your office, Sherry. Okay?" She backed away, then waved. "Nice to meet you!" she said to Bram.

"Nice to meet *you*," he said.

He watched her back as she scurried away, and I continued to watch him watch. Then, we stood facing each other. I held my coffee cup in my hand, but Bram's cup was empty on the table. He leaned over and said in my ear, "You better not go looking for that other guy, babe. Remember, *you're mine.*" He winked. "See you at your place," he said.

WHILE I waited for Amanda in my office, I could hear my own heartbeat, so loud it sounded like hammering on the walls. I had so much to do—papers to grade, forms to fill out, calls to return, classes to plan—that I couldn't begin to do any of it. I didn't *want* to do it. Doing it seemed meaningless, each one a task for Sisyphus—so much rock-pushing, only to watch the rock roll back down the side of the mountain of such rocks. What I wanted was to be at the efficiency with Bram. Or even at home, with Jon. Or with Chad. At a movie. Or at the park, where we spent so many years and then never went back. I could still see

Chad, swinging too high, defying gravity, terrifying me. I turned on my computer. I opened my e-mail and composed a message.

Sweetheart, hope you're doing well. Daddy and I can't wait to see you. Two weeks? Have you made your plane reservations? Better start shipping the stuff you're not going to store. Grandpa's not feeling too well, so when you get home we'll go to visit? I know he'd be happy to see you. Did you know Garrett joined the Marines? I love you with all my heart. Mom

AMANDA seemed subdued, a little shy, when she got to my office. Could she tell? Did she know there was something there, between me and Bram at the table? Had she overheard us talking before she said my name?

Under Dalí's rose in her bright orange dress, she looked like something that had grown out of control in an old woman's garden. I thought of enormous tropical flowers that bloomed only once every fifty years. Too bright, too showy. She cleared her throat and told me that she had Doug Bly in her Composition II class this semester, and she needed some advice. She knew I'd had him for his first-year writing course. Had he been as disruptive in my class as he was in hers? She was, she said, at her wit's end. He badgered her, she said, all through class. He made snide comments about the other students. He mimicked her gestures. She'd turned around at the chalkboard one afternoon and was sure she caught him giving her the finger. She'd spoken to him, threatened to have him dropped from the class, but it had no effect. She was, she said, a little frightened. What should she do?

I couldn't remember Doug Bly.

"Are you sure he was in my class?" I asked.

"That's what he told me," Amanda said. "I looked up his transcript. You gave him a B+."

Doug Bly?

If he was the one I thought I remembered from the year before, he was a perfectly polite young man. He would have gotten
an A except that he turned in his last two papers late. He'd called
me *ma'am*.

I tried to tell Amanda that she needed to be stricter.

I was sure she wasn't strict enough.

She was, after all, only twenty-seven. Doug Bly probably saw
her insecurity, that she was young, inexperienced, and he didn't
like it. Maybe underneath his polite demeanor in my class, it had
been there all along, a bit of shark, and with Amanda, he had finally smelled blood. I told her that the next time he interrupted,
she was to walk over to the door of her classroom, and hold it
open for him. If he refused to leave, she should call security.
After that, she was to go to the dean of students and demand to
have him withdrawn from the class. She should tell the dean that
she was fearful for her personal safety—which always got the
wheels turning, fast.

Amanda seemed pathetically grateful for the advice. She sat
up a little straighter, I thought. She squared her shoulders. She
said, "It's so great to have an older teacher to talk to about this.
A mentor. Thank you, thank you, thank you."

That dress.

I remembered a goldfish Chad had won one year at the
Brighton fair, an award for tossing a rubber ring over the neck of
a Coke bottle. At first, that fish had been no larger than Chad's
thumb, but by the end of the year it had grown out of its bowl.
We had to buy an aquarium for it. We all laughed about it, but
something seemed wrong, too. It couldn't go on. Jon had told
Chad, "You need to stop feeding that fish," but Chad was only
six, and couldn't stop himself. Whenever he got the fish-flake
can in his hands, he gave the goldfish as much as it could eat—
which was extraordinary. Finally, we came home one afternoon,

and the fish was floating at the surface of the aquarium, its fins fluttering like scarves around its bloated body. Chad wept, and I comforted him with ice cream and a description of fish heaven (ceramic castles, seaweed), but I was secretly relieved. It couldn't have gone on, that growth, that fish.

Amanda said, "I feel so young and inexperienced."

Without thinking, I patted her arm. I said, "It'll be over soon." Neither of us really knew what I meant by that, but we laughed a little. We relaxed a bit after that. She asked about Chad. I asked about her dog Pretty, whom she'd adopted the year before at the pound. Amanda had said that although Pretty was perfectly happy around Amanda, she would bark and snarl at anyone else. The neighbors had complained that they were afraid the dog would break her leash and bite their children. So, she'd taken Pretty to obedience school, but Pretty had been so threatening to the other dogs and their owners that she'd had to quit. The last time we'd talked, Amanda had been afraid she was going to have to take Pretty back to the pound.

But Pretty was doing wonderfully now, Amanda said. Pretty had calmed down. Totally. She was like a different dog. A happy dog. "Pretty even likes Rob," Amanda said.

Rob?

The face that flashed through my mind at the mention of the name was my brother's. He was holding a handgun to his temple. I asked, *"Who?"* too loudly.

"Rob," Amanda said. "Robert."

"Robert Z?" I asked.

Amanda giggled. "Yeah," she said. "Didn't you know? We're dating?"

I swallowed.

I felt my heart in my chest.

It had, I thought, skipped a beat, hadn't it? Now, it was working hard to catch up, to reestablish its regular rhythm. I said, "No. I had no idea."

"Since January," she said. "It's been"—here, she looked at the ceiling, and inhaled—*"so nice."*

"I had no idea," I repeated.

Amanda looked at me. She must have seen something there, because she stopped smiling. She said, "Oh, you're not upset, are you?"

I exhaled through my nose. A kind of snicker, maybe, because she looked surprised. I shook my head in quick little snaps and said, "Of course not. Why would I be upset?"

"Well, maybe, because we're in your department. Maybe— political reasons?"

"Political reasons?" I sounded incredulous, I thought, but also bitter. What was wrong with me? *Was* I upset? I remembered Sue implying that I would be jealous if Robert Z and Amanda got involved, that I would be jealous if Robert Z had any girlfriend at all. ("You seem," Sue had said, "really invested in him being gay. We have no reason, you know, to think he's gay.")

But I had honestly thought he was.

And, if he wasn't, I would never have thought, anyway, that Amanda Stefanski would be the type of woman, of *girl,* he'd have had any interest in.

I looked at her.

Those eyes—they were so large, they were like a bug's, a *calf's,* eyes. Her hair was thin, but glossy. Her jawline had a rough stripe of pimples along it, which she'd tried to cover up with foundation. She looked so young, so pliant, so overly accommodating. Could Robert Z be in love with *her?*

Then, I thought of Bram, looking at her, from her waist to her neck. In this ridiculous dress! I could see the tag on her bra through the sheer fabric. I could see the little roll of fat on her belly pushing out beneath the sash at the center of it.

But Amanda had small, delicate hands, I noticed for the first time. The skin on them was utterly white and smooth. Her nails were trimmed plainly short. She brought one hand to her mouth and began to chew on those nails. I looked up at her face. Was she, after all, *attractive*?

I stood up. I took the hand she did not have in her mouth and said, "Amanda, I'm truly happy for you. And for Robert." I forced myself to smile. I said, the smile aching a little on my face, "I'm even happy for Pretty."

"Oh," Amanda said. "Thank you so much, Sherry. That means so much to me. I couldn't bear it if you disapproved."

I continued to smile until I'd closed the door behind her.

CHAD returned my e-mail within the hour:

Sorry to hear about Grandpa, Mom. Yeah. Heard that about Garrett. He's gonna get his butt blown to bits. Gotta go to physics. Will call tonight. Luvya2.

BRAM was at the efficiency already when I got there. I'd had a key made for him, left it in an envelope in his campus mailbox, and he'd used it to let himself in.

Before I even opened the door, I knew he was there. I could feel him—a powerful shadow, an impression of energy—on the other side of it. He was standing by the kitchen sink, drinking a beer. When I walked in and looked at him, he said, "Hey," in a way that made the back of my knees feel as if a feather, or a breeze, or a breath, had passed over them quickly.

"Hey," I said back.

I dropped my purse on the floor and went to him.

On the futon, we were quicker than we had been before. I came easily under him, his mouth on my neck, my hand reaching between us, cupping his testicles. "You're so wet," he said. "I like how wet you get."

We fell asleep on the futon in one another's arms before eight o'clock, then woke up just past midnight. The alarm clock I'd brought from home glowed on the floor, a murky blue, the second hand seeming to whirl too quickly, too smoothly, around the dial to be keeping actual time.

This time, he rolled me over on my side and pushed into me from behind. It took longer than it had the first time, and when we were done, the sheets were tangled and sweaty, and we were both panting—Bram on his back, and me still on my side. After a few minutes of just breathing together there in the dark, in the moonlight from the window and the glow of the alarm clock, he reached over and put a hand on my hip. "Are you okay, babe? Are you happy?"

I rolled onto my back.

The length of him was pressed against me, cool and blue in the darkness. I said, "I am, Bram. I'm happy."

"So am I," he said.

Without having to look at his face, his deep eyes, it was easier to talk to him, to ask him, "Bram, how did this happen?"

"You hit a deer," he said. "And then I saw you. And then I had to have you."

"Is that it?" I asked. "I mean, you'd seen me before, hadn't you?"

"Maybe," he said. "But not like that. In that skirt. Smelling like roses. I really noticed you then, babe. You were impossible not to notice."

But Garrett had said he'd spoken of me. The hot teacher in the English department. They should all take classes from her. Garrett had been so sure he'd been talking about me.

If not me, then, who? The other women in the department, except for Amanda, were older than I was. None of them could have been described, without being sarcastic, as "hot." Could it have been—

"Had you ever seen Amanda Stefanski before today?" I asked.

"Who's Amanda Stefanski?" he said. He was stroking my hip. He'd rolled onto his side.

"The woman who came up to us in the cafeteria. The English teacher."

He rolled onto his back again. "Sure," he said. "I've seen her."

"How would you describe her?" I asked.

"She's pretty easy on the eyes," Bram said. "She's pretty hot," he said. "But not like you," he said, pulling me into his arms again, pressing his erection against me.

Afterward, I got up to get a drink of water from the bathroom sink.

I turned on the light, looked at myself in the mirror.

There were bite marks on my right shoulder.

BETWEEN classes in the morning, I went to the women's room to look at those bite marks. Every time I did, I felt breathless— a deep electric surge between my hip bones. Because it was Tuesday, and tonight I would be sleeping at home, I wasn't sure if that deep magnetic longing was for Bram, or Jon. Did I want to be bitten by my lover, or to show my husband that my lover had bitten me?

"He *bit* you?" Jon asked, his eyes widening, slipping my blouse off my shoulders to look. I nodded.

He saw the mark there, which had gone from pink to purple during the day.

When he saw it, I could feel his whole body go rigid against mine. He put his mouth over it, then yanked my blouse—my good white blouse, the one that went with all the skirts and pants I wore to teach in—straight off of me, the pearl buttons scattering between us on the floor.

GARRETT.

I woke up beside Jon in the middle of the night—achy, stiff, as if I'd been sleeping for many hours on a train—and I had to pee, a sharp pain at the center of my pelvis that spread into a wider, duller pain.

I peed in the bathroom, in the dark, and then stood up from the toilet, and turned on the light, and looked at myself in the bathroom mirror. I was again a stranger, of course (I'm never, any longer, the woman I expect to find in the mirror), but not unpleasant-looking, I thought:

A woman with a husband who fucks her on the living room floor.

A woman with a lover who was jealous that another man had written her love letters.

My hair was dark and messy, and the eye makeup I was wearing had smeared smokily across my lids. If I blurred my eyes, peering into that mirror, I looked, I thought, young enough to be myself, years before, when, crossing the street, men would whistle at me from either side, from passing cars.

I would, then, hearing their whistles, look down at my feet, somehow ashamed to have called such attention to myself, but deeply in love, also, with that attention.

When I focused my eyes, I was myself again.

Jon's wife.

Chad's mother.

Bram's lover—

And then I realized, suddenly and completely, who it was if it wasn't Bram who'd written those notes.

It was, of course, Garrett.

Garrett.

Poor lost Garrett, whose bony little body I'd held in my arms when he fell down hard in the driveway, chasing after Chad, and who'd stood up then with both knees streaming blood.

Garrett's little-boy blood all over my Asian-print skirt, and his tears on my blouse.

He was small, then, even for his age. His hair was always sticking up in back. He smelled like Corn Flakes, and sun. He'd pressed his face into my stomach as he wept. I put an Elmo Band-Aid on each knee and gave him an ice-cream sandwich.

Garrett, of course.

His own mother, possibly a drunk, then dead. His father, dead.

Garrett had seen me in the hallways, I supposed, and some dim memory of that comfort from years before, that physical closeness, had come back to him, and he'd thought, wrongly, that he was in love with me—because I'd been kind, once, because he was alone. It was why, of course, he'd told me the notes were from Bram. He was embarrassed to have written them. He was trying to throw me off the track.

Oh, Garrett, I thought, sitting down on the lid of the toilet, and thought of him sitting across from me under Dalí's rose, telling me he'd joined the Marines. Had he been trying to impress me? (*The first to fight.*)

Oh, god, no.

Poor little Garrett with a truck bumping against the legs of my coffee table, his small butt in the air, making *vroom-vroom* noises.

Please, dear God, don't let poor little Garrett go to that war and die.

I WOKE in the morning to Jon breathing into my neck, "I want you to bring him here. I want him to fuck you in our bed." He rolled on top of me, his penis rigid between my legs.

"How?" I asked.

"I don't know," he said. "Tell him I'm out of town. I'll *go* out of town. I'll just come back early."

He pushed my legs farther apart with his own.

The look on his face was serious, I thought. Dangerous, again. And stupid, too, I thought. He didn't know Bram. He didn't understand what he was asking.

Or, he simply didn't care—about me, about our marriage, about anything but himself and his sexual fantasy.

"No," I said.

He looked surprised. He said, "Why?"

"Why? *Why?* Why would you ask me to do that?" I asked.

"Because, I—I—" He seemed not to understand the question. He seemed hurt that I would ask it. He was *whining,* I thought.

"No," I said, pushing gently against his chest with my palms. "I'm not bringing him here, Jon. I'm never bringing him here."

Jon rolled off of me then, onto his side — although he was still looking at my face. He was pouting. Sulking. But there was a stubbornness to it, too. I thought of Chad, with his arms crossed at his chest at Toys "R" Us, refusing to leave the Hot Wheels display without another miniature car.

"This is our bed," I said to Jon, enunciating each word carefully. (*No — I'll buy you three cars, young man, no more. Let's go.*) "I will not bring a stranger into our home."

"You won't bring a stranger into our home." Jon snorted. "You think you haven't already brought a stranger into our home?" At that, he laughed. He said, "You think this hasn't already come into our *home?*" His eyes were wide, as if it were mostly amusing, as if my stubbornness were the issue, not his.

I said nothing.

We were at the threshold of a room I didn't want to enter. I didn't want to talk about what this meant — about our marriage, about our lives. I didn't want Jon to say anything that would mean that this had happened, really, ever, or that it had made any difference between us, that it had brought something new into our marriage, something that might now always be there.

But then, as if my saying nothing were an agreement to his plan, Jon rolled back on top of me and said, "Come on, Sherry. I want you to fuck him in our bed. I want his come stains on our sheets when I get back." He pressed the tip of his penis to the entrance of my vagina. "Okay?" he said. "Okay? Say yes. *Please?*"

I saw, then, in my husband's face over mine, that there would be no talking him out of it. (*Okay. One more. But that's it, young man, and then we're leaving.*) And it came to me, looking into his stubborn, boyish expression, lit up with sexual energy, that there would be nothing left for us after this.

All those nights of ordinary pleasure, twenty years of them, after a long day, after Chad was in bed, after the dishes had been unloaded from the dishwasher and the lights had been turned out, and our teeth were brushed—those nights when we had quietly and companionably taken off our clothes, touched each other, kissed each other, then had uncomplicated, undangerous sex—those nights were over.

And what, if anything, would replace this edgy game when, as it had to, the affair with Bram had ended?

Another affair? The memory of the affair?

Or nothing?

"*Okay?*" he asked again. "Okay?"—louder this time, as if I hadn't heard him already, and a little more like a threat. He said, "Look, Sherry, I let you fuck this guy. You owe me, don't you?" He pushed himself into me so hard and fast that I cried out from the pain of it, and then he fucked me for a long time, as if he hadn't heard that cry of pain, as if he couldn't tell, or didn't care, that, beneath him, I was exhausted and uncomfortable and a little afraid.

When he was done, I said, "Fine. Okay. Okay."

"Great," Jon said, standing up, headed toward the bathroom. "Good girl. Friday?"—so casually he might have simply suggested having another couple over. Sue and Mack. Or going to a movie.

And then he was in the bathroom, and I was surprised to find my hands clenched in fists at my sides. I was surprised to find myself thinking, *Fine.* I lay in bed listening to the sound of the mourning doves outside as Jon showered and got ready for work, and to the sound of something making what must have been a nest under one of our bedroom windows (a fussy ticking, a flustering, something intricate and exhausting being prepared) just as they did every year—wrens, finches, building their nests in the eaves troughs, under the windows, in the hanging plants on the front porch, any sheltered nook they could find, as if the house were no longer ours, but theirs.

He was right, of course. Who was I to think I hadn't already brought a stranger into our home?

When Jon came back into the bedroom wearing his suit, smiling, smelling of soap, I thought, *Yes, okay, all right.*

ON THE drive into work, I saw her, at first, from a distance, and mistook her for an old coat in the median—a camel's hair coat—empty, tossed out of a passing car, a nice coat, the kind my mother used to wear, and I thought, *Now why would someone toss out a coat like that?* before I recognized her for what she was, and what I'd done.

"How HAVE you been?"

Sue, on the other end of the line, sounded much farther than a few offices away.

"Why are we talking on the phone?" I asked her. "I'll be right down."

When I got there, she looked papery, and shiny, sitting at her desk. There was something strangely poreless about her skin— the way Chad's skin had looked a couple of years ago when he'd been prescribed Accutane for his acne.

Yes, the acne had gone away, but what was left was a mask-like perfection that scared me. It was unnatural. When I read about a boy in Illinois who'd killed himself, and the parents had blamed the Accutane, I made Chad go off of it. "Fine," he'd said. "You were the one who didn't like my zits, not me."

And he'd been right. It *had* been me who'd worried over those red eruptions on his flesh, and it had been, hadn't it, because they meant he was not a baby any longer—his flesh hairless, poreless, blemish- and perspiration-free?

But after he went off the Accutane, Chad never got a single pimple again.

Sue, now, was the one who looked as if she were wearing some kind of mask. She looked as if she would be dry to the touch. "Are you okay?" I asked.

Her side of the office was a mess, which was unusual. Usually Sue was the one who complained about the bad habits of her office mate, an eccentric old woman from Alabama who taught English as a Second Language and whose students—Syrians, Koreans, Nicaraguans—came out of her class speaking their second language in a long aristocratic southern drawl. "Look," Sue would say, pointing to a cup of coffee that had been left undrunk on MayBell's desk and molded over, "someone needs to teach her to clean up after herself. She's still waiting for her slaves to come back from the fields."

A stack of old newspapers had slid off Sue's desk onto the floor, and no one had bothered to pick them up. I bent over to do it for her.

"I'm great," she said. "I guess you must be, too. But, I'm only guessing." Her tone was frankly angry. It surprised me. I took a step backward.

"What?" I asked. "What do you mean?"

"Well, you asked me how I've been. I wonder *where* you've been."

"I've just been—*here*," I said, pointing to the air around me. "I haven't been *anywhere*."

Sue laughed under her breath. It sounded brittle. "Oh," she said. "Well, I guess in the last twenty years I was getting kind of used to hearing from you every few days, so when two weeks go by . . ."

"Oh, no," I said. I put my hands to my heart. "Oh, Sue. Has it been that long? I'm so—"

"Don't be *sorry*, Sherry. I'm not trying to make you feel guilty. I'm just surprised."

"Oh, dear," I said. "Sue, I've been—"

"You've been what?" Her eyes were narrowed. She was, I thought, studying me closely.

"I've been—I don't know. Sue." I stood for a moment, feeling the closed-up air of her office embrace me too warmly. I inhaled. I sat down across from her. I exhaled. I said, in a different voice, a deeper voice, "How can I tell you, Sue?"

"What is it, Sherry? What's been going on with you?"

I opened my mouth.

She was waiting.

I had to tell her.

I inhaled again, and this time I could feel the dust particles in the air enter me, settle in me. I said, "Oh. Oh, Sue. How can I tell you this?"

"Try me," she said. "What is it?"

"I don't know," I said. "Midlife crisis? Sue, I've—"

I realized I was using my hands as I said these few, vague words, churning them in the air—something I usually did only when I was teaching, when I was actually trying to show the enormity or complexity of something, or to point to something I'd written on the blackboard. I saw my hands in the air in front of me and realized that Sue was looking at them, too, seeming annoyed.

"I'm sorry," I said again, and put them in my lap.

She exhaled raggedly. "Forget it, then," she said. "I don't have to be privy to all your secrets, if that's how you feel. Friendships change. I—"

"No!" I said, my hands leaping to my throat this time. Why did I say it so loudly? Was the idea of the friendship between us changing, *loosening,* that unbearable to me—so unbearable I couldn't even stand to hear the words come out of her mouth?

Yes, I realized, it was. For two decades, she'd known me. I'd known her. It was sacred. I *couldn't* bear it. I said, "Sue, I'll tell you the truth. But, you'll think badly of me."

She turned her hands up on her knees and said, "Try me," as if she'd been waiting for this information, as if she'd brought me to her office to receive exactly the news I was going to give her.

"Sue," I started. I looked down into her empty hands. I said, "I've been seeing someone." I looked up at her face. "A man."

Sue opened her eyes wider, but then glanced away from me quickly, looking over my shoulder, at the bulletin board behind me. There was nothing on it—just tacks, and the holes left behind by previous tacks. Then she looked back at me. "Oh. My," she said, and seemed to be unable to say anything more.

Now, I had to tell her.

The silence between us was full of the sound of the fluorescent lights burning too brightly over our heads. The hallway outside her door was empty. The phone sat on her desk without the slightest indication that it had ever rung, that it would ever ring again. That silence simply hovered around us, waiting for me to fill it. I bit my lower lip, and then I said, "It started, you know, with those letters—"

At this, Sue snorted, and I sat up straighter, feeling stung. I looked at her for some explanation, but she just shook her head, looked down at her own shoes, flat, black, rubber-soled—the shoes of an older woman, nothing like the sandals and stilettos she used to totter around on in the halls between classes.

"They weren't from Bram," I said. "You know—Bram?"

"I know *Bram*," Sue said with such sarcasm it sizzled for a minute in the emptiness between us. "We all know *Bram*," she said, more softly this time.

"Well, the letters weren't from Bram, but, I thought they were, and then I met him, and—things started."

"Shit, Sherry. You're having an affair with Bram Smith?" Her mouth hung open for a moment. She was shaking her head in disbelief. She said it again. "Shit, Sherry. Are you—"

I couldn't stand to hear her say it again, so I said, "Yes, yes. Sue, I'm—I am."

She kept shaking her head for what seemed like a very long time, as if to clear something, or see something, or to deny something completely, and then she stopped and leaned toward me, her eyes narrowed, as if trying to see me through some sort of mist, or brilliant glare. She said, "Are you kidding?"

This time, I shook my head, but only a little.

She sat back and looked up at the ceiling. I would have followed her gaze, but I knew what was up there. Nothing. Ceiling tile. Gray, institutional, weightless.

I looked, instead, at the floor.

Neither of us spoke until Sue said, "Oh. My. God."

"Sue," I started, but could think of nothing to follow it with. "Sue," I said, making it sound, this time, like a statement, or an appeal.

"So," she said, in a more sober tone, as if we were discussing lesson plans or wallpaper choices. "So, are you going to leave Jon?"

"No!" I said. "No, of course not."

"Well," Sue said, "I'm sure Mr. Auto Mechanics is great in bed, Sherry, but have you ever tried *talking* to him?"

"No," I said. "I mean, yes, Sue, I've talked to him. He's a fine man. He's a really very gentle, and—"

She stood up then, quickly, deliberately, as if to silence me—
and for a crazy moment I thought she might strike me. But, of
course, she didn't. Her hands were on her arms. She was gripping
her own arms so tightly I could see that the flesh on her biceps
was turning white. She licked her lips, swallowed, then looked at
me. She said, "I just don't think I can hear about this, Sherry. If
you're going to start telling me you're in love with Bram Smith . . .
I mean—I just don't see myself sitting here taking this seriously.
I think, honestly, that you should grow up, Sherry. I think this is
disgusting, if you want to know the truth."

I flinched, as if she *had* struck me. I said, "Sue, please. I'm—
I'm sorry. I'm—"

She said, "Please, quit saying that, Sherry. You say 'I'm sorry'
way too much. And, hey, don't apologize to *me*. But I do think
you might owe *Jon* some kind of apology."

"It's not like that," I told her. I put my face in my hands. I said
into them, "It's not like that. Jon knows."

"Oh my god," Sue said. "So you *are* leaving Jon?" She began
shaking her head so fast this time that her earrings—two little
black ships on hooks—rocked wildly around her neck. They
looked dangerous, I thought. Furious.

"No," I said, shaking my own head now. "Jon knows. And
he's—he's not upset."

"What?" Sue asked, sinking back down in her seat. "Jon
knows? Jon *approves*?" I said nothing. Sue opened her mouth.
Nothing came out. Then, she said, standing up again, "Now I
have heard enough, Sherry. I'm the one who's sorry now. We've
been friends a long time, and I'll be there for you when this is
over, but right now, I just—"

"I know," I said. "I know, I know, I know. I shouldn't have
told you. It's just, I wanted you to understand why I've been out
of touch. It's not *us*, Sue. I love you. You're my best friend. I'm

just"—I shrugged, I tried to smile—"I'm just—really stupid right now. A stupid middle-aged woman, doing something incredibly—stupid."

Sue blinked, then opened her eyes widely, looking more amused, perhaps, than angry this time. She said, "Lord, Sherry Seymour. I thought I knew you, woman. I mean, you'll always be my best friend, but it's going to take me a while to get to know you again." She stepped over to me and put her arms around me. The act pinned my shoulders to my sides so I couldn't embrace her back. She stepped away, looked at me, and said, "I've got to go now. The boys have a dentist appointment. Just"—she hesitated—"just keep me posted, huh, I guess?"

She walked over to the door and opened it, then stepped out into the hallway, reached back in and flipped her light switch, shut the door behind her, leaving me still sitting on the edge of her desk in the dark.

I CALLED out when I saw him in the cafeteria in the morning, "Garrett!"

He was standing in the spot where he often stood in the mornings before his first class, Auto II. Again, he was talking to the boy who resembled Chad, and the boy was wearing, as usual, his red nylon jacket. When I called out Garrett's name, this boy looked over at me, too, and I could see a flicker of something like resentment cross his face as I walked toward them. I was a teacher, an old woman, someone's dull mother, interrupting something interesting. But Garrett looked pleased. He brightened, turning toward me. "Do you have a minute, Garrett?" I asked. "Can you come to my office?"

"Sure!" he said.

We walked together through the gathered groups of students, through the cafeteria. The chatter was deafening, the colors so vivid—jackets, scarves, skirts. Spring had come to the cafeteria. All the black down jackets, the heavy flannel, the browns and grays, had been discarded or packed away.

Now, it was like passing through flocks of tropical birds, through the furious mayhem of nature. Here and there, someone's iPod or Walkman, turned up too loud to be healthy, leaked a scrap of music from an earphone—a symphonic buzzing, a wailing teenager, the sad angry chant of rap. At one table someone was telling a joke, and although I couldn't hear the words, the rhythm of narrative unfolding was familiar enough, the building of a story, *and then he said* . . . A small crowd of boys in T-shirts emblazoned with the names of football teams huddled around the joke teller, waiting with anticipation for the punch line. A female voice shouted, *Fuck you!*

Garrett walked ahead of me, making a path I could follow, parting the students as he walked, and then—I saw her coming, knew what would happen before it happened but could do nothing to stop it—a pale girl in a white dress, walking backward, quickly, while waving to her friends, bumped into me with a strange force, more like a car traveling at a high speed hitting me than a teenage girl wearing a white dress slamming into my side, knocking me off balance. I stumbled forward in my high heels. Two steps, three steps. Garrett reached out to catch me by the elbow, and he almost steadied me, but it was too late. I fell to my knees at the pink ballet slippers of the girl, who was apologizing profusely before she could even have realized what had happened.

From the floor, the crowd around me seemed monstrous. Tropical birds—but hungry, wild ones. I couldn't, at first, stand up, then Garrett took my hand and pulled me to my feet, and the pale girl (*Oh my god, oh my god, I'm so sorry, I'm such an idiot*) brushed off my skirt with her hand.

"Thank you," I said to both of them when I was standing again.

I looked down. My panty hose had been torn, and both of my knees were skinned, bleeding, long stripes of blood already dripping from my knees to my calves.

"Mrs. Seymour," Garrett said, looking at the blood. "Jesus Christ."

The girl, again, *Oh my god, oh my god.*

But, truly, there was no pain, and the wound was superficial, I thought. That's why there was so much blood. I knew. I'd spent years and years tending to such scrapes. I assured them I was fine, that I just needed some paper towels, that no serious damage had been done.

And it hadn't.

I'd simply been knocked to the earth by the spirit of spring, which had continued its colorful, raucous babble — completely indifferent, uninterrupted, just as it would have, I thought, if it had killed me.

AFTER I'd cleaned myself up in the women's room, stopped the bleeding with damp paper towels, thrown my panty hose in the trash can (luckily it was warm enough I didn't need them anyway), I went back to my office. Garrett was outside it, reading, again, the poem on my door. (*But the guts were out for the crows to eat.*) "Mrs. Seymour," he said. "Are you okay? I—"

"I'm fine," I said. "Really. I'm fine."

He looked at my knees.

The bleeding had stopped, but the skin was torn, a brightly

raw pink on my left knee, a bruise-colored scab already forming on my right. He winced.

I opened my door, and he followed me in. We sat down across from one another, and I said, "Well, Garrett, before all that, I just wanted to talk to you about your plan. Your enlistment. I just wondered—is it too late? I mean, have you really thought this through? Don't you think you should finish school first, and then if you still want to, you can join then? Maybe after things, after the war, assuming it *ends,* ever, maybe you can—?"

"It's too late," Garrett said. He was nodding, smiling. "It's really nice that you're so worried. But, yeah, it's too late, and I feel really happy, really sure. I'm completely committed, Mrs. Seymour. It's what I want to do."

Garrett was wearing a gray T-shirt with MARINES written across his chest in what looked to me like incongruously girlish script. The T-shirt was so new, so fresh and stiff, it could have stood up by itself. It had never been worn until this day, I could tell—never been washed, never been put in a dryer. Inside it, Garrett's shoulders looked narrow, and bony, and I remembered the feel of them, pressed against my skirt, his tears on my blouse, his skinned knees bleeding on both of us.

I said, "Oh, Garrett," but he was smiling.

He said, "I'm really sorry, but I have to go to class, Mrs. Seymour."

He stood up, and I opened my door for him, and before more than an inch of light from the hallway had cracked between the door and the frame, I knew what was on the other side.

A scent, a vibration, a shadow, Bram.

He had his arms crossed. He said, "Hi, Mrs. Seymour, I was just reading your poem here. Hey, Garrett. Gonna be late for class, aren't you?"

Then Bram looked from my neck to my knees and said, "What the hell happened to you?"

"I DON'T like him. I don't want you alone in your office with him," Bram said later over dinner in the efficiency.

Chinese. I'd picked it up on the way over from work. Bram liked Mongolian beef, like Jon. I got chicken fried rice for myself. We hadn't turned the lights on. Outside, it was not yet dark, but there was a steady icy rain pouring down. Over the course of the afternoon, something cold and purple had blown in out of the west—winter back for one last blast—and the temperature had dropped, and this frozen rain had started. In the shadows, Bram's face looked featureless across the table from me, nothing but eyes and teeth.

"Bram," I said. "I've known Garrett since he was five years old. He's my son's best friend"—which wasn't true, but sounded, I thought, reasonable enough—"and there's *certainly*—"

"Have you been getting any more love notes?" Bram asked. He'd finished his plate of food. He'd put his fork down at the edge of that emptiness.

"No," I said. "I haven't."

"Well," he said, "since you know now that the notes weren't from me, who do you think wrote them?"

"I don't know," I said.

"Yeah, you do," he said.

I put my own fork down. I asked, knowing the answer, "Who?"

"Garrett Thompson, obviously," Bram said.

I inhaled. I said, "Well, Bram, even if it was—"

Bram stood up. He said, "Whether or not it was, that motherfucker better watch himself."

Bram came over to me at the table and took my hand, pulled me up to stand against him. His erection against me felt uncomfortable, insistent. He put his mouth to my neck, one hand at the small of my back, pinning me to him, and the other on my breast.

WHEN I woke, I realized it was much later than I should have slept. I'd forgotten to set the alarm, and the sun pouring through the window was high and bright. I could barely open my eyes, and when I finally did, they were filled with water, a landscape of brilliance and tears before me, painted on the blank space of the ceiling.

I didn't bother to hurry out from under the sheet, or to rouse Bram. Without looking at the clock, I knew it was already too late. My first class on Thursdays started an hour and a half before the sun could have gotten this high in the sky.

I lay there, resigned to it.

(*Too late, too late, no hurry now.*)

And, with my eyes full of water and sun—too bright to see—I was reminded of how, when Chad was only three years old, Jon and I took him to Lake Michigan after a trip to the west side of the state, after visiting my father. It had been July, a day so bright blue that, even with my sunglasses on, to glance toward the water was blinding—that vast, frothing nothingness, impossible to really look at, shining as if it were generating its own super-radiance, a kind of white fire all the way to the horizon.

Before we'd gotten to the beach, I'd imagined laying our towels down, then taking Chad by the hand, walking him down to the edge of the water, letting his pudgy little feet baby-step themselves across the damp shingle of sand, over the layer of pebbles between the shore and the water, then his toes into the lake. Maybe we would make our way farther, up to his tummy, until he got scared, and then I'd take him in my arms, or pass him over to Jon, and we'd reassure him that if he stayed with us, he was safe.

But, while I was spreading the towels out, and Jon was taking his shoes off, shoving his car keys into the toes, tying the string around his bathing shorts tighter, each of us thinking the other was watching our son, Chad ran straight to the lake, and into the waves. I looked down at my side, where my son had been standing, and there was nothing.

When I turned and saw that he wasn't with Jon (two seconds having passed, really, or maybe only one), I opened my mouth and heard the words *Where's Chad?* come out, and then the bright empty shock of it crossing Jon's face. He looked toward the lake and said, pointing, "There!"

But what did *there* mean on a day of such luminous nothingness?

The water, an illusion, the sun smeared over it—*there* did not exist.

It was as indistinct as *nowhere*.

I was a blind woman in a bathing suit looking for the silver glint of a needle, and then both of us were running toward the water.

"There!" Jon continued shouting. "There!"

But there wasn't *anything* there. Water, sun; sun, water. *Nothing.*

And, then, suddenly, I saw him—a silhouette at the edge of the world, just before the world crashed over him in layers of brilliance and darkness, a huge flume of it snatching the silhouette off the edge of the horizon.

And then I was in the water, too, searching it wildly, unable to see anything but my own fingernails, painted red, and the pink back of Jon's neck as he bent over searching the water, still shouting, "There! *There!*"

White foot—or fish?—I lunged at it.

Grabbed it.

A miracle.

Something nature had snatched away, then tossed back up to me. My baby. Dragged out of Lake Michigan, laughing. I held his squirming happy form to me for too long. He started to cry.

After we dried off and calmed down enough to even speak to one another again, Jon and I packed up.

We drove home, in stunned silence.

In bed that night, we spoke of it in monosyllables.

"God."

"Lord."

"If—"

"I know."

"Fuck."

"Oh. Jon."

"*So* close."

"I can't—"

"I know."

Whenever I closed my eyes, I saw it:

That nothing, *there,* blazing, with my baby at the center of it.

"What are you thinking about, babe?" Bram asked. He'd propped himself up on one elbow and was looking down into my face. The shadow he cast there made it possible for me to open my eyes. I looked at him, and said, "I'm thinking we're too late."

"What difference does it make?" he asked, pulling me to him. "I can't think of anywhere I'd rather be than here."

"What about your class?" I asked.

"Fuck the class," he said. "They'll figure something out." He kissed me. He pushed the sheet away from my body, ran his hand from my neck to my hips. "You're so beautiful," he said. "You're like a sculpture."

His kissed my shoulder, where he'd bitten me before. He ran his tongue down the inside of my arm to the elbow. He moved down to my legs, kissed the skinned knees—first the left, which had begun to heal, and the right, which stung under his lips and made me flinch. "I'm sorry," he whispered, then moved back up, kissed my shoulder again, and then moved down my arm, from the elbow to my wrist. He kissed it. He bit it lightly. He took the wrist in his hand and pinned it over my head, then the other. He said, "I want to tie you up and make you come."

It surprised me how my whole body was electrified, involuntarily, at this suggestion—a tuning fork struck somewhere in my stomach, which caused my back to arch toward it, my nipples to harden without even being touched.

Bram got up and picked his pants up off the floor, and took from his pocket a length of rope so obvious I couldn't believe he'd been carrying it there and I hadn't noticed.

I looked at it.

He turned, smiling, and held it up so I could see it better— a laundry line, the kind my grandmother always kept strung between two trees in her backyard. I saw her, incongruously, suddenly, in a pink dress—the kind of dress she would never have worn, with big pockets stuffed with clothespins. My grandmother, twenty years dead. Bram snapped the rope and said, "Your husband ever tie you up?"

"No," I said. I was breathing so hard I could barely get the words out.

"Well," he said, and smiled. "I'm going to tie you up."

At first, despite the desire, the flicker of fear, I felt a little foolish, lying there quietly on my back, patient and naked, waiting for Bram to secure my wrists over my head, and then to tie the rope to the leg of a chair he'd hauled over to the side of the futon. I thought that, to give this anything more than symbolic significance, shouldn't I be struggling to get away? Or at least pretending to struggle?

Instead, I lay still, with my eyes closed, thinking, despite myself, about the office, about my class. It would have started and ended already. How long, I wondered, had my students sat and waited? Had they finally huffed in exasperation? Or did they high-five each other, hurrying out the door? (*Yeah! No class!*) Did someone go to the English department secretary and tell her that Mrs. Seymour hadn't shown up? Would Beth try to call me at home, or simply e-mail me, or just shrug?

But when I realized that the rope was tight enough around my wrists that, to get away now, I would have to knock the chair over, scramble away on my injured knees—that I would be awkward, trying to get away, and easily overpowered, and that Bram was spreading my legs, and moving between them, kissing my thighs, so that I could feel his hot breath there, and I opened my eyes and looked straight at the ceiling, I forgot about class, about my skinned knees, about Jon, Garrett, Chad, my father, about being a middle-aged English teacher on a futon—and my hips strained skyward, and it was all sky then, as he eased two fingers into me, and I thrashed against the rope despite myself, futilely, and Bram hardly needed to touch me with his tongue before I started to come.

AFTERWARD, still with my arms tied above me, as Bram slid in and out of me, I thought—is this what it is? To have sex purely for pleasure? Is this the great gift of growing older, of having procreation and marriage and the future over, to be with someone without grasping for *more*, without wanting anything in exchange for what I was giving—the negative capability of it. This pure pleasure was all there needed to be between us.

But, as I was thinking it, Bram looked down into my face and said, "Remember, babe, you're all mine."

I TRIED to slip into my office without being noticed, but Beth whirled around at her computer the second I stepped in and shouted, "Sherry! Are you okay? Why weren't you in class?"

"Oh," I said. "I overslept. I'm—not feeling that well."

She looked at me for a second, then said, "Well, you look great."

On my voice mail, there were seven messages.

Two were from Beth—the first one checking to see if I was in my office, the second confirming that I wasn't and that I'd missed my class. One was from a student telling me she'd left her paper in my mailbox. One was Sue, who'd heard from Robert Z that I'd missed my class, wondering if I'd be missing my afternoon class as well, and saying, "I hope you're okay," with the cold concern of a colleague, not a friend. And two messages from Jon.

"Jesus, Sherry. You missed your class. What's going on?"

I felt happy to hear the edge of worry in his voice. It seemed familiar, spousal—the reaction a husband in an ordinary domestic situation would have upon hearing that his wife had not gotten, that morning, into work on time.

But then, the second message from Jon was half whispered:

"I hope what's going on is what I think is going on. When you get home, I want to hear all about it."

The last message was from Summerbrook. "Just calling to tell you your father's doing much better. Give us a call if you'd like an update." The woman's voice on the message was unfamiliar. Chirpy. Childlike. Full, I thought, of false cheer.

I needed to return these phone calls, but I did not yet feel I would be able to speak without revealing myself, where I'd been, what I'd been doing. It had to be in my voice, the long morning in bed with my lover. Surely, anyone hearing my voice would be able to hear it, too.

I turned on my computer.

In my in-box, an e-mail from Chad:

Ma, So. Hey. If you and Dad aren't too busy you think you could pick me up from the airport? Week from Sunday. I'll be the guy at baggage claim formerly known as your son. Remember me? You're my mother?

Chad.

PS. Talk Garrett out of his warrior ambitions yet? I say go for it, chump. More food for the rest of us . . .

After I turned the computer off, I picked up the phone to call Summerbrook, where it didn't matter what the physician's assistant thought of me or my extramarital affair. Who cared what she could hear in my voice? When I asked for her, they said she was in and transferred me to her.

"Hello?"

She answered the phone cheerfully, musically, the same tone of voice with which she'd spoken in her message, to a machine. I told her who I was, who my father was, and she sang out, "Oh, yes, yes, yes!" He was, she said, doing much, much better since they'd started him on the Zoloft. Yesterday, they'd managed to talk him into coming down for arts and crafts (I thought I heard her flipping through papers here, as if consulting her files on my father, on his relative happiness or despair—files full of papers I imagined blank, white, the thinness of onion skin) and he seemed very, very happy. He'd made Easter baskets with some of the ladies. He was eating again. (I had to pull the phone away from my ear, she was speaking to me so loudly, so excitedly.) "You should see him!" she said—and I felt the guilt of it stab me somewhere near my sinuses, the tears starting there, trickling behind my face, into my throat, where I could taste them, a little sweet, with the lingering taste of the peppermint I'd eaten in the car on my way into the college, as if something sharp, but also sugary, had stung me between my eyes. I said, "I'm sorry. I'm sorry I haven't been in to see him. I've been so—"

"Busy!" she said, as if it had been a contest, as if she were pleased with herself for having shouted out the correct answer, having filled in the blank for me with the very word I'd been searching for. "Mrs. Seymour," she said, "that's what *we're* here for. It's our job to take care of people who don't have anyone with the time to take care of them."

I sat up straighter in my chair.

Was she criticizing me—brilliantly, subtly, with this pretend-cheerfulness, this friendly reproach—or was this simply the brutal truth?

It didn't matter. I wanted to apologize more. I wanted to tell her, *Look, he's always been a hard man. Even when I was a child. Years would pass when he hardly smiled. We were really never close. It was my mother I was close to; my father, he was like a shadow on the wall, he . . .*

I wanted to tell her that I'd had a brother. My father and he were much closer than he and I had ever been, and my brother had killed himself, had taken his own life—and wasn't that the ultimate act of abandonment, hadn't he deserved some blame for that, shouldn't he, having bowed out so completely with no concern whatsoever for our father, for *me*, shouldn't he bear some responsibility now, too? *Why should it always be the daughter who—*

And then she chimed in, as if with good news, "There's

nothing you can do for him, Mrs. Seymour. We're taking great care of him ourselves."

She sounded proprietary, I thought—as if my father now belonged to her.

Over the freeway, two sandhill cranes were flying low, looking prehistoric and determined, like long smooth crucifixes in the sky—one obediently trailing the other, making loud trilling sounds as they flew.

Were they speaking to one another? Or were they, I wondered, calling out to the rest of the world?

"So," Jon said, greeting me at the door. "What happened to you last night to make you miss your class this morning?"

There was a splash of light from the window on his face, and it washed his features so brightly that I would never have been able to pick him out of a lineup, or recognize him on the street. I could see that he was smiling, but I had no idea whether or not the smile was forced, or sincere.

"The alarm clock was unplugged somehow," I said. "I overslept."

His smile faded. He took a step toward me, out of the spotlight of sun from the window. "I don't believe you," he said. "I think you were with your lover."

I tossed my purse onto the floor, shaking my head.

"Yeah," he said, taking me in his arms. "I can smell it on you, Sherry." He put his face in my hair. "It's okay. You can tell me."

I felt a dull pain tapping me at the base of my skull—some vein beating against a nerve, I supposed. I felt the tears well up in my eyes again, but I blinked them back this time and said, "You're right." I swallowed. I said, "He tied me up."

"Jesus Christ," Jon said, pulling away from my hair to look at me. "He tied you up?"

"Yes," I said.

"Oh, Sherry," Jon said, putting a hand on my breast. "That's good," he said. "I want to go upstairs, and I want you to tell me exactly what happened."

WE'D ALREADY made love, taken a shower, and gotten back into bed, but Jon instantly had an erection again. While we were having sex, he'd made me say Bram's name. *Say his name,* Jon had said. *I want to hear you saying it when I come.*

I'd said it, and when I did, I saw Bram's face over mine, looking down, saying, *Remember, babe, you're all mine.*

How had this happened, I wondered, that my lover had become jealous, possessive, while my husband was trying to give me away? I said his name again, and Jon pushed into me hard, and came.

Afterward, Jon pulled me to him and said, "Did you tell him you want him to come over here? That you want to fuck him in your sacred marriage bed?"

Jon was laughing and serious at the same time, and it cut through me, the sarcasm.

It *was* all a game to him, I thought at that moment, bitterly. Not only the affair, the marriage. I remembered my mother standing over my brother when he was twelve or thirteen. He'd just said something vile to her—one of those things he so often said. *You bitch* or *I hate you* or *You smell like piss,* and he was smiling up at her, and she said, "I should slap that smile right off your face, buddy."

"So? Did you ask him?" Jon asked.

"No," I said. "I forgot."

"You *forgot*?" Jon thought for a minute, but he was still smiling. "You've got to be kidding me, Sherry. How could you forget a thing like that? Come *on*. You *forgot*."

In truth, I hadn't forgotten. I'd thought about it all day—Bram in our house, in our bed—and most of the night. I'd thought about it while I was teaching my class. I lay beside Bram on the futon and thought about it. On the drive home, I'd thought about it. And again, that echoing tunnel:

Did I want—*could* I want—to bring Bram to my home, to my bed? Did I want it because Jon wanted it? Or *not* want it because Jon wanted it? Did I want Bram to want it?

And why did it feel, despite my husband's insistence on it, like more of a betrayal than anything else—of the marriage, of our life?

Was it?

No. I thought, no, of course, it wasn't.

How could it be more of a betrayal of our marriage than spreading my legs for Bram? Taking him into my body? Sleeping beside him?

In truth, even before Jon had brought it up, I'd wanted to bring Bram here, hadn't I? I'd wanted to show him where I lived, who I was. I'd begun to feel that the efficiency was the place, the *way*, he thought I lived—who he thought I was—a woman with nothing but a futon and two sets of dishes, no history, no family or possessions or taste. I'd wanted him, I thought, to see my garden, my woodstove, my *life*. I'd imagined taking him on a tour through my house. *See. I live here, these are my things* . . .

"You better tell him tomorrow," Jon said.

I looked over at him.

His erection was still pressed against my hip.

I'd almost forgotten that he was there. He said, "Chad's home next Sunday, and after that it will be too late."

Chad.

Sunday.

I'd nearly forgotten about Chad, too.

I hadn't even returned his e-mail.

The mention of his name at that moment sobered me entirely, and I inched away from Jon and his erection and his heated whisperings, and suddenly the whole pathos and absurdity of the situation washed over me, *through me,* all blood, and shame — and also the sense of desperate, pointless urgency. "Okay," I said. "Okay. I'll tell him."

BRAM came around the corner of the hallway to my office while I was standing outside my door, unlocking it, with a student beside me — Merienne, flunking out of my Intro to Lit class, a blond in a top cut so low it would be impossible for anyone not to stare into the shadows into which it plunged. She was gorgeous, and when I saw Bram behind us, I wanted to throw a blanket over Merienne so he couldn't see her, couldn't compare her dazzling firmness to me.

But, he did see.

How could he not?

And, before I could turn back to my door, I saw his eyes travel over her, and a surge of humiliation coursed through me — chemical, fluid, smelling of household cleaning products, formaldehyde, opening every pore of my skin at once.

"Hey," he said to me, looking at her.

I stepped into my office and Merienne followed.

"I'll have to talk to you later," I told him, closing the door.

———

"So," BRAM said, later, in the cafeteria. "Am I truly forbidden to come to your office?"

"No," I said. "But it's awkward. I have students I have to see. And, seeing you—"

"Does it distract you?" Bram asked. His hand hovered for a moment over the Styrofoam cup of coffee in front of him, and I realized that he was, perhaps, looking for some kind of reassurance. He was asking about his own power over me, checking on it.

"It definitely distracts me," I said.

"Well, I don't want to distract you at work," he said, and reached across the table with his hand, ran his fingers over my knuckles. "But I'd like to distract you elsewhere."

I pulled my hand away and looked around. The cafeteria was nearly empty, but Derek Heng was at the table next to ours. He was looking at me. He hadn't been in class since the day we'd discussed the first act of *Hamlet*, when he'd asked me what the point of reading it was if they couldn't understand it.

Derek nodded at me noncommittally. I nodded back.

I turned to Bram again.

He was looking at me. The smoky darkness. Something right behind his irises, smoldering. I could feel the blood pulsing in my neck. I put my fingers there. I opened my mouth to speak, but just as I did, something landed on the table between us. A hornet? Something buzzing and golden. I pushed my chair away from it as it tripped through a bit of stickiness that had been left to dry on the table. Bram waved his hand over it, and it flew away, making the sound of a very tiny, stifled alarm as it did.

I looked back up at him. I said, "Can you come to my house?"

"Sure," he said, still looking at me. He didn't blink. "I'll come to your house, babe. Are you sure your husband won't walk in on us?"

I said, "He won't."

"Okay," he said.

Bram followed me from the cafeteria back to my office. When we walked into the department together, Beth raised her eyebrows, but then turned back to her computer, a line of clubs and hearts on her screen.

After I'd shut the door behind us, Bram moved around, touching my things.

A paperweight. The stapler. A box of paper clips.

He picked up a photograph of Chad and looked deeply into it, looked at it so long that I had an impulse to snatch it out of his hands, but didn't. I let him look. I looked over his shoulder. In the photograph, Chad was eleven years old in a baseball jersey and a green cap. His smile was so wide and eager it was almost too bright to look at. That moment, I always thought when I looked at that picture later, was the last part of his childhood. After that, he learned, as we all do, how to hide his naked enthusiasm for life from the world, and especially from the camera. After that, there was never a photograph of Chad again in which he did not have a half-ironic smile. A bit of a smirk. An expression that said, *Yeah, this is me, I'm smiling.*

Bram put the photo of Chad in its little brass frame back down on my desk gently, then he picked up a picture of Jon. He looked at it for only a second, scoffed, put it back on my desk, facedown. He turned to me, put his arms around my waist, and pulled me to him. "You're mine now," he said, kissing me deeply, bending me backward, until we were against my desk, and he was between my legs.

He moved the crotch of my panties to the side with the fingers of one hand, then took himself out of his jeans with the other, and pushed himself deeply into me. I stifled a gasp against his shoulder, but he moaned loudly enough, I thought, for Beth to have heard from her desk, for anyone passing by my door to have heard as they passed.

But I did nothing to stop it. We both came there, like that, quickly, and then he stepped back to look at me, his pants still unzipped, the underarms of his white shirt damp, his lips parted, his eyes narrowed. "Don't forget it," he said. "All mine." He zipped up his pants, tucked in his shirt, and left.

I sat for a long time at my desk, not daring to leave the office. I waited until I thought it was lunchtime, and Beth would have left for an hour. I wanted to see myself in the bathroom mirror before anyone else saw me.

AFTER the women's room—where I stood looking at myself for a long time in the full-length mirror—I went down to the cafeteria. There, I saw Garrett from a distance, and I called out to him, but he didn't turn around. And then, from behind me, I heard Sue say, "Hey, girlfriend."

I turned to find her standing a few inches behind me with a cup in her hand. She was wearing a blue dress with a wide tan belt around her waist, smiling.

"Sue," I said.

She looked good, I thought, rested. She'd gotten a new haircut, and the little curls on her forehead seemed girlish, optimistic. I said, "Sue, you look great."

"I *am* great," she said.

"You look better than ever," I said. "You look—radiant."

"Well, how are *you,* Sherry?" she asked.

"I'm fine, too," I said—feeling suddenly prudish, exposed, knowing she knew what she knew about me, that I myself had told her. Now, I wanted somehow to take it back, to tell her that what I'd told her about Bram, the affair—that I'd made that up. That it had been a fantasy, a story. It had not actually happened.

Could I? Could I somehow laugh, and lie, and turn it into a little joke?

No.

If I'd ever lied to Sue, I didn't remember. Of course, I'd told her on several occasions that I'd liked a pair of pants or shoes she'd bought, when I didn't really—but did that count as a lie? And, anyway, what possible explanation for having made up such a story could I give her? She knew me better than that. She knew it all, now, all about Bram. I'd told her myself, of course—but, still, I felt some resentment about it, as if she'd borrowed something of mine she was refusing to return. I'd given it to her, of course, but she was holding it now against my will—or we both knew she could if she wanted to.

Maybe to distract us both from what hung between us, I pointed in the direction of Garrett, who was standing in his usual spot in the cafeteria, talking to his friend in the red nylon jacket, and I said, "Do you remember him? He used to be Chad's little pal in elementary school. Garrett."

"The one whose dad died?"

"Yes," I said.

"Whew," she said. "They grow up fast. Will my boys get that big someday?"

"They will," I said. "In the blink of an eye."

"In the meantime," she said, "I have to go because I have to take cupcakes into their classes today. I'm Snack Mom today."

"Snack Mom," I said, and remembered it. The weight of a tray of cupcakes, the challenge of covering them with tinfoil or plastic wrap without ruining the frosting and the sprinkles on top. The little paper napkins. The children at their desks. The

smell of cake in a small room. The perfume of something sweet
having been made by someone's mother. The great simple pleasure of being the mother who'd made it.

"He's joined the Marines," I told her.

"Oh, no," Sue said. She took a sip from the cup of coffee in
her hands, and we started to walk slowly together toward our offices. I saw Robert Z on the other side of the cafeteria as we
passed through it, but I looked away, not wanting to have to talk
to him, especially in front of Sue, about where I'd been yesterday,
why I'd missed my class.

"Yes," I said. "I tried to talk him out of it—"

"There's no talking them out of it," Sue said. "Some of these
boys—I've had them in my classes, it's like moths to the flame.
They don't believe in death yet. And they believe in what they're
doing."

"I know," I said. "With Garrett though—I feel responsible.
I feel—"

"Why?" Sue said. "You're not his mother." She stopped to
sip her coffee again. "It's got nothing to do with you."

I stopped, too, and turned to her. I said, "I feel as if it does."

"Why?" she asked. She started walking again. "You don't
even really know him, do you?"

"A little," I said. "I do know him a little."

"Well," Sue said. "A little is nothing. You can't go around
feeling responsible for every kid you know a *little*."

I stopped then in the hallway and turned to her. I said, "You
know those notes I got?"

Sue kept walking, nodding, and didn't turn to look at me. I
followed her.

I said, "You know, I thought they were from—Bram?" I
pronounced his name under my breath, and she stopped then,

turned around to me, but didn't look up. She was looking into the black pool of her coffee as if she'd lost something in it. "But they weren't," I said. "They were from Garrett."

Sue snorted and looked up, shaking her head.

She wasn't looking into my eyes. She was looking at my neck. She kept shaking her head, and a bit of black coffee spilled out of her cup, trickled down the side of it onto her hand, but she didn't seem to notice. She inhaled. She said, as if it exhausted and relieved her at the same time to say it, "No, Sherry. The notes weren't from Bram, and they weren't from Garrett."

"I know," I said. "I know it sounds ridiculous, because Garrett's so young, but I think he may have, I don't know, projected some feelings, maternal feelings maybe, onto me, and—"

Sue sighed then and looked straight into my eyes. She smiled—a smile that looked weak, I thought, apologetic, and she said, "I was going to tell you eventually, Sherry, but I guess I really have to tell you now, because this has gone too far. I guess it was a mistake. I had good intentions, but it was obviously a big mistake. The notes"—she inhaled—"were from me."

I put my hands instinctively to my throat.

A little sound came out of my mouth.

Sue looked up as if she expected me to say something, and I tried, at first, but no words would come out. She opened her own mouth then, and closed it, then shrugged, and looked down at her feet.

I looked at them, too, and thought I saw the floor move slightly under us. A shifting of light on the linoleum. A trick of the eye. But I moved over to the wall, to lean against it, to steady myself. My hands were still at my throat. I swallowed. Finally, I said, "Why?"

Sue said nothing.

I asked again, more insistently this time, "Why?"

Again, Sue shrugged. She said, "I felt sorry for you, Sherry. I thought Chad leaving for college had really taken a toll. You always looked so tired, like you weren't taking care of yourself anymore — sort of washed up. I wanted to spice up your life a bit. I thought it would do you good to think you had a secret admirer. I guess it worked just a little too well."

BACK in my office, I gathered up the notes from my desk drawers and the filing cabinet and, without looking at them, crumpled them up and threw them away.

In the hallway, I had stood speechless before her for what seemed like a very long time, and even after all that time during which I might have gathered my thoughts, the only thing I'd managed to say was, "Oh."

Oh.

Oh.

She was observing me, I felt, from a distance, with a look on her face that I recognized, I thought, as *satisfaction.*

What else could it have been?

She did not look sorry, or sad, or empathetic. She was standing very straight, looking into my eyes, and her gaze never wavered. She had done something, and had meant to do it, and she'd kept the secret of doing it long enough, that gaze seemed to say.

And that was all there was to it.

But, standing in the hallway, being looked at by her, I'd felt myself zooming backward, at great speed.

A woman strapped to the mast of a ship.

No, a woman strapped to a *rocket.*

A woman growing smaller, being observed. All the years of our friendship, then, telescoped in a few heartbeats, in the hallway, and suddenly I was a million miles away. She couldn't possibly be seeing me, I thought, although she was looking straight at me, *seeming* to see me. But if she *were* still seeing me, I thought, she would need to be squinting. She would need to be holding binoculars up to her eyes—and, even then, I would have been an ant. I would have been a dot. I had been propelled away from her over the years in only a few seconds. I'd completely disappeared. I'd been blotted out by the sun in the Writing Center the day we first met. I'd been obliterated with the speed of my own propulsion—blown backward over a landscape strewn with Styrofoam cups, and discarded clothes, torn envelopes, white flowers—the ones she'd worn in her hair at my wedding—and all the Christmas and birthday cards she'd signed in that fluid, youthful script. Her handwriting, I should have recognized it immediately—why didn't I? *Be Mine.*

Love, Sue.

How had I missed it, all those years, in that *Love,* the hatred, too?

"Come on, Sherry," she'd said, "don't overdramatize this, okay?"

Three

On Jon's side of the bed, lying on his back, his head on Jon's pillow, Bram looked like the stranger he was.

Underneath him, in our bed, I'd felt hollow. Stupid. Fat. It had been weeks since I'd fallen out of my usual routine of going to the gym every evening. While Bram was moving in and out of me (that pained, erotic expression on his face seeming, in the too-bright afternoon light, almost cartoonish with pleasure) I could see that the lip of flesh I'd been so proud to have lost by dint of all those miles traveled nowhere on elliptical machines was back.

Jon had sounded shaky and exhausted that morning on the phone from work. "What time do you think you'll get there? What time do you think you'll be fucking him in our bed?"

The night before, he'd presented me with a tape recorder he'd bought at Best Buy. It was slim and silver, and he'd said, "I'm going to set this up under the bed."

"No!" I'd said. "What if it clicks? What if Bram hears it?"

"I thought of that," Jon said. His eyes were shiny. The pupils small as pinpricks. "I asked the salesman and double-checked it myself. It's digital. It doesn't click."

"Get that away from me," I said, heading for the bathroom, for a shower.

"Why?" He followed after me with it in his hand, holding it

toward me as if it were a present—an engagement ring, a sum
of cash—that should mean as much to me as it did to him.

"What," I said, whirling around, "you need proof, Jon? You
can't just believe me, that I'll bring him here, you need *proof*?"

"No," he said. "I don't *need* it, Sherry. None of this is about
what either of us *needs*. This—"

"This has gotten completely out of control, Jon. This has
gotten sick, and offensive, and—"

"Offensive? What? What are you talking about? It's *offensive*
that I want to have hot sex with my wife? It's *offensive* that I want
to think about her fucking another man?"

"It doesn't feel as if you're trying to have hot sex with me, it
feels as if—as if you're trying to *resurrect* me. When did I get so
dull to you, Jon, so—so *asexual* that you have to titillate yourself
this way to even *see* me, to even—?"

"Well, Sherry, Jesus. You know, we've been married for two
decades, if you haven't noticed. I'm sorry if—"

"—if you have to think about another man fucking me in
order to fuck me yourself?"

"But, Sherry, we've *always* fantasized about this. Right from
the beginning. Before we were even married, we were always
talking about—"

"That was different," I said. "That was about *us*. This is
about *you*."

Jon laughed then—one quick burst, but then he kept laughing. Laughing as if he'd been keeping it bottled up for a long
time. As if he'd been an actor in a comic skit for years, suppress-
ing it, and now the show was over. *Heartily*, I thought. The word
that would have described the way Jon laughed, then, was *heartily*.
He let the arm, still holding the tape recorder stretched out toward me, drop down to his side as he laughed. He leaned up
against the wall as he laughed. When he'd finally stopped laugh-

ing he said, "Okay, Sherry, then don't do it. I didn't realize. It
seemed to me that having a little fun with a fantasy, with a tape
recorder—" He shrugged, his eyes still teary from laughter. "I
didn't realize, I guess, that you were such an unwilling player in
all of this. You could've fooled me."

Again, I saw my mother standing over my brother.

She never did it. She never *slapped that smile* off his face. She'd
only ever threatened to do it, and he'd been smarter than that.
He'd seen straight through that.

Defeated, I said, "Okay, Jon. Just do whatever you want with
the tape recorder. I'm taking a shower now."

"Okay, Sherry," Jon said. As I walked away from him he said
to my back, "You're still going to bring him here, aren't you?"

I HADN'T stayed at the efficiency Wednesday night, as I usually
did, because I hadn't, myself, slept at all the night before. After
the argument about the tape recorder, I lay wide awake all night,
but with my eyes closed, listening to the sounds moving around
in the darkness outside.

A coyote calling out.

The Henslins' spaniel answering.

A car driving too fast through our intersection.

Breeze. Leaves. The spring peepers trilling in the Henslins'
scummy pond.

How full of themselves they were!

It was, wasn't it, all about sex?

Did they have any idea how brief their lives would be, how
shallow and dirty the pond into which they'd been born was, that
this pond was not the only pond in the world, that it was just one
of millions of ponds, not even one of the *better* ponds?

I imagined them in it. Trilling. Swimming. Fucking. I'd read somewhere that male frogs, during mating season, would happily make love to a fistful of mud if it were shaped like a frog.

They'd fuck the mud. They'd fuck other males. Presumably, they'd fuck sick frogs, old frogs, dead frogs. Theirs was just a blind instinct, directed at nothing in particular. Nothing personal. Nothing that mattered. I pictured all of this in the Henslins' pond—all the fuming and anxious groping—and, at the edge of it in the darkness, Sue, with that look on her face:

I wanted to spice up your life a bit.

Oh, I'd said, my voice sounding as if it were coming from somewhere far away from me. And then, weakly, walking away from her, audible only to myself, *That did cross my mind.*

But it had *never* crossed my mind.

As I walked back to my office, Robert Z passed me in the hallway again, only looking over for a moment, raising his hand in a soft hello. He'd seen something there on my face, I could tell, which kept him from stopping, kept him from teasing—*"Playin' hooky yesterday, Sherry?"* And it occurred to me suddenly then, sickeningly, that *everyone* knew—knew that I was having an affair with Bram, that the notes had been from Sue, that I'd fallen for it, the whole thing, that I was vain and stupid enough to continue to fall indefinitely as they watched.

Had that been what Sue had wanted all along?

Had I betrayed her somehow so deeply—not listened to her attentively enough, not called her often enough—that finally she'd devised a plan to humble me forever?

Had she, over the years, grown to have so much contempt for me—my worries about my weight, my taste in clothes, the way I talked, the books and movies I liked or didn't like—that she wanted to end our friendship this way?

All these years, had I simply overlooked it, as I talked on and on about Chad's accomplishments, about Jon's good humor, about the hollyhocks in the garden, about what I was making for dinner, or what I'd just bought at the mall, the signals she was sending?

I remembered noticing, once, the look on her face, one afternoon, showing her photographs from our week in Costa Rica. It had honestly puzzled me, that expression. I'd said, when I noticed it, "I'm sorry, Sue. Am I going on and on?"

"No," she'd said, but her expression had stayed the same, and I'd gone on, then, about the ocean, about the tropical flowers. I had totally failed to see it for what it was—boredom, disdain. Deepening, widening.

Maybe.

Or, maybe it had occurred to her suddenly, one morning. Maybe she'd simply woken up one morning and realized that she hated me.

Or, perhaps, was she only telling the truth, there in the hallway that afternoon? That she'd only felt sorry for me? That I'd looked *washed up*. That she only wanted to spice up my life?

And, which of these possibilities would be the least painful to believe?

WEDNESDAY afternoon, when I'd called Bram from my office and told him I had to go home that night, not to the efficiency, he said, "You're kidding, right?"

Why would I be kidding?

"No," I said. "Bram, I have things I have to do, and I'm tired—"

"What do you have to do?"

I said, "Chad's coming home on Sunday. I have to do laundry.

I have to —" I could think of nothing else to say, so I told him the truth. "I'm exhausted," I said. "I couldn't sleep all night."

There was a silence on the other end of the line that, it occurred to me, could quite possibly contain a third person, listening. Suddenly, then, I felt sure of it. Who were the phone operators at the college? I'd never even seen them, as far as I knew. I'd had the impression that they'd all been replaced years ago by a tape recording, but that couldn't be true, could it? Someone had to be there to talk to the people with more questions than a machine could answer.

So, where were they? *Who* were they? And did they, perhaps, get bored wherever they were and listen in on the conversations zigzagging back and forth across the campus?

"Oh," Bram said.

"But I'll see you tomorrow," I offered.

"Whatever," Bram said.

Behind him I could hear an engine start up, and something metal — flimsy and heavy at the same time — crashing onto cement.

Now, he was lying on his back on Jon's side of the bed. Looking up at the ceiling, he said, "So, what are we going to do about this, Sherry?"

I was relieved, I realized — a weight rising from my chest, as if a large bird had been perched there — hearing him say something that had to do with what was happening between us, the little door it opened into the possibility that this was wrong, that it had to end. In that crack of light I thought I could still see myself in my old life — maybe carrying a basket of laundry up the stairs. Going for a slow walk with Jon through a park, holding hands, growing older, placing a plate of sliced beef and onions on a table between my husband and my son. I said, "Oh, Bram, you're right. This *can't* go on."

He said, "I want you to leave this motherfucker, baby. I want you to be mine."

I couldn't move.

I couldn't breathe.

The word *mine* seemed to echo around the bedroom, peeling itself down to the essentials of hard consonants and the single bright vowel (*eye eye eye*) bouncing from one white wall to the other—while, outside, what had sounded like thousands and thousands of spring birds making noises about their territory, about their fears, about their plans for the future in the trees, went completely silent.

I sat up.

What was I doing here, with this stranger, in my marital bed? Whether Jon had wanted it or not, it *was* a complete betrayal, and I'd done it simply out of vanity, hadn't I? It hadn't been for *Jon*. I couldn't even pretend to myself that it had been. It had been for *me*:

See, Bram. I am a woman with a lovely home. I am a woman with things, and people, and—

No.

It had been for *Sue*.

See? No one needed to spice up my life.

It had been for all of them. It had been for Beth at her computer, playing solitaire, watching me out of the corner of her eye. Amanda Stefanski in her orange dress, telling me what a wonderful mentor I was. Robert Z, who wasn't gay at all, but who still had no interest in me. My student Merienne with her misspelled name and plunging neckline. Derek Heng. *What's the point of reading* Hamlet *if we don't understand it?* My mother, who'd died when she was my age. My brother, who'd gone to a Holiday Inn in Houston to shoot himself in the head and never even left a note. I'd done it for *them*.

But, in doing it, I realized now, listening to Bram breathe on Jon's side of the bed, staring at the ceiling, I had plucked out my own eye. I had taken a knife to my own hand.

"We have to go," I said to Bram, and got out of the bed.

He got out of bed more slowly than I, but he did get out, and as he pulled his clothes back on behind me I brushed the pillowcases and the sheets with the palms of my hands. There was nothing there, but I brushed anyway. Skin cells. Molecules. The dust and detritus of us. My hands were shaking. I made the bed, pulled the sheets up, tucked them in—and the white comforter, heartbreakingly familiar and plain, a blank page upon which I'd written all of this, I pulled that up, too, smoothed out the creases, sweeping the surface, patting it down until it looked exactly as it had—although, I knew, stepping back, that it was no longer the same bed in which Jon and I had slept the night before, and the night before that, and all the nights remembered and forgotten stretching behind me, through time. It had been changed, forever—the subtle alteration having taken place, it seemed, at the level of its atomic structure, a few rearranged particles that had turned it into another bed entirely, the bed of a couple I'd never met, a couple I would not have recognized, passing them on the street. A couple I would have failed to recognize mainly because the woman, passing by me with her husband, would have borne such an uncanny resemblance to me.

"Are we going, babe," Bram asked, "or are we going to stand here staring at the bed?"

I didn't turn to look at him.

I couldn't tear myself away.

I was stunned, frozen in time, over my own bed. There was

something, I thought, that I needed to remember about this bed — but then Bram, behind me, cleared his throat impatiently, and I turned away from the bed, while, under it, the tape recorder continued its digital whispering, which either I didn't hear, or I chose not to hear.

BRAM drove my car back into the city. We'd left his red Thunderbird in the parking lot of the college, ostensibly so that my husband, who was supposed to be out of town, wouldn't hear from the neighbors about another man's car parked in our driveway.

Being beside him in a car was a lot like being with him in bed. He knew what he was doing. He was absorbed completely in the task of doing it, the mechanics of it.

But I felt strangely shier beside him here in my car than I had been even the first time with him in bed — self-consciously pulling my seat belt across my chest, awkwardly adjusting the visor so that the sun, which had begun to slide out of the sky already into the west, wasn't in my eyes.

I crossed my ankles on the floorboard, and, when that seemed matronly, I crossed my legs.

Bram looked down at them, put his hand briefly on one of my knees — the one that still bore a deep blue bruise and a patch of raw skin from my fall in the cafeteria — and then put both hands back on the steering wheel as we merged onto the freeway.

As he drove, I watched the side of his face. In profile, driving, he looked, I thought, like a man who loved nothing, no one, more than a complicated engine, and the stab of terror I'd felt beside him in bed — *no*. He was passionate, yes, but he was, surely, a reasonable man. When I told him that the affair had to end, he would be understanding, and discreet. He would be polite when he saw me in the hallway at the college. He would slip

politely out of my life, as quietly as he'd slipped into it. What
Bram Smith really loved was just this—a car, driving it, completely absorbed, utterly lost in the world on the other side of it,
while, at the same time, completely attentive to the network of
belts and cogs and oiled steel that was the motor of the thing he
drove, which was, at this moment, my car.

I could see that in his eyes, and felt relieved that he was looking into the windshield, not at me, with that intensity.

Then, listening to something, Bram said, "This car's sprung
too tight. These Jap cars—"

He shook his head. He suggested that I get something (the
timing belt?) checked. He said there was a clicking sound when
the gears shifted, a bit of grinding, and the car pulled a little to
the left. How long since I'd had my tires rotated?

I told him I had no idea. Was I supposed to have my tires
rotated?

He snorted, nodded. He said, "Doesn't your fucking husband know anything about cars?"

No, I told him. My husband knew about computers, he designed software, important—

"*Soft*ware," Bram said. "Pussy."

I inhaled at the word, and my mouth stayed open, waiting for
the breath to return from inside of me to the world—shocked
at how sharp it had felt, hearing that word, meaning Jon. It was
as if I'd been slapped on the top of my hand with something thin,
but solid. Defensively, I said, "He shoots, too. He hunts . . ." but
I let it trail off, picturing Jon outside the house in his orange coat,
taking aim at a squirrel on the roof.

"Well," Bram said, "he ought to be taking better care of his
wife's vehicle." He touched my knee again and looked over. "Not
to mention some of his wife's other needs."

———

MILES passed before we spoke again.

It was a parody of a late spring afternoon. Stone-blue sky. All the flowering trees in bloom. The grass was emerald green. I unrolled my window a few inches and could smell damp clay, new leaves. Even along the freeway, daffodils and narcissi were holding up their sugary torches in the ditches—their proof of the triumph of beauty over decay, their perfumed suggestion that, under the earth all winter, something had remade them, turned their deaths into something frivolous, lighthearted, and sent them back into the world wearing it.

We passed the place where I'd hit the doe, but when I looked into the median, I saw nothing there.

Had the grass simply, finally, consumed her—nature washing her out of this world, reabsorbing her, the fur and the blood and the bones, bringing her back into the earth? Or had someone come along with a truck, a pitchfork, and, in an orange suit and plastic gloves, disposed of the evidence?

Did it matter?

She was gone.

We were close to the exit we needed to take to get to the college, and I wasn't sure if Bram had ever approached it from this direction, and I was about to point it out when he cleared his throat and said, "I had a word with our friend Garrett."

I turned to look at him.

His mouth was open. His nostrils were flared. Both of his hands were on the steering wheel, holding it more tightly than he needed to hold it. I said, "What?"

"I told Garrett that if he continues to bother you in any way, there will be serious consequences."

"Oh my god," I said. "Bram," I said. I put a hand over my mouth. In only the span of a few heartbeats, I'd broken into a sweat. I could feel a cool droplet of it run from the back of my neck straight down my spine. I said from behind my hand, "You shouldn't have said anything to Garrett. I—"

"That's between me and Garrett," Bram said, passing our exit. "I don't want to talk about it. I just thought you ought to know."

I took my hand from my mouth and looked down at my lap. My hands felt loose, distant—like parts of me that could easily slip off, be lost. I could feel my heart beating behind my ears, a low voice coming from my blood, insisting (*was was was*), and opened my mouth to try to say something, but before I could, Bram looked around and said, "Where the hell are we? Fuck. Did we miss our exit?"

I managed to tell him that we had, that we needed to take the next one, go back, turn around.

The traffic had thinned to nothing—just one wobbly truck in the driving lane, which Bram passed smoothly. Before he did, I saw the stenciling on the side of it (TWO MEN AND A TRUCK) and caught a glimpse of the young man behind the wheel, who was either singing or talking to himself. Chad flashed in front of me then as Bram made his way to our actual exit:

Chad, in the photograph in his baseball uniform.

Chad, eleven, unblinking, uncensored, pure enthusiasm looking into a camera.

The pounding of my blood behind my ears softened and grew more insistent at the same time.

It was Chad's little-boy voice now.

Ma ma ma.

DRIVING back home, I remembered it:

The tape recorder.

I'd never put it under the bed, but I'd also never checked to see if Jon had put it there.

A heavy rain had come out of the east, carried across the sky in a single massive blue-black cloud, and the windshield wipers made the sound of heavy, congested breathing as they cleared the torrents of it from the glass. I pulled into the driveway, turned the engine off, and sat, trying to prepare myself—for the rain, for the run to the house, for Jon.

No, I thought.

It could not have been under the bed.

Surely, after our argument, Jon had taken it back to Best Buy, or put it away in a drawer.

And, even if he'd put it under the bed, even if he'd switched it on, in the morning, himself, it would have run out of tape long before Bram and I had gotten into the bed.

But, I also thought, what if it *had* been there, what if it had recorded everything?

Would Jon have heard what he'd wanted?

The sound of me fucking another man.

And what about *I want you to leave this motherfucker, baby? I want you to be mine.*

What about that?

What if the machine had recorded that?

I remembered Bethany Stout, in class on Thursday, raising her hand as we labored through a final discussion of *Hamlet.* "Mrs. Seymour, isn't this business, when Hamlet gets kidnapped by pirates, a really good example of deus ex machina? I mean"— she tossed up her hands here as if she'd completely had it with Shakespeare—"give me a *break.*"

Where, I wondered, had she learned the term?

Deus ex machina.

This was the same girl who, earlier in the semester, had asked why I couldn't have assigned a more recent translation of the play.

I opened my own hands, then, as if to catch what she had tossed up, and Todd Wrigley said, "What the hell is *day us Mackinac?*"

Bethany turned in her seat to address him directly. "It means," she said, "'god comes from the machine,'" and, despite her own shaky translation, she went on to explain the literary concept to Todd Wrigley far better than I could have.

No.

There had been no machine.

And, even if there had been, I was ready, I thought, to go inside, to see Jon, to explain to him, as simply as Bethany Stout had explained herself to Todd Wrigley, what we had let happen, and why we had to make it stop. I was ready to get out of the car, to walk up the steps of my house, to sit down with Jon, to talk. I really was—but there was also so much rain pounding on the roof of my car and the ground around my car that it sounded like a herd of deer, stampeding, close by, their delicate hooves thundering in unison, in panic, hurrying past the house, tearing up the yard, altering forever the very landscape upon which we walked. I sat behind the wheel of my car for a long time, listening. In a trance of listening. I might have sat there, like that, in the driveway, for a few minutes, or for many hours, staring straight ahead, listening to those hooves. When I finally got out of the car, ran through the rain, stepped drenched onto the porch, Jon was standing in the doorway.

I could see that he'd been crying.

"Were you just going to stay in your fucking car all night, Sherry? Were you afraid to come in here and talk to me?"

"How COULD you do it, Sherry? How could you cheat on me, *lie* to me? How could you bring another man here? How could you fuck him in our *bed*?"

"What?" I said.

I put my purse on the floor, slowly. There was a puddle of rain already at my feet. My dress was running with water, and my hair. Jon's hands were in fists and he was holding them up against his chest like a prizefighter getting ready to punch. I stepped backward.

"The tape recorder, Sherry. It was under the bed. I heard *everything. I heard it all.* You can't tell me you faked *that*?"

"Faked what, Jon?" I said, as gently, as quietly, as I could, trying not to startle him into any kind of action. I said, "Jon, why would I fake anything?"

His mouth opened, as if in astonishment, and he let the fists fall then, in slow motion, in front of him. Sudden and enormous tears fell out of his eyes, onto the floor at his feet. They looked like cartoon tears. Illustrated tears. How could real tears be so large, fall so quickly? He said, as if he'd been completely defeated, "Sherry. Do you hate me that much? Do you really hate me that much?"

I stepped toward him carefully. I put my hand on his arm. I tried to caress it. I tried to look up into his face, but then he yanked away, snapped to attention, and glared at me.

Again, I stepped backward, away.

"You fucking cunt," he growled, and I put a hand to my throat. "You sick bitch," he hissed.

"Jon!" I said, holding my hands out to him. I said, "Jon, why are you acting like this?" I said, "Okay, okay, the tape. You heard it. You heard it all. But this isn't something you didn't already *know*. This isn't something you didn't tell me over and over to *do*."

Jon sprang at me then, pushed me with the palms of his hands on my chest, and I stumbled backward onto the love seat with my mouth open in surprise, and he shouted—loud enough, I thought, for the Henslins to hear all the way down the road—"You bitch! You lying bitch! Don't you blame this on me! That was a *fantasy,* and you know it. I never told you to do *anything.* What kind of husband do you think I am? What kind of a fucking monster do you think I *am?*"

I continued to watch him with my mouth open.

The roped veins in his neck.

The terrible burning flush on his face.

The baffled, wild rage.

His eyes—pure black, but flashing.

"Jon," I said—and I felt it, again, as I had in the hallway with Sue: that telescoping. Back this time through the weeks, the sex, the whispered insistences—was it possible? Had it all really been a game? Had he somehow never known? Had he thought—?

No.

"Jon," I said. "What did you think, then? What did you think would be on the tape recorder if—"

"I thought you would *invent* something, Sherry. I thought you would *play along.* Like the bite marks. I thought you'd *fake* something. For the fantasy. I thought you'd—"

He stopped talking, sank to his knees, began to sob—horribly, inconsolably—into his hands. Outside, the rain had stopped, and the sudden, total silence out there was startling, disorienting, maddening. I put my hands to the side of my head to cover my ears, to block it out.

CHAD at the airport:

I saw him from the back, first, watching the baggage carousel.

When he was little, I could scan a room full of children, or the pool, or the park, and find him instantly.

It had nothing to do with what he was wearing, or any of the details of him—haircut, height. It was everything, all of it, all at once—the whole of him set absolutely apart from all other children. My gaze could pass over a hundred others in a blur, land on him with perfect accuracy (*mine*) and with a swiftness that never failed to surprise me.

But this young man at the baggage carousel, with his head bowed, watching its slow revolutions, could have been any young man. My gaze slipped past him the first time and settled mistakenly on a laughing boy with a bag of golf clubs, and then an older man with Chad's build, and then a little boy—ten? eleven?—before I saw him, my son, watching the luggage traveling past him, waiting for his. I had to catch Jon's arm to steady myself, seeing our son—a wash of fear moving through me so swiftly it felt like something that had been injected directly into my veins.

Did he know?

Could he know?

Could Garrett have told him?

A phone call? An e-mail? (*Your mother's lover threatened my life.*)

Or were there, perhaps, others who knew, who might have told him—out of spite, or concern, or self-interest?

Sue? Beth? *Bram?*

Or, was it possible that he was so much a part of me, my body, still (my baby), that, somehow, he simply *knew*?

But then Chad turned around at the luggage carousel as if he'd heard or felt us behind him, and he smiled, stepping toward us, his arms open—and the wash of it in my veins rose from me, a cool and floating sensation in my limbs, in my chest. No, I thought, he doesn't know. Garrett, the good boy, the patriot, the loyal friend—Garrett would go to his grave with a secret like that. And there was no one else who would want to hurt us that way. And it was impossible to simply *know*—with that distance of the continent between us. *Chad didn't know.* I let him take me

in his arms, my face pressed into his denim jacket, the smell of
fuel, ozone, airport on him. Behind us, Jon stood with his hands
in his pockets, and when I turned to look at him I saw that there
were tears—slippery and iridescent—in his eyes.

I MADE spaghetti for dinner. Garlic bread and salad. Chad was
starving, it seemed. He ate so much that I didn't take seconds
for myself, afraid there wouldn't be enough for him if I did—
although I was also strangely hungry, as if I'd gone days without
eating (had I?), or run a marathon.

Jon and I asked him the usual questions about school.

Grades (all As). Dorm life. Cafeteria food. Friends.

But the conversation was exhausted early—the long flight,
for Chad, I supposed, and the time change.

And, for Jon and I, the last two days since Bram had come to
the house spent huddled in anxious conversation with one another, reassuring ourselves about our marriage, about our lives.
Two sleepless nights. Two long days of oblivion, limbo—conversation, grief.

There'd been weeping, screaming, stunned silences, and, at
one point, Jon had stood over me, shaking his fist. "How could
you do it?" he'd shouted. "How could you do it, whether you
thought I wanted you to do it or not, you fucking *whore*."

But that was the last name he called me, and it had surprised
me how quickly his anger had softened into sadness, into pain,
and then we were holding on to one another, kneeling together
on the floor, both of us sobbing, clutching at one another, weeping, stammering.

He stroked my hair, and said, over and over, "It's my fault.
It's my fault. It's my fault."

"Of course it's not your fault," I sobbed. "How could it be *yours*? It's *mine*."

"No," Jon said with such conviction that I didn't argue with him about it anymore. "It's all my fault," he said.

For hours that first night we groped and clawed at one another on our knees—lovers drowning in a shallow lake—sobbing, sobbing, talking, talking, talking. And kissing. Tasting one another's tears. We went to the bathroom sink together and took turns washing our faces. When Jon rose from the basin, water running off his eyelashes, down his cheeks, he looked up at me, and said, "Sherry, how could I not have known?"

I put my hand to his forehead, as if checking the temperature of a child, or baptizing one.

I said, "Jon. Jon. You never suspected? Not at all?"

"No," he said—under his breath, sounding awestruck, amazed. "It never even crossed my mind, Sherry," and there was a look of such ravaged pain in his expression that I had to look away. I looked at his chest, focused my eyes on some vague place around his heart, and I said, "And, you—"

I couldn't say it.

—*forgive me?*

Because what if he said *no*?

"Of course I forgive you, Sherry. You're my whole world, Sherry. What good would it do me not to forgive you?"

He stood up straighter then and went to the towel rack, put his face into the towel, leaned against the wall, heaving into the towel for a few minutes while I stood, motionless, watching, frozen in place, in time, and then he looked up from the towel— and when he turned around, I was shocked to see that he was smiling—distantly, sadly, but he was smiling, and he said, "I didn't know you, did I?" He said, shaking his head, but still smiling, "It's embarrassing. Really, Sherry, that's what it is. It's embarrassing. I was in an imaginary world, all these weeks—no, all these *years*—while you were living in the real one."

I didn't smile.

I went to him.

He took my head in his hands. He looked at me closely, as if trying to read an answer to a question in tiny print on my face. He said, "But it's over, now, right? Now, it's over?"

"Oh, yes, Jon. God. Yes. It's over," I said.

He kissed my forehead then. He inhaled. Kissing my hair, he said, "I just want everything exactly the way it was before. The way it's always been," and he wrapped me more tightly in his arms.

We stayed in that embrace for two days.

We stayed in the same room at all times, kept our hands clasped together, our knees touching, our shoulders. We lay down together on our bed at night, but we didn't sleep, we didn't make love, we never even got under the covers. We stared at one another for long, lingering moments. For hours. Occasionally, I saw Jon squint, or grimace, as if he were remembering something, but then he would see that I'd seen it, and he'd try to smile. He'd kiss me—my lips, my eyelids, my ears. We cried, and the crying turned to laughter, and we laughed, which turned to crying. We didn't answer the phone. We didn't leave the house.

We made plans.

We were, Jon said, in this now together. He was willing to take the blame, because he believed, completely, that I would never have had the affair without his goading, that I wanted as much as he did for this to be over. It was *our* mistake, he insisted—a misunderstanding born out of complacency, out of blindness, out of sheer ingratitude for the great gift of our long marriage, our perfect life. So, in ending it, we were conspirators, partners in a high-stakes game. As we held one another and made plans, I realized that we had never before been (had we?) so passionate, together, about anything—not even the house, not even our child, and never our marriage—as we were in determining the way we would deal with the problem of my lover.

I would meet Bram, we decided, at the coffee shop around the corner from the efficiency on Tuesday (*not* at the efficiency) and tell him that, because the semester was over, I had broken my lease, that we no longer had a place to meet.

And I *would* break the lease. Right away. There would be no more efficiency. In the fall, Jon and I would find a condo closer to our jobs, in the city. No more commuting, or separation. ("I don't care about the house, Sherry," Jon said. "The house is nothing without you.")

On Tuesday, at the coffee shop, I would tell Bram that I'd made a terrible mistake, that my son was home now from college, that my husband was suspicious, that I had too much to lose. I would tell him that people at work might find out, that maybe some of them already suspected, that our jobs could be in jeopardy. If I had to, I would tell him that my husband had a rifle, that he was a hunter, that he could be violent—impressing upon Bram that the danger was great, that the affair *had* to end.

Even Jon agreed that I couldn't, *shouldn't,* tell him that my husband knew.

Who knew what Bram's reaction might be?

Outrage? Humiliation?

Jon, like me, had been shocked by the weight and the conviction of that sentence (*I want you to be mine*) and we'd agreed that we didn't know this man at all. We had no idea how he might react to any of this. We agreed that I could never be alone with him again, that I'd have to be gentle, but completely convincing. Stalwart. Not the slightest wavering in my conviction. I would end it, and everything would be as it had been before.

Everything would be as it had been before.

"So," Chad said, putting down his fork after finishing his third plate of spaghetti. "I've told you all about *my* life. What's new around here?"

"Not much," Jon answered, quickly.

"Nothing new here," I said, and shrugged.

"Okay," Chad said. "So much for that."

We talked about the weather. We talked about the war. And, after Chad and Jon helped me clear the table, we said good night, and Chad went to his room, and we went to ours—where, for the first time since Bram had been in it, Jon and I got into our bed and fell asleep in one another's arms.

IN THE middle of the night I woke up from a dream that Chad, as a little boy, was wading at the edge of what I thought was a shallow lake. I was relaxed in the dream. Completely content. The sky overhead was overcast, but I felt happy about that, too. We didn't need sunscreen. Things were hazy. The lake was shallow. Everything was fine, I thought, the way it had always been. We were completely safe.

But, even in this dream, I knew that if I were feeling these things, so conscious of them—the goodness and security of it all—something bad was going to happen. This was, after all, a dream. So, I stood up from the chair I'd been reclining in on the beach in my dream, and forced myself to wake up before the bad thing could happen.

Afterward, I lay awake beside Jon for a long time, and felt the relief of the near miss, the averted disaster, even if it would only have been in a dream.

It must have been, I thought, about three in the morning, but I could hear Chad in his room—the stereo a dull thumping through the wall.

Jet lag.

A boy from a different time zone.

A boy from another life.

It was comforting and unnerving at the same time to hear him in there, I realized—our little boy, back home.

But, also, a stranger in the house.

I'd grown used to the privacy of having him gone, I knew. Making love with Jon on the living room floor. Walking naked from the bedroom to the bathroom.

Now, I put on my robe after slipping out of bed—something I hadn't bothered to do since the last time Chad had been home. I pulled it around me. I headed for the bathroom. When I passed Chad's room, I paused in the doorway and looked in. The light above his bed was on, and Chad was sprawled on top of the covers in his boxer shorts, reading a book with a black cover.

"Hi," I said.

"Hi, Mom," Chad said, and put the book down on his chest so that it rested there, wings spread, like a crow.

His suitcases had been opened, and various items—books, a towel with a Corona beer bottle on it (something I'd never before seen in Chad's possession), and a few faded T-shirts—were scattered around on the floor.

Since spring break, I'd only gone into his room to straighten, to dust. I'd only vacuumed once. Without Chad there, it had seemed like no one's room. I'd mostly ignored it.

But, now, already, it was Chad's room again, reclaimed completely. Without thinking, I felt a pang of annoyance — the dirty laundry on the floor — and he must have seen it on my face, or simply noticed me looking at the mess on the floor. He said, "Don't worry, Mom. You can clean up in here and do my laundry in the morning. I'm in no hurry."

I looked up from the mess to the boy and smiled, rolled my eyes. I said, "Did you get enough to eat for dinner?"

Chad shook his head and said, "No, actually, Mom. Can you make me some pork chops now?" then laughed.

I nodded. I understood: *Why are you asking?*

I said, "I just wondered if you couldn't sleep."

Chad propped himself up on his elbows and said, "I can sleep, Mom. I just choose not to sleep."

This sarcasm (irony?)—where had it come from, when had it started? I liked it, actually, but it was the attitude of someone I didn't really know. A clever clerk at the video store. A student from the back row of the class. I said, "I'll leave you alone, now, Chad."

He nodded, and said, "Good night, Mom. I'll see you in the morning."

I said, "Maybe after you're settled in and caught up on your sleep, we'll go to visit Grandpa?"

"Sure," Chad said. "But it'll have to be Saturday, okay? I work this Tuesday and Wednesday"—the lawn service for which he worked last summer—"so tomorrow I'm going to visit Ophelia if Dad'll let me take his car."

"Ophelia?"

"Yeah, Ophelia," Chad said.

"Where is she?" I asked.

"She's staying in Kalamazoo for the summer, in her sorority house."

"Oh," I said. "So, are you—seeing her? Ophelia?"

"Well, I'm *seeing* her tomorrow, Mom. Otherwise I haven't *seen* her since spring break. Why do you pronounce her name like that, like it's some kind of tropical disease?"

"I don't!" I said. Too loud. I would wake Jon up. "I say it like everyone else says it. *Ophelia.*"

"*Ophelia,*" he said, correcting me, although I couldn't hear the difference between his pronunciation and mine.

Ophelia.

He was already visiting her, his first day home from college?

What was there, I thought, about this girl, who'd seemed neither particularly pretty nor bright, that could be of such interest to Chad? Surely, the girls at Berkeley must have been infinitely more sophisticated, more interesting. I'd imagined Chad finding, there, someone slender, and bookish, I supposed—an English major, maybe a writer, someone, frankly, more like me.

But, Ophelia?

I remembered that her feet, flat, shoved into too-tight shoes, had looked painful as she tottered around in the grass in our front yard while Jon arranged her with Chad in his camera lens. "Smile," I remembered Jon saying—and then the casual distant smile Chad offered beside the overeager, too-wide smile of Ophelia Vanriper—who, I thought now, wasn't only plain, but was one of those girls who balanced so precariously between plain and ugly that it would be only a matter of lighting between one and the other.

And, at the same time I thought these things, I was surprised to find myself thinking them, so viciously, about a nice girl my son liked.

Since when did good looks in a girl matter so much to me?

Hadn't I always been the one who'd told Chad, when he was little, not to make fun of the chubby girls, not to assume that just because a girl wasn't pretty that she wasn't a lovely person? When he was in seventh grade and I found the *Sports Illustrated* swimsuit issue on his desk, I took the opportunity to tell him about the objectification of women, about how it was a fine thing if someone looked nice on the outside, but it was the inside that mattered.

What reason did I have to dislike Ophelia Vanriper, who'd only ever been polite to me?

"Okay," I said, trying to smile with sincerity—generously, warmly. "If Dad won't let you take his car, you can take mine."

"Sweet!" Chad said. "You're still my excellent mother." He winked.

BUT CHAD and Jon were both gone when I woke up. I looked outside to see that Jon's car wasn't in the driveway and that, either overnight or in the few hours of morning sunlight I'd slept through, the lilac bush at the edge of our yard had burst into purple blossoms.

I opened the window.

I could smell it.

The perfume of it was so familiar and redolent of home, of peace, of domestic certainty, that I felt filled with blind optimism—such a complete faith in the future that I had to sit down on the edge of the bed to catch my breath.

I looked around.

There, on my dresser, my jewelry.

There, on the wallpaper, those roses.

The lace curtains. The white lampshade. That braided rug on the floor. Outside, as usual, Kujo was pawing around in the scrubbrush. The birds sang. A nest, built by house finches in the hanging fern on the back porch, was full of baby birds already, and from where I watched I could see the mother come and go busily. I could smell the musk of them (damp feathers, bird shit) and hear the brilliant cheeping as they called her back to them when she left. And, overhead, and from a great distance, miles and miles into the sky, I could hear a jet traveling from one edge of the world to the other, flying at great speed, with no feathers at all. *Everything will be fine,* I thought:

I will make a pot of coffee, take a cup, and drink it on the porch. I will pick up that book I put down so many weeks ago, the one about Virginia Woolf. I will read it. I will call Sue, to whom I haven't spoken since the afternoon, in the hallway, when she told me about the notes. I will tell her she's my best friend. That she will always be my best friend. I will forgive her completely. What choice do I have? Haven't I, in these weeks, proven myself to be someone capable of hurting those I love the most? Haven't I, in these weeks, proven myself capable of harboring secrets—harmful, bitter, painful secrets—and did those not exist right beside the deep, complete devotion I had for those I loved?

And Garrett.

I'll call Garrett.

I'll try to explain to Garrett that it's all been a misunderstanding. A terrible misunderstanding. Whatever Bram had said to him—please, please forget that. I'll invite Garrett to dinner. I'll tell him that Chad's home from California, and wants to see him. I'll make burgers, or nachos, or sloppy joes—some kind of big, young-man meal. They can drink all the beer they want.

And then I'll call Bram and explain that my life is the life of a simple woman.

A woman here.

A mother. A wife.

That I belong to this life, have always belonged to it, can never belong to him.

I will stand up.

I will inhale.

Lilacs.

Morning.

Ready to begin my ordinary day. Return to my ordinary life.

BUT THEN the phone rang—loud and insistent, like an explosion in the silence of the house. I stood up from the edge of the bed fast and hurried down the stairs in my bare feet to answer it. My voice sounded breathy, I thought, and formal, and unfamiliar to me when I answered. "Hello?"

"Hey, babe."

Bram.

I swallowed.

For a moment I could say nothing, and then I said, "Bram. You're calling me at home."

He said, "Well you're not in your office. Where am I supposed to call you?"

"You can't call me here," I said. "My son is home from college. He could have answered the phone."

"Yeah," Bram said. "Well, I'll tell him I'm selling encyclopedias. Or I'm the plumber." There was a scratch on the air between us. A laugh?

"Where are you?" I asked.

"I'm at your efficiency," he said. "I'm on my cell phone. I'm lying on your futon."

"Oh, Bram," I said. "I'm going to have to let the lease on that go. The semester's over. I—"

"Being here, thinking of you, is making me hard."

"Bram."

"Sherry. What are you wearing?"

I hesitated. He asked again. I told him. My nightgown. It was white.

"Push it up over your thighs," he said.

I didn't do it, but when he asked if I had, I said yes, I had. It seemed, at the moment, the easiest thing to say, the thing that might end this conversation the most quickly. I took the phone and sat down on the couch.

"Are you wearing panties?"

"Yes," I said.

"Pull them down. I want them down around your ankles." He paused. "Are they down yet?"

"Yes," I said. "They're down."

"Spread your legs. I want your knees apart. I want those sweet thighs open. Are they open?"

"Yes," I lied.

He said, "I'm touching myself now, baby. I'm hard as a rock."

I listened.

All I could hear was his breathing. And then the rhythm of him touching himself, growing stronger. A moan. And then he said, straining, "Wrap your lips around it, baby. Put your mouth on it. I want to feel your tongue on it. That's right, that's—" And then he was quiet.

Wind in a tunnel between us.

On the roof I heard a scurrying of clawed footsteps.

A squirrel. Maybe two. They were back. The children of the squirrel Jon killed in February? Or a new family of squirrels, nesting in the eaves? They sounded wild up there. Busy, frantic, making a nest for themselves on the roof of ours. I listened, until finally he was moaning, loudly, "Oh, babe. I love you, babe. I need to be inside you now. I need to be between your legs. I need to be fucking you, fucking you hard, right between your fucking legs, right now, babe, right now. I'm coming, babe. I'm coming all over us, sweetheart."

I said nothing. I was shaking. I held the receiver away from my mouth, afraid he could hear the chattering of my teeth. Bram said nothing for what must have been a full minute afterward— just the sound of the second hand of the clock in the kitchen, dry and static as those squirrel claws on the roof, and then he sighed, and said, "I just came all over your face, baby. I just came in your beautiful mouth, Mrs. Seymour."

"Bram," I said when I could speak again. "Bram." I could think of nothing else to say. Everything around me had lit up— foreign and silver. The stack of magazines in the corner. The vase full of dried flowers on the mantel. The Oriental rug, its dizzying geometric designs, its disorienting patterns. Far off, I could hear an ambulance wailing its way somewhere. Someone's ordinary day, over.

"Bram," I said again. "Are you still there?"

"Yeah, I'm here."

I cleared my throat, pressed the phone harder to my ear, passed my free hand across my eyes, and said, "I have to tell you, Bram, this has to end."

"No," Bram said.

I said, "But—"

He said, "How long is it going to take you to get your pretty little ass over here?"

Then, there was the small digitally silent snap of his cell phone cutting me off.

I TRIED to go on with my morning. I made the cup of coffee. I picked up the book about Virginia Woolf. I put it down. I passed the phone, afraid it would ring. I went to the back porch with my coffee cup, out of which I had not yet taken a sip. I didn't bother to take the book with me. I stepped off the porch, onto the grass. It was damp.

In the distance, from the Henslins', I could hear cows lowing. One insistent bird in the maple tree would not stop shrilling at me—a steady torrent of singing that sounded both angry and ecstatic. It must have had a nest nearby. It must have been trying to warn me away from it. I couldn't see the bird, could not find the branch from which it was threatening me, because the tree was so blinding with brand-new leaves, but, after listening for a few minutes I realized that the sound of it (*weak-weak-weak-weak-weak*) seemed to be coming from my chest.

That bird, inside me, seemed to be my heart.

I went back inside.

I put the coffee cup down.

I took out the phone book and looked up *Thompson,* letting my finger travel down the inch of them until I came to the one on the street on which Garrett lived. He answered on the first ring.

"Garrett," I said.

He cleared his throat. He said, "Mrs. Seymour?" His voice sounded hesitant, I thought, a reticence that had become the very syllables of my name.

I said, "Garrett. I need to talk to you about something."

"About what, Mrs. Seymour?"

Behind him, I could hear music. (Handel? Was it possible? Could Garrett be listening to the *Messiah*?)

And then I couldn't say it, what I'd called to say to him. I could not mention Bram, or the threat. I could think of no excuses to make, no explanations that would explain anything at all. Instead, I inhaled, exhaled, swallowed, and said, "Chad is home from California, Garrett. We'd like to have you over for dinner tonight."

"Okay," Garrett said, as if I'd given him instructions rather than an invitation. "When, Mrs. Seymour?"

LATE in the afternoon, Chad pulled into the driveway in Jon's Explorer, fast. I could hear the gravel crunching, spinning under his tires. The brakes squealed when he stopped, and then the sound of his shoes kicked off on the back porch. "Ma? You home?"

I'd taken a shower. I'd gotten dressed. A pink T-shirt, a faded pair of jeans. I'd made the bed. But then I'd done nothing but lie on it for hours, until I realized that morning had blurred into afternoon, and that eventually they'd come home, Chad and Jon, and that I could not be lying on the bed when they did, so I'd gotten up, gone to the kitchen, measured the flour and the water into a bowl for a loaf of bread.

"Yes," I said. "I'm here."

I stepped out of the kitchen. Dough on my hands. I'd been kneading it and hadn't put enough dry flour on my hands to keep it from sticking to them. I was holding my hands in front of me, trying not to touch my T-shirt, and when Chad looked at them he said, "Hey, are you my mother?"

It was a joke left over from a picture book I used to read him as a child — the baby bird, hatched while his mother is away, tries to imprint on cows, on planes, on steam shovels, in search of a mother, and then, in a moment of recognition, finds his true mother and knows her instantly for who she is.

As a little boy, Chad had been endlessly entertained by that book. "Look, *there's* the mother," I would say, tapping at the illustrated mother bird, and he would laugh and clap.

He'd been, all those years ago, truly a mama's boy, I supposed — not in the sense that he was girlish or particularly needy, but because he seemed to feel that he should be (that he *was*) the center of his mother's world. When something distracted me (the phone, a book, or even his father) he was quick to get my attention again. He had a million tricks for doing it. Something in the house would break. A vase, a cup. He would suddenly be hungry, or thirsty, or would have lost his shoe.

But, then, in a few heartbeats, he'd grown up, and it became just a joke he told (*Are you my mother?*) whenever I was doing something he meant to imply was out of the ordinary for me, his true mother—like baking bread.

"I am," I said, still holding up my doughy hands, "your mother," and tried to smile.

He smiled back.

He looked disheveled.

He was wearing khaki shorts so long and with so many pockets, many of them looking heavily filled—with what? rocks? coins? jewels?—that they hung down nearly to his calves. He had on a pink polo shirt, and it was half tucked in, half untucked. On his left wrist he wore the watch I'd given him for graduation (Swiss Army, black) and a macramé bracelet with a single brown bead on it, which I'd never seen before. He looked, I thought, flushed, excited, as if he'd been running a race and had won it.

"Did you have fun with your friend?" I asked.

"Ophelia," he said with emphasis, as if I'd purposely refused to say her name.

"Ophelia," I said.

"Yeah," he said, but he smirked. Had I again mispronounced her name?

I went back into the kitchen, and, once there, tried to call as casually as I could back to Chad, "Is she a girlfriend now?"

"Yes," Chad said, following me in. He opened the refrigerator and took the jug of orange juice out.

"So," I said, "you like her a lot?" I sank my fingers into the dough again, which felt too cold, and stiff, and grainy. I'd done something wrong.

"I do, Mom. I like her tremendously."

He drank from the jug then—something he knew I hated. I turned to watch him. He put the cap back on and said, "Sorry," but I wasn't sure if he was apologizing for drinking from the jug, or for liking Ophelia Vanriper tremendously. "I'm gonna take a nap, okay?" he said.

"Sure," I said. "Okay." I said, "Garrett's coming for dinner, but not until eight o'clock."

Chad turned around and looked at me.

Did he smirk again?

He said, "So, are you *Garrett's* mother now?"

"No!" I said, too quickly. His tone had surprised me. (Contempt? Accusation?) Less insistently, I said, "He's your friend, Chad. I—"

"Garrett's not my *friend*," Chad said, crossing his arms. "Apparently he's *yours*."

"Chad—"

"Really, Mom, where'd you get this 'Garrett is your friend' business? When have *I* ever invited Garrett over? When was the last time you saw me hanging with Garrett? Fifth grade? *Third* grade?"

"Chad," I said. There was an expression on his face I'd never seen before. Was he exasperated with me? Was he *tired* of me? "I just—"

"You just like Garrett Thompson, Mom. It's okay to say it. You like Garrett Thompson, and you've invited him over. That's fine. But don't tell me it's because he's *my* friend, okay?"

I could think of nothing to say except, "Okay," but immediately wished I hadn't.

It seemed to confirm something in Chad's mind.

He looked away from me.

He said, "I have to take a nap now, Ma," and turned out of the kitchen.

I stood where I was and listened to his footsteps on the stairs, ascending, and wanted to call after him, wanted to tell him to rest, to sleep, that I loved him, that he was my son, not Garrett Thompson, or anyone else. I wanted to call out to him that I was sorry.

But I didn't. I finished kneading the dough. I washed my hands. I heard Chad's bedroom door close. I heard the bedsprings when he lay down. I put the dough under a clean dishrag in the corner of the kitchen. I turned the ringer on the phone off in case Bram tried, again, to call while Chad was home, and I was about to sit down again, with a cup of tea this time, to pick up the book about Virginia Woolf, when I heard tires in the driveway and went to the window instead.

Bram's red Thunderbird.

"BRAM," I said, leaning down to speak into his unrolled window. "What are you doing here, Bram? My son is home." I was whispering. Chad's bedroom looked out onto the driveway, and his window was open.

"I don't care," Bram said.

He didn't bother to whisper.

He opened the car door and stepped out, then slammed it closed behind him and leaned back against his car. He looked at me for a moment, then up at the sky, and then directly into the sun with his eyes open. Was he drunk?

"I can't have him see you," I said. "You have to leave." I took a step backward, under the porch eaves, where Chad wouldn't be able to see me. I made shooing motions with my hand toward Bram, his red Thunderbird.

But Bram just shook his head, then looked from the sun to me, blinking, squinting. What could I have been to him after that incandescence but a silhouette, a black paper cutout?

He said, "No, babe. You're the one who has to leave."

I took another step backward. I could feel the tears spring unexpectedly into my eyes—burning, *scalding.* I said, "Bram, *please.*"

"Well, Mrs. Seymour," Bram said. "If you didn't want me to come here, you should have come to the efficiency. Like you said you were going to." He swept his hand out in front of him. He lifted his eyebrows. He said, "How was I supposed to know what happened? I thought maybe you had an accident. Maybe you hit another deer. You told me not to *call* here, so what could I do but *come* here?"

The tears had spilled from my eyes to my cheeks. Bram took a step toward me and wiped them away matter-of-factly with his thumb. I caught his hand, looked into his eyes. I said, "Bram. You—"

"Is your husband here?" Bram asked. He nodded toward Jon's Explorer. "Is this his piece of shit?" He looked hard at the SUV as if he were planning to take it apart, to expose it for what it was—as if he were trying to decide where to start.

"No," I said. "My son is here. Bram"—I took a step backward, up the stairs to the porch—"I'm going into the house now, Bram. Please, if you care about me at all, you'll go. I'll call you later. We can meet somewhere and talk, but now you have to go."

But Bram took a step toward me and pulled me to him by the waist. Standing on the step, I was eye level with him. He did not, at that moment, look like a spurned lover, but like an angry child (*Are you my mother?*), or like a child who was holding his mother hostage (*You* are *my mother*). "I'll go," he said, "if you kiss me."

"Bram," I said.

"Please," he said.

I couldn't speak.

If I kissed him, would he leave?

What choice did I have but to kiss him?

I motioned for him to come up on the step, under the roof, where Chad, if Chad was looking out his bedroom window, couldn't see — and then I stood still, my face toward him, and let him kiss me.

It was a deep kiss — tender at first, his lips even seemed to be trembling, and then he pulled me closer to him, his arms so tight around my hips and sides I couldn't break away, even with my hands at his chest — and then the kiss became harder, and deeper, his tongue in my mouth, his hand on the back of my neck, and then he let go, and pushed me backward, gently, but it was a push. "Thanks," he said. "You call me. Tell me where we're going to meet."

I opened the door to the back porch and hurried in, and shut the door behind me.

Bram started up his car — that huge motor roaring — and let it idle loudly in our driveway for a few minutes before backing out and peeling into the road, leaving the smell of rubber burning behind him.

SHAKING, I sat down at the kitchen table, and listened.

Had Chad gotten out of bed? Had he looked out his window? Had he heard Bram? Seen him? Or (*dear god, please*) had he slept through it all?

I sat where I was for over an hour before I heard Chad walking above me.

The sound of bedsprings. Footsteps.

By then, the bread dough under the dishrag had bloomed horribly—a distorted, gigantic, mushroom cloud of flour and air. I stood up when I heard Chad on the stairs, took the dishrag off, and punched it back down. It surprised me how quickly that mound collapsed, but I kept punching.

Chad came into the kitchen behind me and said to my back, "Hey, what did that bread dough do to you?"

I felt the relief of it collapse around me. He *hadn't* heard. I felt the relief of it spread through me like cool water. He'd heard nothing. He'd slept through it. Somehow. He didn't know. I said, turning, "Chad—"

He said, "Yeah, Mom?" as he went to the refrigerator, going for the jug of orange juice again.

"I love you, Chad," I said.

"Hey," he said, "I love you, too, Mom."

He took the cap off the jug.

For my sake, I suppose, he took a glass out of the cupboard and filled it, then raised it to me as if in a toast before drinking it all without taking a breath.

As soon as Chad pulled away in the Explorer to pick his father up from work, I called Jon. The sound of his voice, answering the phone—steady, sober, patient—brought something up from my throat that had been there since Bram had driven away in his red Thunderbird two hours earlier. It caught there. A bit of barbed wire. A piece of broken glass. I couldn't speak except to say his name, but Jon knew it was me.

"Sherry," he said. "What's wrong?"

I said, "Jon, something happened."

"Are you okay?" he asked. "Is Chad okay?"

"Yes," I said. "But, Jon, Bram came here."

"What?"

"He came here. To the house. Chad was asleep, but—"

"Did he touch you?" And then he qualified it, asking, "Did he hurt you?"

"No," I said. "He just wanted me to talk to him. He wanted me to kiss him."

"Jesus Christ," Jon said. "Did you? Did you kiss him?"

"Yes," I said. "I had to."

"Sherry," Jon said, sounding angry now. There was a thinness to his tone, an implication that his patience was running out. He said, "You have to end this, Sherry. I know I played a part in it, and I'm willing to take full responsibility for that, and I'm being honest when I say that I'm not angry at you. But this game's over. You have to tell him that."

"I didn't *want* him to come here," I said. (Was I whining?) "Do you honestly think that I would *want* him to come here, after everything that's happened, with *Chad* here?"

"I don't know," Jon said, and the flatness of his tone took my breath away.

When I could speak again, I said, "You don't *know*? Jon, if I'd wanted him to come here, would I be telling you about it now?"

There was a silence. In it, I imagined Jon taking stock of everything he'd ever known and thought about me. I felt as if a flock of invisible birds had descended on me—so much fluttering and heartbeat and breathing, searching around in the bones and clothes of me for flesh to eat.

"Jon?" I said. "Do you think I *wanted* him to come here?"

Jon said nothing. I said, more loudly—maybe I was shouting—"Jon, are you there? Are you listening? I've told you, haven't I, over and over—you *know* how sorry I am. You're not going to pull away from me now, are you? You're not—"

"No," Jon said. "No. No. Sherry, calm down."

"Calm down?"

"Yes, calm down. No. I don't think you wanted him to come to the house today, Sherry. But I also think that if you'd told him, Sherry, like I told you to, that you were ending this, he wouldn't have come over. You certainly didn't have to let him kiss you. Don't patronize me, Sherry. I'm not a child."

"Jon," I said. "You don't know. You don't know Bram like I do," I said, and regretted it immediately.

"No," Jon said, and I could not have mistaken the sarcasm in it for anything other than what it was. "No, I don't know Bram like you do, Sherry. But I know *men*. They don't come around if you haven't given them some sort of encouragement to come around. And he won't come again if you make it clear, Sherry, that there's nothing in it for him. Just tell him you'll call the cops, or that your husband will shoot him, or something, if he comes to the house again. Make it very plain.

"Now, I have to go, Sherry. I have someone waiting for me. Call him now, Sherry. End this *now*."

I'D NEVER had Bram's cell phone number or his home phone number. He'd never even given me his address, never even told me if he had roommates, a house, a pet. What did I know about Bram Smith? I called the only number I had, his office number, expecting no answer—hoping, I suppose, that there would be no answer—but Bram answered the phone on the first ring. "Bram Smith," he said.

"It's Sherry," I said.

"Yeah," he said.

"I'm calling—to talk, Bram."

"I'm busy right now," he said.

"Should I call you back?"

"Yeah," he said, "you should."

"When?"

"I don't know," he said. "How 'bout after dinner?"

"I'll try," I said. "It will be—"

"Yeah, I know," Bram said. "Want to know how I know?"

"What?"

"Want to know how I know all about your plans for dinner?"

"What are you talking about, Bram?"

"I'm talking about your dinner guest, Mrs. Seymour. I just saw him, in the shop. Heard all about how he's coming to your place for dinner tonight, babe. Sounds like you've got a regular thing going here. Kind of a revolving door, huh?"

"Bram. Garrett? You saw Garrett?"

"Yeah, Mrs. Seymour. It's a real small world. You really can't go around fucking every guy in it and not expect them to cross paths now and then, can you?"

"Bram." I stopped speaking for what seemed like a very long time, the words eluding me entirely. The *idea* of words was something I'd seemed to have lost. Then, I said, "Bram, there's nothing between me and *Garrett*. For god's sake, Bram. He's my son's *friend*."

"That's not what Garrett says," Bram said. "I mean, you really got to twist the little fucker's arm to get the truth out of him, but when he finally spit it out, it kind of turns out, babe, that he's *not* such hot pals with Chad. I think *you're* the hot pal. I think *you're* the one who wants Garrett to come to dinner. Am I right?"

"No, Bram."

"Well, like I said, Mrs. Seymour, I'm pretty busy here. Why don't you just give me a ring after your lovely dinner, 'kay?" He hung up.

On the dead line, there was a hush so total that it seemed animate—a breathing, pulsing silence into which I could project the sound of myself, into which I could tumble, listening, as if it were not silence, but space. I stood with the phone in my hand, listening to it for a long time, that silence inside me, traveling over the phone lines toward me, until Jon and Chad came in the door and called out loudly to me—*H'lo, Sherry! Hey, Ma!*—and the sound of their voices slapped me back to myself, and I put the phone in its cradle, and, without being able to respond to their greetings, headed to the kitchen to begin making dinner.

GARRETT arrived at the back porch door at 8:00.

Jon let him in. Chad greeted him without standing up from the love seat, with a salute. I came out of the kitchen and said, "Garrett. Hello."

His hair had been shaved down to a fine dark dust. He nodded in my direction, but didn't look at me. He was wearing a clean white button-down shirt. Chad stood, finally, slowly, then clapped Garrett on the shoulder. "What's with the hairdo, guy? I thought you weren't going anywhere until September."

"I changed my mind," Garrett said. "I sped up my induction. I leave for boot camp in two weeks."

"Oh, Garrett," I said.

But Chad turned and looked at me so fast I said nothing more. The expression on his face, was, I thought, either suspicious or annoyed. He laughed, turning back to Garrett, and said, "So you're really doing it, old pal. You're off in defense of the homeland. Well, let me be the first to shake your hand."

They shook hands.

If the sarcasm had registered, it didn't show on Garrett's face. He neither smiled nor looked defensive. He simply nodded soberly when the handshake was over.

I said, "Chad, Garrett, you boys can have a beer while I finish getting ready for dinner. Does that sound okay?"

Chad followed me into the kitchen.

I opened the refrigerator, and he took out two Coronas, un-
capped them with a bottle opener we kept hanging from a string
and a hook on the wall, turned back toward the living room with
the beers in his hands, but before he stepped out of the kitchen
he said, so quietly under his breath that I wasn't sure I was supposed to hear or if I'd heard him correctly at all, "Are you my
mother?"

Chad and Garrett went out on the front porch with the
beers. The screen door banged shut behind them. Jon was in the
garage. From it, I could hear things clanging — dropped, or
tossed. He was upset. Before Garrett had come to the door,
while Chad was reading the newspaper on the love seat, Jon had
whispered to me in the kitchen, "Did you call him?"

I said, "Yes. He wasn't there. I'll call him later," and Jon had
stomped upstairs.

While the meat for the nachos sizzled in the frying pan, I
shredded lettuce. I cut an onion into fine pieces, stopping to
wipe my eyes on my forearms. I cut up one tomato, and then the
second — which, although it looked perfect on the outside (a
deep, false red), was, at the center, black. Rotting from the inside — or had it, all along, been swelling and ripening around this
rot? I tossed it into the garbage can, which was full, then pulled
the bag out of the can, tied the drawstrings, took it to the back
door.

Passing through the dining room, I could hear Chad or Garrett cough on the front porch.

The front door was open. Something large and buzzing
bumped against the screen. One of them, Chad or Garrett,

cleared his throat. I stood for a moment, listening, with the garbage bag in my hand—eavesdropping, I supposed, but there was nothing to hear. Either they'd quit talking because they'd heard me passing through the dining room, or they hadn't been speaking to one another at all out there—not one word—on the front porch.

I tossed the garbage near the back door for Jon or Chad to take out and went back to the kitchen to finish preparations for dinner. I set the table, and put the food out, and called them in. And, when they came, I smiled as if nothing had changed, as if I were the wife, the mother, the friend of the mother, inviting them all to the table I had prepared for them—exactly the woman I had been two months before, the year before that, the decade prior to it, the woman I had been for half my life.

But the silence between Garrett and Chad was carried with them to the table.

They passed food to one another, but didn't look at each other.

Jon seemed conciliatory toward me, however. He complimented the smell of the food, its abundance. Chad and Garrett nodded in agreement. I said thank you. I asked if anyone needed anything.

No. No. No.

Everything was fine.

Everything was great.

We ate for a few minutes in silence, and then Jon cleared his throat and asked Garrett a few questions about the military, about his induction, which Garrett answered politely, finally saying, "I decided there was no reason to just hang out here all summer, that I should go."

I looked over at Chad, who was nodding. He said, "Hey, bro, want another beer?"

Garrett wiped his mouth with a napkin, and looked at me.

"Chad," Jon said. "How many have you boys had? Garrett has to drive home."

"Yes," Garrett said, "thanks. I shouldn't have any more."

Chad snorted at this. He said, "I don't have to drive anywhere," and stood up from the table, went to the kitchen. Jon and I both watched him walk away, but neither of us said anything.

"So," he said when he returned, open bottle held in his hand by the neck. "So, Garrett, how's that Thunderbird of yours going? Got it fixed up yet?"

Garrett put his fork full of nachos down, and said, "What?"

"Your Thunderbird, pal. You know, I thought you were fixing up an old car in your garage?"

"Mustang," Garrett said.

"Mustang," Chad said. "Whatever."

Thunderbird.

I put my own fork down.

My breath felt knocked out of me, knocked into another room.

"It's still in the garage," Garrett said. "The transmission's not in it yet. I'm still driving my mom's old station wagon. But not for long."

"Awesome," Chad said, and took a long drink from the bottle.

I stood up from the table, and went to it—the kitchen. I said nothing as I left.

Thunderbird.

It had been a slip, Chad had simply misspoken, but it had run straight through me like a knife.

He *had* seen.

He'd been awake.

He'd seen Bram's Thunderbird.

He'd seen *Bram*.

He'd seen *me* with Bram.

I held on to the edge of the kitchen table for a moment.

"Mom?" Chad called out. "Can you bring me another napkin while you're out there?"

I ran my hands over my face, as if to compose it, then turned back toward the dining room. I took a napkin with me. I gave it to Chad, who looked up at me as I did, and asked, "You okay, Mom?"

"Yes," I said.

Jon looked at me. Instead of concern on his face, I thought I saw an admonition. (*Pull it together.*) I sat back down. Chad was still looking at me. He said, "Say, the last time we were all together, Mom was getting love notes from some grease monkey over at the college. What's up with that, Mom? Still getting propositions, or what?"

Garrett looked down, too fast, I thought, at his plate. Chad looked over at him.

"Hey, Garrett, didn't you say your auto instructor was hot for my mom back then?"

I opened my mouth, and nothing came out, but Jon, as if he'd been rehearsing for his moment for weeks, said in a voice so casual and convincing I almost believed his offhandedness myself, "We don't know what you're talking about, Chad. Your mother's been the object of so many lovesick fellows, we can't be expected to keep track of them all."

"No," Chad said, and went back to eating his nachos. "You're right. Of course," he said with his mouth full.

We finished eating in silence, and when we were done, I stood up to clear the table, trying to take Garrett's plate away first. He'd only eaten half his dinner, but his napkin was beside his plate. He'd put his fork down, his hands in his lap, and before I could take it from him, he stood up with the plate himself and said, "Mrs. Seymour, let me help."

"Thank you, Garrett," I said.

He took Chad's plate, too, and Jon's, and I followed him into the kitchen with the glasses, a handful of silverware.

"Mrs. Seymour—," Garrett said when we were alone in the kitchen. "There's—"

"Garrett," I said, whispering. I tossed the handful of silverware into the sink and turned to him. "I'm so sorry, Garrett, that you had to be involved in this. Please forgive me, Garrett. I promise you, no one will hurt you. It's all been a terrible mistake."

Garrett took a step toward me, and he said, "Did Chad tell you then? You know he thinks—" He nodded his head in the direction of the dining room, where Chad and Jon were talking about something clinical, it seemed, abstract—*mismanagement . . . precision . . . opportunity for growth and development . . .*

"No," I said. "Not Chad. *Bram.*"

Garrett looked as if he were simply, purely, confused. He put our dishes down on the counter. He looked, I thought, with that buzz cut, in that starched shirt, so vulnerable and young I couldn't help it, I went to him, and took him, as I had so long ago (those skinned knees, the blood running in dusty rivulets down his shins) in my arms. He let me hug him for only a moment, and then he pulled away, glanced toward the dining room, and we both saw him at once—Chad, standing behind us in the doorway to the kitchen.

Those voices had been the television, in the living room, not Chad and Jon.

Chad said, "Am I interrupting something here?"

Garrett stepped backward, away from me.

I said, "No, Chad. Garrett's just helping me —"

"Yeah," Chad said. "I can see that."

I stayed in the kitchen after that, cleaning up. When I finally came out, Chad and Garrett were gone.

"Where are they?" I asked Jon.

Jon shrugged. He was still watching the political debate on television. He looked up from it and said, "They went out. They didn't tell me where they were going."

I LAY awake long past midnight, waiting for the sound of Garrett's car pulling into the driveway, dropping Chad off—but, eventually, I simply fell asleep to the sound of a coyote, far away, howling, over and over.

The sound of it was mournful, but not desperate — a wild and melancholy dog singing a tuneless song, not a cry for help or an appeal to God. The sound of it made its way into my dream. I was rocking a baby (Chad?—no, this was a new baby, a girl) in my arms. As we rocked, she made those soulful, uncomplaining sounds against my breast, and after a while, I joined in, and it was oddly comforting, and beautiful, rocking together, howling quietly and distantly, in unison, into the night. When something loud (a car door slamming?) punctured the silence outside, I woke up and realized that I was actually humming aloud. Whatever it had been, the noise from outside, it didn't wake Jon any more than my humming had.

I lay in the dark and listened to the silence.

Now, there was nothing out there — as if the night had *im-*

posed silence upon itself, as if it were holding its breath, tiptoeing, a finger to its lips, *shhhh.*

I tried to return to my dream (the lulling hum of that baby in my arms), but it was gone.

When I fell asleep again, finally, I didn't dream at all.

IN THE morning, I woke to the sound of Chad's alarm clock, shrill and insistent, and remembered that it was his first day back at the lawn service. I got out of bed and went to his room, and when I got there I saw that he had one hand on the alarm clock, which he'd managed to turn off, but that he'd fallen asleep again—on top of the bedspread, fully clothed in the same things he'd been wearing the night before. His room was suffused with the smell—stale and familiar and redolent of the past—of beer and cigarette smoke.

"Chad," I said from the doorway. "You've got to go to work, don't you?"

He blinked, and the alarm clock slipped out of his hand to the floor.

"Yeah," he said, then sat up and looked at me. "Oh, Mom," he said. "I'm a very hungover boy. Do you still love me?"

"Yes," I said, blinking at the sudden tears in my eyes as I said it.

I went downstairs and made a pot of strong coffee, eggs, bacon, toast, while Chad showered. When he came downstairs I gave him a sympathetic and disapproving look. He was wearing jeans and FRED'S LANDSCAPE CREW T-shirt.

"Please," he said. "Mom, don't look at me. It hurts."

"What time did you get home last night?" I asked.

"I don't know," Chad said, spreading strawberry jam on his toast.

"That late," I said. "Did Garrett drink as much as you?"

"Garrett drank a lot," Chad said. "Once word got around the bar that Garrett had joined the Marines and that I was his friend, we got so many rounds bought for us we couldn't keep up."

"Where were you?"

"Stiver's."

"Stiver's? How? You're not twenty-one."

Chad snorted. He said, "Mom, we've been drinking at Stiver's for years. They don't care how old you are."

"Oh," I said. It was not, I decided, the time to interrogate him about the past, about Stiver's, about drinking, but I wondered—when? With whom? Where had I been? How could I not have known? Instead, I asked, "Then Garrett drove you home, afterward?"

"Yeah," Chad said.

"Drunk?"

"Please, Mom. We made it, okay? Don't scold me." He looked up at me, and what I saw there made me take a step backward. It was like a little threat, I thought, the expression on his face— eyes narrowed, lips parted. What was he telling me with that expression? What did he know?

Bram?

Had Garrett told him after all?

Or, that red Thunderbird—was it certain, then, he had seen it?

Or, did Chad know, simply, that his father and I had, ourselves, driven home from Stiver's, drunk, only two months ago?

I said nothing more.

I poured more coffee into his cup.

"Thank you, Mom," he said.

————

ON THE drive to Fred's Landscaping, Chad kept his head against the passenger-side window, his eyes closed, but when we pulled up to the enormous garage that is Fred's, he leaned over and kissed my cheek (toothpaste, soap) and said, "Love ya, Ma," and got out.

Fred—a fat man in jeans that hung so low on him that not only did his belly pour out from under his T-shirt, but I could also see where the pubic hair began to ride down into his pants, curly and black—waved to me before he and Chad high-fived each other. Chad turned then and blew me a kiss before disappearing with Fred into the garage.

He still loved me.

Everything was the same.

The blown kiss. The summer job.

Just like last summer, I thought, I would pick him up here at five o'clock, and he'd get into the car. He'd be speckled with damp green bits of shredded grass and leaves, smelling of lawn, fair weather, hard work. He would kiss me on the cheek. He would take a shower at home. We would have dinner when Jon got home from work. If the subject of the Thunderbird came up, we would think of something, Jon and I together. If Garrett had told him, we would sit down with Chad. We would have a long talk. We were his parents, and we'd find a way to explain.

WHEN I got home, I poured the last inch of coffee from the pot into a cup, and brought it with me outside, to the back porch.

The sun all over the backyard had lit it up.

Out there, in the scrubbrush, Kujo was barking, howling, so consumed with whatever he was doing that he didn't notice a small white-tailed rabbit hopping mindlessly across the green lawn toward the road. When the mail truck came down that road, blowing up dust and dirt as it does, it had to swerve to avoid hitting that bunny, which continued its straight line right into the truck's path.

THE MAIL:

A sporting goods catalog for Jon, a phone bill, a credit card solicitation, and a white envelope with my name and address written on it in an unfamiliar hand.

Inside, a white sheet of paper, and, in black pen, *Sherry. I wish now I'd written you a love note sooner. I'm sorry I waited this long to tell you how beatiful you are. I can never let you go. Your mine forever. Call me please. Bram.*

I had never seen his handwriting before—cramped and masculine, as if writing with a pen on a piece of paper were oppressive, feminine. My name in that writing looked foreign to me, a name belonging to someone else—to a woman who had brought her lover into her home, made love with him in her marriage bed. To a married woman who had kissed her lover on the back porch of her own house as her son slept in the bedroom over them. To a woman who might weakly pretend that she had ended her affair but who, in truth, had made nothing clear to the man who had written her name on that envelope.

What, I wondered, had made her think it would be so easy to undo sins of such magnitude?

Why, I wondered, had she expected that, with no real effort, she could simply return to her ordinary life after departing from it so blithely, so completely?

Looking at my name, captured in Bram's unfamiliar handwriting, I heard Jon's voice say, *End this now,* and I put the envelope, with Bram's return address written in the left-hand corner, in my purse, got my keys, and headed for the car.

BRAM's neighborhood was an area of small houses only a mile or so off the freeway. It was easy enough to find his street, Linnet Drive, but more difficult to find his house, because there were no numbers visible from the street. It was as if, here, someone had come through the neighborhood and painted over the addresses, or stolen the numerals from the mailboxes, as an elaborate prank. Always the postman's daughter, I wondered how the mail got delivered, how often it wound up at the wrong houses, if the neighbors returned the misdelivered mail to one another, or simply threw it away.

Then, I saw it:

The red Thunderbird.

My hands began to sweat, seeing it. Cold and damp on the steering wheel, they slipped as I turned into the driveway behind that car. I hit the curb, but managed to park, to step out of the car, to walk toward the front door.

It was a light blue house. There was a white birch tree in the front yard. Bandages of white bark had peeled from the trunk, near the roots, and fallen onto the lawn, revealing raw, pink flesh underneath. There were crows in the top branches. They cawed when I stepped out of the car, but went silent, looking down at me from their high branches as I passed under them. Somewhere down the block, a cat yowled, but other than that, the neighborhood seemed deserted, dead quiet. I climbed the two steps to Bram's front door.

It was painted red. There was a peephole in the middle of it, like a single, brass-rimmed eye. The curtains in the front window were heavy and white, and pulled closed. I took a breath, knocked on the storm door, which rattled in its frame. I stood still, then, and listened. I heard nothing from inside the house.

I knocked again.

Nothing.

I looked around until I found a doorbell behind the branches of a forsythia bush—its yellow flowers already having bloomed and faded—and rang it, and the bell was so electrical and loud, even from where I stood on the other side of the door, that I imagined it rattling the walls of the house, blowing the curtains open, knocking cups and plates from the cupboards—and still I heard no movement from inside. But when I turned and began to walk back to my car, I felt something behind me, and whirled around to look.

The front door was open, and a woman was standing at it.

She said, "Yes?" from the other side of the storm door.

I took a step toward her, and she disappeared in the glare on the glass. I squinted, but still couldn't see her. I said to that glare, "I'm looking for Bram." I said, "Are you—"

"Yes," she said. "I'm his mother."

I felt my heart stutter, then start. I opened my mouth to speak. I said, "Oh."

The woman opened the storm door a crack then, and I saw her even more clearly. Yes. This was Bram's face—female, older, but she had Bram's deep-set eyes, the eyebrows, the facial structure. She was wearing a white robe. Her eyes were dark, but not suspicious. Was I wrong, or did she look, somehow, amused? Did she know Bram had told me she was dead? (*Why* had he told me she was dead?) When I managed, finally, to say, "Do you know where he is?" she smiled and shook her head. She said, "No, hon. No, I sure don't."

"He's not here?" I asked.

"No," she said. "He's not here."

"His car?" I said, nodding toward the Thunderbird.

"Yeah," she said. "Well, his car's here, and all his things are here, which is certainly a mystery. But *he's* not here. I haven't heard a word from him since yesterday. I must have been at the store when he came home with the car. Amelia is going crazy. He was supposed to have the kids last night. She had to get a sitter."

I took a step backward, told her I was sorry to have bothered her, that I worked with Bram at the college, that—

"Well," she said. "If you hear from him, tell him we don't know what he's up to, but it's time to check in with his mother. Boys," she said, shaking her head. "They never grow up, do they?"

She smiled again. I tried to smile back.

CHAD smelled like sunlight and grass when he got in the car. He sighed, sitting down in the passenger seat. He pulled off his T-shirt and wiped it across his face. When he leaned forward to do it, I saw a long scratch on his back. Had a branch, or a rake, or some other hazard of the landscape torn the flesh there during the day? I said, "How are you, Chad? How's your hangover?"

"Better," he said. "I sweated it out."

On the drive home he told me about his day. A hedgerow they planted at a country club. A lawn they mowed and edged just outside of town. He told me that Fred had gotten even stranger since the summer before, when Chad would regularly find him talking to himself, sometimes crying, in the back of the truck they used to haul the landscaping equipment around. "Today he asked me if I believed in alien abductions," Chad said.

"What did you tell him?" I asked.

"I told him, no, I definitely did not, and I didn't ask him why he was asking me."

"Good thinking," I said.

"He's got nothing for me tomorrow," Chad said. "They haven't worked me into the schedule quite yet. We can go see Grandpa if you want."

"Oh, yes," I said. "Yes, let's do that, Chad. Let's go tomorrow."

"Sure," he said. "Good."

The car, with Chad in it, felt lighter.

Full of spring, green.

We pulled into the driveway, and I saw that the lilacs were still wildly in bloom, that they had not even edged to the other side of their full perfection. They shimmered with it—purple, swollen, fragrant.

It couldn't last, I thought, more than another day or two, but for now, they were at the height of their beauty.

In the scrubbrush, Kujo was still wrestling with something, pawing around in the weeds. Either he'd been there since morning, or he'd left and come back. When Chad got out of the car, he called Kujo's name, but the dog ignored him.

DURING the drive to Silver Springs, Chad and I talked about books. We talked about movies. We talked about California, and the weather, Grandpa's depression, the traffic, and then I asked about Ophelia. "What's she like?" I asked.

"You've met her," Chad said.

"I know," I said. "But I've never really talked to her."

"She's great," he said. "She likes to read. She plays tennis."

The legs, I remembered. The sturdy, athletic legs.

"What do her parents do?"

"Her dad killed himself when she was four. Her mom's a dental hygienist. Her stepfather's a cop."

"Her father killed himself?"

I looked at the side of Chad's face.

The beautiful, strong jaw. The gentle curve of it—neither Jon's nor mine. He turned to look back at me, and then I saw it in his eyes. *He's in love with her,* I thought—this plain, tragic girl, who reads, who plays tennis, who has the lovely teeth (although I couldn't remember them) of the daughter of a dental hygienist.

He turned away from me again, and said, "Yeah. He shot himself. *Ka-bam.*" He held his index finger to his temple, and I gripped the steering wheel tighter. *Rob, the gun, the hotel in Houston.* Had anyone ever told Chad how my brother had died?

I hadn't.

Had Jon?

Would Chad have made such a joke if he'd known?

I said, trying to control the tone of my voice, "Has she been able to get over that? Has she —?"

"No," he said. He said it like a challenge, as if I'd asked an insulting question. "No," he repeated. "She most certainly has not."

"Is she happy, though?" I asked. "Is she a happy girl?"

"No, Mom," Chad said, and laughed out loud this time. "She isn't *happy.*" Again, the sarcasm. I'd asked him a ridiculous question, which he refused to take seriously. He was refusing to give me the answer he knew I wanted, which was that his girlfriend was a sane and stable person. He said, instead, "But I wouldn't exactly call myself a 'happy person,' Mom. Are you?" He turned to look at me again, and I felt it burn straight through me, like a laser, like an X ray, and thought it again, *he knows.*

I couldn't answer.

I looked straight ahead, out the windshield, and said nothing. After a few miles, I changed the subject. I said, "It's a beautiful day, isn't it?"

In my peripheral vision I thought I saw Chad shake his head, but when I looked over at him, he was nodding yes.

I<small>T WAS</small> too late by the time we got to Silver Springs to go to the nursing home, so Chad and I checked in to the Holiday Inn and then went to dinner across the street at a place called the Carousel, which had a motif of painted horses and an all-you-can-eat spaghetti buffet.

But there were flies hovering over the buffet, flying in and out of the steam that rose from the noodles and tomato sauce under the bright overhead lights, so we made our dinner choices from the menu. I ordered a salad with grilled shrimp, the Hoola Bowl, which was placed before me with a small paper umbrella at the center. Chad had a steak, rare, which bled profusely all over his plate. His baked potato turned pink with it, but he dug into it quickly. I tried not to watch.

Our waitress was a beautiful redhead, maybe eighteen or nineteen years old, and she was clearly smitten with Chad. She could barely look at him. She giggled far too loudly when, after asking him if his steak was too rare, he looked up at her with a dripping slice of it held over his plate and said, "No, I like to hear the heartbeat. It's comforting."

"She's so pretty," I said as she walked away. "Don't you think?"

Chad looked in her direction, as if he hadn't noticed her before, and said, shrugging, "She's okay. Not my type."

"What is your type?"

"Well, I don't like girls who giggle," Chad said.

"Doesn't Ophelia giggle?" I asked.

"Ophelia most definitely does not 'giggle,'" Chad said, returning to his steak. It was almost entirely eaten, just a long bone with some scraps left on it. Chad sawed at those scraps.

"It's sweet," I said, trying to keep my voice steady, noncommittal and magnanimous at the same time, "that you've known

Ophelia as a friend all this time, and now you see her as a girlfriend."

"Mom," Chad said. He put his fork down on his plate, his knife balanced on the bone. He cleared his throat and looked up at me, a half smile on his face, and said, "Ophelia and I have been dating for two years."

I said nothing.

I looked down at his plate.

I looked back up at him.

He was no longer smiling.

I said, almost in a whisper, "Why didn't you ever tell me this, or your dad?"

"Dad knows," Chad said. "Dad always knew."

I put my own fork down. I swallowed. I said, "Why didn't I know?"

"*You* know why," Chad said.

I inhaled.

I put my hands on the edge of the table, and held it. I said, "I do?"

"Yeah," Chad said. "You do. You know."

"*What* do I know?" I asked. I was trying to picture it—the two years. It was all there, seven hundred and thirty days crammed into a space the size of a postcard, misaddressed, still traveling from post office to post office, accumulating postmarks, and messages, and meaning, about to arrive in my mailbox. Just now arriving in my mailbox. "What?" I repeated. "What do I know?"

"You know you would have hated it," Chad said. "You didn't like Ophelia. But not just Ophelia, Mom. No girl would have been good enough. Even Dad always said it would be better just to keep the information about Ophelia to myself." He laughed then, and reached across the table, took my hand. "But I love you

most, Mom. I always will. Don't worry. If I get a tattoo, it'll say
MOM."

I looked up at him. He was joking, he was laughing, but he
wasn't smiling.

I let go of the table, pulled my hand out of Chad's, and put
my hands in my lap. I said, "So, why are you telling me now?"

"Because it's time for you to know," Chad said. "You should
know about me, Mom. I know about you."

"How do you know?" I asked under my breath.

"I saw the fucking car in the driveway," he said, and the
harshness of it made me sit up straighter. "I *saw* it, Mom, you
know, and what was going on down there, and I finally got Garrett to spill the beans at Stiver's, and, anyway, it was obvious. I
knew it even when I was in California. Let's face it, Mom, you're
not the world's greatest bluffer."

It began to spin then—the table, the restaurant, Chad across
from me. I closed my mouth. I opened it again, and Chad said,
casually, picking his fork and knife back up and beginning to cut
again at the ragged bits of bloody flesh on the bone, "Don't
bother to say anything, Mom. I'm not going to tell Dad or anything. Your secret's safe with me. And it's over now anyway."

"It is," I said. "Chad. It's—"

"Yeah," he said. "Let's not ever mention this again. Okay?
Mom? I mean it. I never want to talk about it again. It never
happened."

The waitress brought our check. I took it. Chad never looked
up at her, but he looked at me. He said, "I don't blame you entirely, Mom. It was his fault, too. I know it. He was an asshole.
But you're too old for this shit, Mom. And that's the last thing I
ever want to say about it."

———

AFTER dinner, we went back to the Holiday Inn, and Chad fell asleep on the double bed closest to the television while we were watching a made-for-TV movie about a man whose secret identity had begun interfering with his love life. When I saw that Chad's eyes were closed, his mouth open, I tiptoed across the room and turned the television off. He was fully dressed, and not under the covers, so I took the bedspread off my bed and put it over him. When I did, he snorted a little, then rolled onto his side.

He'd always slept on his side. I could still see him—a newborn propped between pillows on our bed, deeply asleep on his side, his tiny pink hands pressed together near his cheek, as if in prayer. I had a photograph of him like that, his little rosebud lips puckered. It was in an album.

But if I hadn't snapped that photograph, put it in an album, would I have remembered?

And what pictures of the past had I *not* taken—forgotten, lost?

What details had slipped away from me over the years, into the limbo of memory, forever?

In the end, at least, I wondered, would they come back to me? Would that be the consolation prize for having to die—a brilliant replay of all of it, every moment fresh, in perfect light, relived, with all five senses, again? Could I have it all back, ever, someday, in the last moments of my life? And, if I could only have one thing—one detail, one sense—what would it be?

Oh, I knew.

I knew.

It would be the smell of him as a baby.

Milk and crushed violets and new leaves.

I closed my eyes and pressed my face into that smell. That baby neck. The soft flesh between his ear and his collarbone, and hummed to him. *Hmm, hmm, hmm.* He cooed. And then I knew I was asleep, because I had a baby again, and then a toddler—I was poised above his golden ringlets with a pair of scissors, a scrap of Handel drifting through the windows of a passing car, and then he was a little boy again, running across a green field, scaling a tree. He started climbing higher, and higher. "Chad," I called up to him. "Get down here."

But he kept climbing.

I started, myself, to climb the tree after him.

"Chad?"

He didn't answer.

"Chad!"

He kept climbing until all I could only see was the sole of his tennis shoe. My heart was pounding. Still, I thought, if I could just stretch far enough, if I could reach high enough, I could get ahold of his ankle, and then I—

Then I felt something close around my own ankle, a hand, and I looked down and saw Bram smiling up at me.

"Sherry," he said. "Did you think you could get away from me?"

And then he was pulling me down, and Chad had disappeared entirely, and I was falling, and I saw the truth of it all as I was falling, as if it were a photograph, as if it had been in an album all along but I'd never really looked at it, never truly seen it:

None of it had mattered.

None of it.

I'd worked at it, motherhood.

The cupcakes. The lessons. All those nights reading to him. I'd read Shakespeare to him. I'd read Whitman. Emily Dickinson. Yeats. I'd volunteered in his classrooms. I'd julienned his vegetables. I'd insisted that he get some fresh air, and then I insisted that he sit down to study. I breast-fed him. I sang to him. I'd gotten to know his teachers. I'd befriended his friends—and then in the driveway with Bram Smith in five minutes on a May afternoon (the lilacs, obscenely perfumed, just on the edge between blossom and self-destruction), I'd ruined it all, I'd run a stake straight through the heart of the life I'd thought I'd been living—the life I thought I'd created, perfected, and I woke up breathless in the motel room in the dark, my hands at my throat as if I were trying to stop myself from screaming—while, outside the door, in the hallway, a child was laughing, and a man said, "*Shhh*. It's late. People are asleep."

I DIDN'T have to get dressed. I'd never changed into my nightgown. I found my card key on the counter in the dark and slipped it into my purse, stepped out of the room, and pulled the door closed behind me.

The light in the hallway was absurdly bright, the carpet wild with geometric designs—too chaotic and one-dimensional to look at in the glare. I took the elevator to the lobby and found the pay phone. I punched in my own phone number, and then my calling card. "H'lo?" Jon said, sounding as if I'd woken him. And the sound of his voice—open and willing—brought tears to my eyes. I said, "Jon."

"Sherry," he said. "Is everything all right?"

"No," I said.

Behind me, at the desk, the receptionist was, herself, talking on a phone. She was arguing with someone about money. *I told you I'd pay my half, but not a penny more. The rest is your responsibility.* Jon said, "Sherry, sweetheart. Tell me what's wrong."

"Jon, I've ruined everything." I started to sob. "I've ruined it all."

He was quiet on the other end of the phone, listening to me

cry. Behind me, the receptionist had also grown quiet. She was listening, too, I supposed, to me, speculating about what domestic conflict might have brought a middle-aged woman to the Holiday Inn lobby after midnight and had her sobbing into a pay phone.

"No, you haven't," Jon said. "Everything's going to be all right, Sherry. And *you* haven't done it, Sherry. Whatever mess we're in here, we're in it together."

"No," I said. "It's my fault, Jon. It's all—vanity. It was all—"

"It doesn't matter now, anyway," Jon said. "It's over, Sherry. Whatever happens next, we'll handle it together. But it's done now. It's done. You need to get a grip on yourself. You need to get some sleep. You'll—"

"Jon," I said, "Chad knows."

There was a silence for what must have been a full minute on the other end of the phone, and then Jon said, "Fuck."

"Jon," I said. "I've ruined it. Our whole life. Everything. Can you imagine what he must think of me? I've wrecked it. I've wrecked the *past,* Jon. All of it. He'll never forgive me, he'll—"

"Yes, he will," Jon said.

"No." I was sobbing.

"Yes, he will, Sherry," Jon said again. He said, "Chad's smarter than you give him credit for. He's older than you think he is. He—"

"But *this,* Jon. He always said how lucky he was, that I was the perfect mother, that he would marry me himself if he could. Remember? He would send me those cards, even after he was sixteen, seventeen years old, telling me how much he loved me, that I was everything to him. And, also, *us,* Jon. *Us.* Always. He was always saying how lucky he was that his parents loved each other so much. Remember? He always said we were the perfect couple, that—?"

"No," Jon said. "He knew we weren't."

Something in his voice.

I held the phone a little tighter in my hand. I said nothing. And then I asked, "What do you mean?"

"Sherry," Jon said. "I want you to know I'm not telling you this to hurt you. This has nothing to do with what's happened now, my telling you this. I'm not mad at you, about this bullshit, with—Bram—" He seemed to choke on the name before going on. "But you're not the only one," he said, "who's made a mistake in this marriage. And Chad knows that."

Behind me, the receptionist had begun to whisper into her own telephone. There was a man standing at the counter, filling out his check-in card. He was in his fifties, maybe, a balding man, but with strong arms, and he looked at me, and for a moment I had the sure sense that we'd been here before, together, this man and I, in this very situation, when we were younger, or in another life. There was such compassion in his gaze. He knew that I was crying. *He remembers, too,* I thought. *He knows.*

Then I turned my back to him and said into the phone, to Jon, "Tell me."

Jon inhaled.

Exhaled.

"Oh, Sherry," he said. "It's been at least ten years ago. At least. Ten years or longer. I don't know. Chad was little. Really little. Third grade? Maybe fourth? I—I was having an affair."

I looked up at the ceiling.

Why?

Had I thought I would see the stars above me? Planets?

What I saw, instead, was a water stain on the ceiling tiles overhead.

To Jon, I said nothing. His breath sounded close and fast in my ear. I could even hear him swallow. It was as if, now, a hundred miles apart, we were standing as close to one another as we ever had.

"Did you know it, Sherry?" he asked. "Have you known it all along?"

"No," I said. "I never knew."

There was a long, concentrated pause.

Years were compressed into the pause.

That pause had the texture, the density, of slate.

Then, Jon said, "I—I thought maybe you knew. I thought it. But I was never sure. I didn't know, I thought maybe Chad had told you. He knew, Sherry, because he came home one day, and she was there, and I had to tell him, I had to explain—"

"Where was I?" I asked, alarmed enough suddenly by my own absence to ask him a question, to sound angry. It wasn't possible! I'd caught him in a lie. I had never, in all those years, not been home for Chad when he got there after school, had I? On the afternoons I didn't pick him up myself, I was waiting for him at the edge of the driveway when the bus dropped him off. How could I have been erased from a day of my own life? How could Jon erase me? Where was I in this new life Jon was describing, the one I hadn't been there to live? Some mistake, surely, was playing out here, some kind of identity theft, a complete misunderstanding—

"You weren't there," Jon said. "You were in Silver Springs. You were moving your dad into Summerbrook."

And then it came back to me.

The boxes. The Realtor. The clothes unpacked and folded in my father's new dresser at the nursing home.

Two days. Maybe three. I would have been here, perhaps, alone, at this very Holiday Inn. Ten years ago, I might have been at this very phone. I would have been calling Jon to check in, to make sure that Chad had gotten home from school, that he'd done his homework, that he and Jon had eaten dinner.

Out of two decades—*three days*. I'd gone away, and those had been the days in which my life, my *real* life, had been lived.

"Chad was supposed to be taking the bus home," Jon went on. "But he missed the bus, and Garrett's mother found him in the parking lot, waiting, and drove him home. You know how slow the school bus used to go. He was home at least forty-five minutes earlier than I'd thought he would be. And she was still here, in the house, when he walked in."

"She was there."

"Really, Sherry," Jon said. "It was nothing. He saw almost nothing. We were dressed, but we were on the bed, and we were kissing, and Chad walked in."

The man from the front desk passed by me then.

A ghost.

A memory of a memory of a lover from some other life-time—a lifetime in which he and I had danced, perhaps, to the song that was being piped in now, too quietly to really hear it, through the ceiling of the lobby of the Holiday Inn. It had been some other May, another night, but not unlike this one. A love-lier hotel. I'd been wearing a silver ball gown, but my feet were bare. Then, he stepped into the elevator, and he was gone.

"Sherry?" Jon said. "Are you there?"

"I'm here," I said.

"Do you still love me, Sherry?"

I said, "Who was she?"

I asked it as if it mattered, as if I were expecting some impor-tant information that would change everything, bring sense and reason to it all—but I already knew it wouldn't. I already knew who it was.

"Sue," Jon said. "It was Sue."

I looked back up at the water stain. It was shaped like a face of a clock. The clock, however, had no hands.

"Sherry?" Jon asked.

I said, "Yes."

He said, "Sherry, haven't you always known? I never told you because, what good would it have done? But I always thought you knew. Sue was so—furious then. She wanted me to leave you. She told me she was going to tell you. She— In my heart, I thought you knew all along, and that you forgave me, that you forgave us both."

I said, "I never knew."

On my way back down the hall to our room, I watched the floor more carefully this time. The geometric shapes were not, after all, haphazard. They were arranged in careful patterns. If I got down on my hands and knees, I could decipher the pattern. I knew I could.

But I didn't do it.

Instead, I leaned up against the wall for a moment before opening the door to the room, and I considered it:

My whole life spinning ahead of me and behind me down that long corridor.

My whole life, spun out there, like a fascinating lie.

My father was asleep in the chair in his room when we got there—chin resting on his chest, a string of spit spilling from his lips to his belly. It wasn't until I knelt down beside him to touch his hand that I realized he was tied to the chair with straps—one around his chest and two at each wrist—but Chad noticed right away. He said, "Jesus Christ. What the hell is this?"

My father woke up then and looked around him, his gaze passing over me, then freezing on Chad. He gasped, and his mouth stayed open afterward, staring. In pleasure, or in shock?

"Dad," I said, squeezing his wrist, but he didn't look at me. He kept his eyes fixed on Chad, who knelt down then beside him, too, and began untying the straps around his left wrist. When that hand was free, my father reached out and touched Chad's face.

"Hey," Chad said, looking softly at his grandfather. "How are you, Grandpa?"

"Robbie," my father said, moving his fingers around on Chad's face.

"No, Dad," I said. "It isn't Rob. It's your grandson. It's Chad."

"Son," my father said, still not looking at me, not seeming to have heard what I'd said. "My boy. How are you? Where have you been, Robbie? Where did you go?"

"I've been at college," Chad said. "I missed you, Grandpa."

"College?" my father said, leaning back as if to see Chad more clearly. "How is *college?*" my father asked—and then a cloudy tear ran zigzagging down his face. He stuttered out, weeping, "I missed you, too. Robbie, I missed you, too."

I got a Kleenex off the bedside stand to wipe away my father's tear, and also the spit that had run from his mouth to his stomach while he was asleep in his chair, and I dabbed at my father's face. As I did it, I said, "No, Dad, this isn't Robbie. This is—"

"Mom," Chad snapped. He gave me a long, cold look.

I put the Kleenex in my purse, instead of the trash can.

Why?

Was I planning to keep it?

IT WAS later, at the front desk, waiting for the physician's assistant, that I realized I still had it—that tear my father had shed for my brother, a little melted diamond, caught in a scrap of tissue, stuffed into my purse.

We'd gone down to speak to the physician's assistant, but she wasn't in, so we had to speak to the head nurse, who seemed so rushed and exasperated to have been called out of a resident's room to the front desk that, when she finally got to us, I couldn't form words.

Standing before her (a beautiful woman in her midthirties, or maybe even younger, with sleek blond hair pulled back tightly in a ponytail, looking like a goddess, molded to perfection at Vic Tanny's) I felt that I would be challenging one of the Fates to ask the question I'd summoned her to ask. I felt that I should bow to her, make offerings to her, not complain to her about my father's treatment. When I opened my mouth, only to have nothing come out, Chad spoke instead. "Why is my grandfather tied up in there? What's the problem here?"

The head nurse looked in the direction of my father's room, then back at Chad with what I could tell was a patience so difficult to feign that if she were forced to do it for very long she might crack straight down the middle, revealing the clean hollow perfection that was inside her. "Your grandfather," she explained, "has started wandering."

"Okay," Chad said. "Okay." There was an edge to his voice — not sarcasm this time, but something else, something so startling and sharp I stepped a few inches away from him. I looked at him. He was staring directly into the eyes of the head nurse. *Where has he come from?* I thought, looking at him—this new man, challenging the Fates, carrying with him this cold blade in his voice? I had given birth to him, hadn't I? I felt awed, and proud, and also afraid.

"So," Chad said, "if he's wandering, is he causing problems for you, or for himself?"

"As you can imagine," the head nurse said, "it's extremely dangerous. We have carts full of medicines here. There are patients here on respirators. Your father wandered into the kitchen one day. He could have burned himself."

"Oh, no," I said. They both looked at me. I felt I should apologize. I wanted to go. My father, I could have told this head nurse if Chad weren't handling all of this now, had been a mailman. He wasn't used to being indoors. He had wandered for a living for decades. If he were going to hurt someone, hurt himself, with the wandering, she was probably right, it was probably best that my father be—

"Well that explains why he's strapped to the chair, I suppose," Chad said, "although it seems like you could handle this by keeping a better watch on things, rather than tying people up. But why are his wrists strapped to the arms of the chair? Why can't he even move his hands?"

She'd been waiting for this, I could tell. What was it the Fates did? They wove the cloth that was your life? They cut the thread that ended it?

"He unzips his pants," she said. (Was I mistaken or did she take a small, threatening step in Chad's direction as she said this?) "He masturbates all day if we don't restrain his hands," she said. I put my own hand to my mouth.

"Well, so *what*?" Chad said. He took, himself, a step in her direction. He wasn't scared of her. It amazed me. *He wasn't scared of her. Nothing* she could say would scare him.

But I was terrified.

I touched Chad's arm, trying to stop him from saying anything else. If *she* said more, I couldn't stand it, I thought. I thought, the physician's assistant, on the phone the other day, had been right. My father belonged to these people now. These strangers were his family now. There was nothing we could do. They knew what was best. His fate was in their hands now. I squeezed Chad's upper arm, and for the first time realized that he was made of pure muscle. He was like stone, himself. Had he been lifting weights? Had he always been so strong?

Of course he wasn't afraid of her. He was a million times stronger than she was.

"It's *his* room," Chad said, "and if he wants to masturbate in it all day, whose business is that?"

"Well," the head nurse said, then licked her lips before continuing. "It's the business of the people who have to work here, sir. It's the business of the people who have to take his food into him, and the families, some of them with little children, who come here to visit their relatives. Obviously, for safety reasons we can't keep his door closed, so it becomes *everyone's* business if your grandfather is in his chair masturbating all day."

"Maybe if you let him walk around," Chad said, "and had the personnel available to keep an eye on him, he wouldn't be so bored that he had to sit in there and masturbate all day. Maybe if *you* were tied to a chair, *you'd* be jerking off all day, too."

"I have to go," the head nurse said. Her face had flushed. She'd turned away. She said, without looking at us, "The physician's assistant is at a conference. He'll be back on Monday, and you can speak to him then."

But I had spoken to the physician's assistant only a few days ago, hadn't I? Then, the physician's assistant had been a woman. I said, "I just spoke to her. She said my father was better, that he'd been making Easter baskets, that—"

"These things progress and change quickly, ma'am," the nurse said, still walking away from us. "I'm going now," she said.

And then she *was* gone — a white blank in the corridor, and then just an absence.

MOSTLY we were silent on the drive home. Chad said he wanted, himself, to call the physician's assistant on Monday, and that if he didn't get a satisfactory response, he would call the director of Summerbrook.

I tried to assume the parental role again, to say that I would do it, but he said no. "You can't, Mom. You don't stand up to these people. You never have."

I didn't ask him what he meant. I said, "Well, maybe your father—"

"*Dad?*" He practically laughed. "You've got to be kidding, Mom. *I'll* handle it."

He fell asleep then for an hour—eyes closed, mouth open, the steady rhythm of his breath.

I fiddled with the radio for a while, and, finding nothing to listen to, turned it off and listened to the silence, to the sound of the road rolling under us, the other cars with their own passengers passing us. Occasionally, I looked over and locked gazes with some other driver, or a woman beside the driver, or the child in their backseat—but it happened too fast to even bother to raise a hand, to wave.

We were almost home when Chad woke, looking like a child again—eyes heavily lidded, the muscles in his face slack. He looked out the car window for a long time, without seeming to be seeing anything, and then he sat up fast, as if he'd glimpsed something that had surprised him traveling on the other side of the freeway.

"What?" I asked.

He still seemed groggy, confused. He said, "I thought I saw Garrett's red Thunderbird."

No. "Mustang," I said, quietly.

"Yeah. Right," Chad said, and let his head drop backward on the back of the car seat again, and closed his eyes.

IT WAS late afternoon when we pulled in the driveway—too early for Jon to have gone to work and come back, but his car was there, parked, and he was standing in the backyard with his rifle, pointing it at the roof of the house. When he noticed us, he put it down. He turned.

When we stepped out of the car he said, "I had to do it," looking from me to Chad, and back to me. "I had to get the whole nest of them," he apologized. "They were moving in. They were going to be living in the attic, chewing up the wiring, living in our house before we knew it if I didn't do something."

They were there, on the ground between the driveway and the house, the fur and blood of them.

I looked at the roof.

Somewhere up there the nest was empty now.

I looked at Jon.

His face was haggard, pale.

"Why aren't you at work?" I asked.

"I called in sick," he said. "I couldn't sleep a wink last night."

SATURDAY.

Chad took Jon's car to visit Ophelia in Kalamazoo again. I spent a few hours in the garden, despite a light and steady rain. My garden gloves, gone from the hook on the back porch where

I'd always kept them, could not be found, so I dug in the dirt with my hands. I packed the earth around a geranium I'd bought last week but hadn't gotten around to planting yet, and when I was done, my knuckles were bleeding. My fingernails had dirt under them.

They were the hands of an old woman, I thought, looking at them.

Unfamiliar, but undeniably mine.

It began to rain harder. In the distance, a very low rumble of thunder. Jon was in the backyard, putting golf balls across the grass. He had no hat on, and the rain had turned his dark hair silver. When he saw me standing in the driveway, watching, he turned and called out, but I pretended I didn't hear him. I went back into the house—not ready to talk to Jon.

Since we'd come home on Wednesday, I'd said nothing to him except that one sentence, *Why aren't you at work?* And I'd answered the few questions he'd asked ("Are you going to bed now?") by shaking my head, nodding it, or shrugging, and slept so close to the edge of the bed that I kept waking up startled from dreams that I was falling.

Once, Jon must have felt me spasm in my sleep. He reached over and touched my shoulder.

Still mostly asleep, I rolled away from him, and he took his hand back.

In the morning, despite the silence between us, we'd had breakfast with Chad, who seemed so jovial and well-rested that I thought, crazily, for a moment, *He's forgotten—all of it, forgotten.* Jon complimented the pancakes so extravagantly and repeatedly that Chad finally laughed and said, "Dad, are you trying to get Mom to sleep with you or something?"

Jon didn't laugh. He gave Chad a disapproving look. He said,

"I just appreciate your mother's cooking, and it wouldn't hurt for you to do the same."

"Point taken," Chad said. "The pancakes are fantastic, Mom."

The subject between them changed to the weather. Rain. All day. Thunderstorms by evening. And, yes, Chad could take the car, but be careful driving home, especially if it was dark, and if there was a storm. Chad said not to worry. He'd be home early. Ophelia had to work.

"Where does she work?" I asked.

"She's a stripper," Chad said. And then he laughed. "No, really, Mom," he said, "she's a waitress at a nice place." He stood up from the table, carried his plate to the sink, kissed me on the cheek, and said good-bye.

I went upstairs, and made the bed.

I heard the Explorer drive away, Chad at the wheel.

Also, outside, a mourning dove, close by, was singing its hollow, throaty song—sounding dry and breathy and underwater all at the same time.

Jon had gone to the garage. He'd tried to talk to me in the kitchen as I rinsed the dishes at the sink to put them in the dishwasher, but when he put his hands on my shoulders, I felt a cold weight settle there with them, and I shivered, and he stepped away, his hands still hovering in the air. He said something under his breath, turning out of the kitchen, but I couldn't hear it, and didn't ask him what it was.

I looked out the bedroom window.

The morning was perfect.

I would never have guessed that in only a few hours it would rain. The air was warm, but light. The lilacs had sagged on their branches, but they had not yet browned. The blossoming trees had begun to drop their petals, but it was beautiful. It left the road and the grass shredded with pearl and pink, as if brides-maids had wrestled with angels in the night, as if spring itself had been passed through the blades of a fan.

In the scrubbrush, Kujo was back. Or had never left. He'd been there constantly for the last few days, and he'd whimpered out there all evening and late into the night. Now, he'd quit whimpering, but was still pawing around and making circles in the scrubbrush, his nose to the ground, relentless in his longing for—what? What terrible appetite was it that could not be satis-fied? Back at the Henslins', a bowl of water and leftovers were surely waiting. There would be a corner with an old blanket for him to sleep on. Mrs. Henslin would put down her dishrag, scratch his ears, when he came in the door. There was, I felt sure, some old rubber ball there for him. A discarded boot that was all his, which he could chew to his heart's content.

But here he was, instead, in the scrubbrush behind our house, still on the trail of whatever it was (deer, rabbit, another rac-coon?) and would not give it up to go home, to rest.

Long after the light rain had turned to a deluge, he was still out there.

CHAD came home later than he'd said he would. I could hear him downstairs in the kitchen. The clatter of silverware. He was hum-ming, opening the refrigerator door, closing it again. I'd left him a pork chop there, some fried potatoes, three spears of asparagus on a plate covered with waxed paper in the refrigerator. I'd made an identical dinner for Jon, and also left it there, but when I went downstairs for a glass of water and an aspirin at nine o'clock and looked in the refrigerator, Jon's dinner was still there, untouched.

It didn't thunderstorm, as they'd said it would. Just that dis-tant threat of thunder, and then torrents of rain. I listened to it from my study, where, for many hours after I was done gardening I lay on my back, listening to that rhythmless pummeling, and then I took them out—the photo albums.

The wedding album first—all those miniaturized smiles, the tiny people, pressed onto paper, kissing one another, arms flung over one another's shoulders. In the background of every photograph, the long shimmering black serpent of the Thornapple River. In the foreground, always a dropped napkin or a flower that had fallen from someone's hair or bouquet. In one, a swan was drifting down the river. In another, Jon's sister (was she ever so young?) was leaning toward the swan, offering it a piece of bread. In another, my father in his tuxedo was toasting what appeared to be the air. He looked stifled in his tuxedo, but also ruddy with good health.

And Sue, in another, with those flowers in her hair, in her low-cut bridesmaid dress, the blond gloss of her. She was talking in this photograph to a man I couldn't recall, a guest I didn't recognize, someone I couldn't remember having invited to my wedding—a man I'd never noticed while he was there, and had never seen since.

And, in another, the cake.

The brilliant frosted tiers of it. Its layers and layers of sweetness. The bride and groom were knee-deep in that sweetness. Behind the cake, there was the blinding white blur of me passing by it, on my way somewhere, or just returned.

Then, I took out the other albums.

Chad's birth. Chad, in the hospital, wrapped in a blanket. Chad at my breast. Chad in Jon's arms—that terrible, beautiful, new-father smile on Jon's face.

And all the years that followed. The red ball, so large in Chad's small arms he could barely hold it. The sandbox. The enormous, stuffed horse. Chad on its back, wearing a cowboy hat. The first day of kindergarten. The zoo. The beach. The park. The swings. The kiddie pool. The county fair.

Chad on the carousel, holding the reins of a lacquered blue stallion with a flowing white mane, looking worried.

A few of the photographs had yellowed or faded despite the protective plastic sheaths they were in.

Some of the pages were stuck together.

The weight of the albums on my knees grew painful. I piled them on the floor at my feet.

Later, I heard Chad in the bathroom. The shower doors opening and closing.

I heard Jon come up the stairs. He came to the closed door of my study. From the other side, he asked, "Do you still love me?"

"Yes," I said, but did not go to the door.

CHAD was rested, happy, talkative in the car on the drive to Fred's Landscaping Monday morning. I'd forgotten to wash his landscaping crew T-shirt, and he had to fish it out of the laundry basket and wear it anyway. "Do I stink?" he asked, coming down the stairs in it as I was putting the eggs on his plate.

I stepped close to him, inhaled—sweat, grass, summer. "No," I said. "You smell good."

"You're just being nice," he said. "I stink."

When we pulled up to the garage, Fred was standing outside it, smoking a cigarette. He was wearing shorts, and I could see that his knees were enormous, deformed. Knees the size of soccer balls. Was it something that had happened to make the bones grow, I wondered, or had fluid accumulated there?

Arthritis? Kidney failure?

Were they painful? How did he manage to walk?

He waved to me as Chad stepped out of the car. I waved back and pulled out into the road. I drove to the freeway ramp, and headed into the city, to the efficiency.

I'd called to cancel my lease, and the woman in the office asked that I have my belongings out of it within the week. Jon said he would do it for me, but I'd said no. I didn't want him to go there. I wanted to be the one to go.

But I felt afraid as I opened the door to it. I hesitated at the threshold. I could feel, I thought, something still in there. I could smell it—his body. The scent of his flesh on his shirts, on my sheets—machinery, tools, the warm suggestion of combustible fuel. I stayed where I was, listening, in the doorway. I said, "Bram?"

There was no answer.

I stepped in and looked around.

Nothing.

A towel on the floor in the bathroom.

A cup in the kitchen sink.

The sheets and blanket had been pulled off the futon and were bunched at the foot of it. I went to it. I lay down.

For a long time, I lay there, smelling him—in the futon, on the pillows. I pulled the sheet and the blanket up over me, and the smell of him, of *us,* was on those, too. I rolled onto my side, and closed my eyes, and a terrible emptiness entered me—*it was over, the affair, this was my life now, altered forever, but also unchanged*—and I fell into a dreamless sleep, swiftly, like stepping through a door, oblivion on the other side. But a familiar oblivion. A place I'd been before. I must have slept for at least an hour because when I woke, it was gone—the scent of him in that nest we'd made. Now, all I could smell was the garbage can under the sink, which hadn't been emptied for over a week—the sweet rotten remnants of our last meal together.

I stood up, folded the sheets, and began the first of several trips to the car.

WE ATE dinner late because Jon got stuck in traffic on the way home. It was already dark, but we hadn't pulled the curtains yet, and, watching my son and husband eat the chicken and rice I'd cooked for them, I imagined the scene from outside the house, what someone would see if he were at the window, looking in:

The small, content family at the dinner table.

The son, almost grown.

The parents, long married and comfortable in their shared life.

The home, tastefully decorated. The food on the table. The easy conversation. The ordinary life being quietly lived. I was imagining that person, at the window, and myself from that perspective. If I imagined it vividly enough, it seemed to me, it could really be the life I was living. Who was to say, I thought, that the life glimpsed from a distance was any more of an illusion than the life being lived? Shouldn't I, of all people, understand that by now?

Then, as I looked out that window, imagining, I thought I actually *saw* someone out there, looking in—a quick glimpse of a face emerging from the dark glass, then disappearing.

I must have gasped, or flinched. Both Jon and Chad looked up at me quickly. "What's wrong?" Chad said, and looked behind him, at the window.

He didn't wait for me to answer.

He said, "Let's pull the curtains, okay?"

He got up and pulled them himself.

After dinner, Chad went up to his room to check his e-mail. I stood up and began to gather the plates from the dining room table. Jon caught my wrist as I reached for his plate, looked up at me, and said, "Let me clean up, Sherry. Please." But I pulled my wrist out of his hand, twisting it to get away, and said, "No."

"When, Sherry?" he asked. "When can I talk to you again? When can I hold you?"

I said, "I don't know."

JON WAS gone already in the morning when I got up. I sat at the edge of the bed for a long time. I could hear, again, what must have been squirrels on the roof. Perhaps some new family had found the abandoned nest already? Easier than starting their own, making a new one, had they simply moved into the one left behind?

No, I thought.

Animals had a better sense of this than people. They would have been able to smell it—that something violent, and permanent, had happened there. They would not have chosen to live in that nest. If there were new squirrels up there on the roof, they were starting over, building a nest of their own.

I needed, I realized, to get Chad up, to drive him to work. The night before, I'd washed his T-shirt, taken it from the dryer, still a little damp, and put it on his bed while he was writing an e-mail. I asked, "Who are you writing to?"

"Ophelia," he said without looking away from the screen.

He was still in his room when I went to bed, and although his door was closed, I could hear the soft rattle of his fingers on the keyboard.

8:00 A.M, I checked the clock, got out of bed, slipped on my robe, went to Chad's room, but he was not, as I'd thought, still asleep in his bed.

I looked in the bathroom, went down to the kitchen, heard something outside, looked out the kitchen window.

He was out there, in the backyard, crouched at the edge of the scrubbrush, making hand motions to Kujo to come to him—but Kujo would not come.

GARRETT.

After I dropped Chad off at Fred's Landscaping (today Fred was wearing overalls, no shirt under them, and I could see that, once, he'd been a muscular man, but now the flesh hung off his arms and chest like old, damp rags), I remembered that it was this week that Garrett was to go to boot camp, to North Carolina.

I have to tell him, I thought, before he goes, how sorry I am, how I never thought, for one second, that my mistake with Bram Smith would have anything to do with *him.*

I wanted him to know that I didn't blame him for telling Chad about my affair with Bram. It wasn't his fault. I wanted him to know that I knew it. I wanted Garrett to know that I would remain his friend, and if there was ever anything at all I could do for him, I would do it.

But when I called his number from home, there was no answer.

I tried again.

And then a third time.

And then I got in the car, and drove to the house I remembered picking him up at, dropping him off at, so long ago, when he was a little boy.

IT WAS exactly as it had been then.

Ramshackle, but pleasant. A small blue modular home with a chain-link fence around it.

Back then, they'd had a dog, I recalled. Some kind of mutt that would bark ferociously when we'd pull in the driveway, and then begin to wag its tail so wildly when we stepped out that it could barely keep its balance.

Had the dog been named *Creek*? Could that be right? Or had I ever even known the name of Garrett's boyhood dog?

Now, there was no dog in the yard, but the grass was green. The garden was without flowers, but tidy. The curtains were drawn, and the garage door was open. In it, I could see what must have been the red Mustang, covered carefully with a tarp. I opened the door to the chain-link fence, and walked up the steps, and rang the doorbell. I heard nothing inside, so I knocked, thinking that the doorbell might be broken, and then I heard something behind me (*"Hello?"*) and turned around.

It was Garrett's friend, the one from the cafeteria, the one with the red nylon jacket, except that today he was wearing a T-shirt (HARD ROCK CAFE, LAS VEGAS). Again, his resemblance to Chad surprised me. The hair. The structure of his face. The shape of his eyes. He was standing in the driveway with a shovel in his hand.

"Oh," I said, taking a step toward him, recovering my composure. "Hello. Does Garrett still live here?"

"He *did*," the friend said. "Do you know where he is?"

"No," I said. "I came here to look for him."

"So did I," the boy said.

"He's not here?" I asked.

"He hasn't been here for a week," the boy said. "I guess. That's the last time he got his mail, anyway. That's the last I heard from him."

I came down the steps, met this boy at the gate. "A week?" I asked.

"Yeah. I guess," he said. "I saw him about ten days ago, up at the school. And then he called me on Monday morning, and we were supposed to put the transmission back in the Mustang on Wednesday, and I came up here, and he wasn't here. And he hasn't been here since. I've come up every day, and there's no sign of him at all."

Monday.

The night he came to dinner.

The night he and Chad went to Stiver's, and Garrett told Chad about Bram.

"Oh, no," I said. "Has *anyone* heard from him?"

"Who would hear from him?" the boy said. "He doesn't have a girlfriend. His parents are dead. He's got one aunt, but he never talks to her at all. Who would hear from Garrett?"

"Have you—done anything?"

"Yeah," the boy said.

He looked younger than Garrett, I thought, younger than Chad. His arms were thin. His teeth were crooked. His eyes were a gray so light they looked colorless. He looked, I thought, like a *shadow* of Chad.

"Yeah," he said again. "I called the cops, actually, and they basically told me that if I wasn't a blood relative to mind my own business. They said it happens all the time, after guys enlist, after they sign the last papers and the plans for boot camp are solid, they get cold feet. They take off. The cops wanted nothing to do with it. But I said, what about the house? What happens to the house if he doesn't come back? It's just sitting there empty. And they said they'd deal with it eventually, when the neighbors complained."

I stood looking at him for a moment. There was a sad light, I thought, shining from this boy. Had Garrett been his best friend? His *only* friend?

In the distance, I could hear a cat crying, and the boy looked behind him then, and said, "I broke a window, to get the cat out"—he held up the shovel—"but she freaked out when she saw me, and took off. I put out some food, but I can't get her to come back. Do you think you could help?"

I put my car keys down on the hood of my car, and said, "I'll help."

The woods behind Garrett's house were thick—pines and birches—and the ground was carpeted with old needles and leaves. We walked a few paces into it, then stopped. I let him call for the cat (*kitty-kitty*—he couldn't remember the cat's name) because, we thought, the cat knew him at least a little. He told me his own name was Mike, and that he'd known Garrett only since the beginning of the fall when they'd met in their automotive class. They were friends, and Mike was helping Garrett with the Mustang, so he'd been to the house, and they'd hung out up at the college, but they weren't close.

Still, Mike was worried. It was weird, to have a guy like Garrett just disappear. "He wasn't scared of the Marines," Mike said. "He was looking forward to it. He wouldn't have bolted."

As we walked together into the woods we could hear the cat, always a few feet ahead of us, her paws snapping twigs, rustling over the needles and leaves.

"Here, kitty-kitty," Mike called, in a voice so soft it seemed impossible that anything would refuse to come to it. He carried with him an opened can of cat food. On the can there was a photograph of a white princess cat sitting on a cushion, wearing a tiara. *"Kitty-kitty?"*

We stopped and listened, and the cat ran on ahead.

We walked farther into the woods, and Mike called again, and the cat scurried farther on. Finally, Garrett's friend said, "Maybe you should call."

I did.

I tried to sing it.

"Here, kitty-kitty," I called.

Nothing. But I could see her behind the spindly trunk of a white birch—a large gray shape with long fur, pausing. I crouched down.

"Here, kitty-kitty."

Still, she didn't come, but she also didn't retreat. She was looking at me.

"Please, kitty. Come here, kitty."

Garrett's friend gave me the can of food, which I held out to her, and I could see her nose lift into the air, smelling it.

"Come here, baby," I said. "Come on. Come on."

She took a step in my direction.

She was coming to me.

She sped up then, hurrying toward me, purring under my hand when I reached out to stroke her.

"Wow," Garrett's friend said. "How did you do that?"

In the car, Garrett's cat howled for a few seconds, and then curled into sleep in the passenger seat. Mike had said that he couldn't keep her at his apartment. Could I keep her?

Of course.

I tore a piece of paper from my notebook and left a note in Garrett's door:

Garrett, Please, if you get this note, call me or call Mike right away. We are very worried. I have your cat. Sherry Seymour

On the back, I wrote my phone number, in case he'd lost it.

"WHAT the hell is that?" Chad asked when he stepped in the house. He'd gotten a ride home from Fred because the job they'd been doing was right up the road, and he was home early. I had only been home an hour. The cat was sitting on the love seat, looking up at Chad.

"It's Garrett's cat," I said.

"*What?*"

"Chad, Garrett's gone."

Chad looked from the cat to me, and then walked past me, into the kitchen.

He went straight to the refrigerator, the orange juice, un-screwed the top, drank long and hard straight from the jug.

"Did you hear me?" I asked.

"Yeah, I heard you. Garrett's gone," Chad said. "Off to the war, I guess, huh?"

"No," I said. "I mean, I don't know. He hasn't been back to his house since—the other night."

"And how exactly do we know this?" Chad asked. He didn't turn to look at me. He was staring straight ahead, with the orange juice jug still in his hand.

"I went to his house," I said.

"I bet you did," Chad said.

"What?" I asked.

"Nothing," Chad said, and put the jug down on the kitchen table, and walked past me. "Nothing, Mom. But I think it's time you stop worrying so much about Garrett." He glanced over at the cat and went upstairs.

JON SAID nothing when he stepped in the door and saw the cat on the love seat. He put down his briefcase. He leaned over and looked at her and then sat back on his heels, held out a hand, which she sniffed, and then licked.

"Hello, beautiful," he murmured. "Hello, kitty cat."

When he realized I was watching him from the kitchen, he looked up at me. He was smiling. He said, "Whose lovely creature is this?"

"Garrett's," I said.

"And what's Garrett's cat's name, and how did she get here?"

"I don't know her name," I said, and proceeded to tell him how we'd come to have Garrett's cat on our love seat.

Jon picked up the cat as I told him the story, and nuzzled into her gray fur, and the sweetness of it—the gentle warmth of Jon—came back to me. The way he used to bend over to scoop up a tiny Chad, loft him into the air, press his face into Chad's soft neck and hair and simply breathe. I had loved Jon all those years, I realized, partly because there was so clearly such a wealth of love *in* Jon. Seeing him with Garrett's cat, perfectly content in his arms, I remembered that. I went to him and put my hand on his arm, and then my face on his shoulder.

"Sherry," Jon said, putting the cat back down gently on the love seat, "do you forgive me?"

He took me in his arms.

He said, "I love you, Sherry." He said, "I'm a deeply flawed man, Sherry, but I love you more than anything in the world. And I swore to God that if ever you would just let me hold you like this, I would never ask for anything else in this life again."

WE MADE love that night without saying anything to one another. The lights out. Our clothes tossed onto the bedroom floor. It lasted for hours. Long, slow, tender hours made of flesh, made of tears. I put my fingers in his hair, in his mouth. He put his mouth on my breasts. He kissed my arms, my neck. When I finally came, it was a sobbing crescendo of pleasure. When he came, I could feel the whole shudder of him like a wing inside me.

In the morning, we kissed good-bye on the porch. A lingering of lips and teeth and tongues. Garrett's cat watched us from the love seat, blinking in slow motion. Chad was still asleep upstairs. He hadn't come out of his room, as far as I knew, all night. Outside, in the backyard, Kujo was asleep, curled up at the edge of the scrubbrush.

"That dog," Jon said, shaking his head. "You better call the Henslins, or he's going to starve to death out there."

"I will. I love you," I said to Jon's back as he stepped out the door.

He turned around.

He came back.

We kissed again. Harder, longer. And then he left.

ON THE way into Fred's Landscaping, Chad didn't speak. He looked out the passenger-side window. I spoke, although I had the sense that Chad wasn't listening. I said, "About Garrett, Chad—he's probably just taken off, maybe left for boot camp early, or maybe he changed his mind about boot camp. Maybe he ran off to avoid it, or went to visit his aunt, but I can't help being worried, Chad. I don't blame you for any of this. This is all my fault, of course, but I need to know, Chad—you didn't *threaten* Garrett, did you? I know he told you about—" I couldn't continue. I swallowed. "But, of course, you know that none of it was his fault. I understand if you were angry at him, Chad, but Garrett didn't leave, did he, because—?"

Chad snapped around and looked at me. "No, Mom, I didn't *threaten* Garrett."

I looked away. I said, quietly, "I know you didn't, Chad. I'm sorry I asked."

We drove for a few minutes in silence, then I cleared my throat and asked how he was feeling, how he'd slept.

He said, "Fine."

Wʜᴇɴ I pulled back into the driveway, Kujo was still there.

I walked halfway down the backyard and called to him, but he was pawing busily around in the dirt and didn't even look in my direction. His ears did not even perk up. I went inside and dialed the number of the Henslins. Mrs. Henslin answered. Her voice sounded fragile, faraway, as if she were answering the phone from much farther down the road than she was, or as if she'd aged greatly since I'd last spoken to her—and I realized that I hadn't actually seen her, except as she and her husband passed in their blue pickup (a glimpse, mostly, of my own reflection in their windshield, and a wave) since last October.

In that voice, she said, "I'll send Ty down when he gets home for lunch, to fetch him. I can't do it, not with this arthritis. And Ernie hardly leaves the house since he broke his hip."

"He broke his hip?" I asked.

"Last October."

"Oh, Mrs. Henslin, I'm so sorry. I had no idea."

I felt more alarmed by how little I knew about the suffering of the elderly couple who lived less than half a mile down the road than I did about Ernie's broken hip. What had I been doing all those months that I hadn't thought to check in on them, had never once stopped by, or called, or wondered more than in passing why it was I never saw them outside any longer?

"Why would you know?" Mrs. Henslin asked. Always, she was practical. "But, anyway, he can't come down there. I'll send

Ty"—her grandson—"and he'll bring a leash and get the dog
back here. And I'm sorry about the trouble."

I told her that it was no *trouble,* that I'd only called because I
was worried, because—

"Of course it's trouble," she said. "We'll take care of it."

She said good-bye and hung up, and I held on to the receiver
for a few moments, feeling somehow dismissed too summar-
ily—reprimanded, or rejected. I wanted to call her back, to explain myself again. Why I'd called. Why I hadn't known about
Mr. Henslin's hip, how busy I'd been, teaching, and Chad having
gone off to college. How I'd thought of them often. How I'd—

But then Kujo began to wail—a famished, cavernous noise.
A cry of such frustration and despair that I put down the phone
and hurried to the door to look out at him.

Had something else happened?

No.

The Henslins' spaniel was just where he'd been for days, his
head thrown back, directing that long wail to the sky.

I went to the refrigerator and got the last of the pork chops
I'd made for Jon and Chad on Saturday, and put it on a paper
plate, and I headed for the backyard with them.

But, as soon as I reached the edge of the scrubbrush with the
paper plate, the pork chop—

As soon as I saw what he'd done—

That the dog had dug a hole at least three feet deep.

And the way, even when I approached him with the meat
held out in front of me on a plate, murmuring his name, calling
his name, finally shouting his name (*Kujo!*) he would not turn toward me, he would not stop howling—

And the scent of it, rising—

And a swarm of sweat bees hovering over the hole that Kujo had dug—

And the flies—

The music of those flies—

I knew.

I understood.

Just tell him you'll call the cops if he comes around, or that your husband will shoot him, or something, if he comes to the house again.

I put the plate with the pork chop on the ground at Kujo's feet, and turned back to the house, running.

AT TWO o'clock in the afternoon, after hours of standing at the back porch door, looking out to the end of our yard, listening to Kujo there, howling, then pacing, then rising up again to howl, I saw Mr. Henslin—his shadow first, hobbling in the dust—coming down the dirt road with a leash.

I opened the back door, and stepped out.

I watched as he approached his dog.

The dog crouched, wagging its tail across the ground—whining, pacing. Mr. Henslin caught him by the collar, and Kujo struggled to get away.

Mr. Henslin clipped the leash to the collar, and Kujo began to cry, and bark, and pull backward on the leash.

But Mr. Henslin was surprisingly strong. He managed to pull Kujo behind him, the dog finally giving up the struggle to pull Mr. Henslin back, but still unwilling to leave, letting his legs scuttle across the ground, refusing to stand, to walk, but having no choice but to let the stronger of the two of them drag him away, out to the road. When Mr. Henslin noticed me standing on the steps of the back porch, he called out to me. "You've got something dead out there," he shouted, then turned his back, pulling his dog behind him, home.

I sat on the love seat with Garrett's cat. I stroked her shadowy coat. There was so much sunlight pouring in through the window on us that I could see nothing beyond this cat, in my lap, and my limbs. It was if we were floating there in a sectioned bit of glare, a bit of roped-off brilliance. The dust around us revolved slowly, galaxies of it. We were space travelers. Time travelers. We had arrived here, in this new world, with nothing. We'd brought nothing with us. We hadn't expected, I supposed, to stay so long, and then hundreds of years had passed, and we were still here, floating, homeless, alone on the love seat—

But when the phone rang, the cat leaped from my lap, straight out the back door, which I'd left open.

I couldn't move, watching her leave.

I tried to follow her with my eyes, but she was gone.

The phone rang so long, the answering machine never picking it up, that I finally found myself rising, despite myself, from the love seat, and going to it. "Sherry? Is that you?"

"Yes," I said. "Jon."

"Sherry. I was worried. I let the phone ring about a hundred times, sweetheart. Were you outside?"

I said, "Yes."

"Sherry. Do you still love me? Is everything, now—is everything okay?"

"Everything is fine," I said.

There was a pause.

He said, "It doesn't sound okay, Sherry. What's happening? Has something happened there?"

"Yes," I said.

"What."

But it didn't sound like a question. It sounded as if he knew.

"Jon," I said. "Did Bram come here again?"

Another pause. Phone lines stretching through cornfields, forests, apple orchards. Soberly, Jon said, "How did you know?"

I said, "I know."

Jon cleared his throat. He said, "You were in Silver Springs with Chad. Do you want me to tell you what happened?"

"No," I said. I felt the blood move from my fingers, my hands, up my arms, into my chest, and then pooling coldly around my heart. I was sweating—my back, my chest, my brow—and had to wipe it from my eyes.

Jon sighed. He said, wearily, "Sherry, I'd say I'm sorry, but I'm not."

My hands were shaking. I dropped the phone. I could hear Jon's voice inside it, still—tiny and a million miles away, calling my name. When I was finally able to pick it back up again, all I could say was that I was sorry. I was sorry, but I'd dropped the phone.

"Jesus, Sherry," Jon said. "I thought you'd passed out. I was getting ready to call 9-1-1. Look, you go lie down, sweetheart. You lie down, and forget all about this, and we can talk about it when I get home."

I heard, then, what sounded like fingers snapping just under my chin, or some delicate bone breaking in my throat. I managed to choke out, "Jon. My god. What now?"

"Nothing *now*, Sherry," Jon said. "That's the beauty of it, sweetheart. *Now* it's over."

———

OVER dinner, he was no different than he ever was at dinner. I'd brought a rotisserie chicken home. Potato salad from the deli counter. I'd walked through the grocery store with a red plastic basket on my arm—a ghost woman, gathering food for the dead. I paid for the food. I carried the brown bag out to the car. I'd driven, without thinking about driving, to Fred's Landscaping, where Chad was waiting for me, sitting under a tree with Fred, both of them with their shirts off—Chad, chiseled and tan beside Fred, whose flesh was the pure white of papier-mâché except for a jagged red scar straight down his chest.

I asked Chad, when he got in the car beside me, what Fred's scar was from.

"Open-heart," Chad said.

He was talkative on the way home.

He'd seen a coyote in the backyard of a house where he was planting saplings. "Right there, in this pretty little suburban area—kind of scouting out their pool, the biggest coyote I've ever seen. It could easily have eaten their poodle, or their kid. It just froze when it saw me looking at it. We stood there staring back and forth for a long time, and then, just like it had made itself invisible somehow, it was gone."

His tone—natural, healthy, familiar, like the smell of grass and leaves and sun on him—brought me back to myself, gradually, until I was an ordinary woman driving a white car, having picked up her son at his summer job, on her way home to her remodeled farmhouse in the country, where everything was the way it had always been, and would continue to be (*that's the beauty of it, now it's over . . .*) forever.

At dinner—the rotisserie chicken, the deli potato salad, some bread from a plastic package full of reassurances about our health (*no saturated fat, heart healthy, high in fiber, calcium*)—Jon and Chad talked about golf, about hunting, about hedgerows and saplings. Now and then, Jon looked across the table at me, and his eyes would linger for a moment. When I looked back, he looked down at his plate, or back at Chad — sheepishly, I thought, like a child who'd recently been reprimanded, who was not sure if he was still in disfavor, who was hoping desperately that he was not.

Is this all it is? I thought.

Jon's sheepish look made it seem that it was, as if almost nothing had happened, as if it were all a regrettable mistake, perhaps, but nothing that a shrug of the shoulders and a mumbled apology couldn't fix.

Is this the beauty of it? I thought.

Was that possible?

For twenty years, Jon had been the one who'd known where to find the fusebox in the basement, how to jump-start a car with a dead battery, when to refinance the house, who to call when the furnace died, how to remove a splinter from a finger, where to go during a tornado warning (interior closet, crouching in the dark among our own coats — the suffocating wool of them, the comforting intimacy of them), what to do to keep the food from spoiling in the refrigerator during an electrical failure.

For twenty years, it had been Jon who'd kept track of our finances, the maintenance of the house. It had been Jon who'd set the timer on the water softener, who'd warned us away from the wasps' nests in the yard, who'd sprayed them with poisons, who'd kept the squirrels from getting into the attic, from chewing the wiring, from burning the house down to fine white ash that would have sifted through our fingers.

Had he known, again, simply, what needed to be done?

Had he known it? Had he *done* it? Was it possible? Had I been married to a man capable of this, and not known it, for twenty years?

Again, he caught my eye when he saw that I was looking at him. He seemed, I thought, surprised by the intensity of it, my gaze. He smiled at me, and it rippled through me like the first smile—the pleasure, the anticipation, this *stranger,* could he be *mine?*

Was it possible, this thrill in the blood despite myself—part horror, part confusion—but also, yes, a kind of baffled amazement that I'd misread him for so long, his passion, so furious and wild, I had never seen it, never.

Jon?

I hadn't, I realized, known him at all.

Yes, he was a stranger. *My* stranger. And he'd killed my lover to keep me.

IN THE morning, I was still asleep when Jon left for work. Down the road, I could hear a dog howling. It was coming from the direction of the Henslins'.

Kujo? Was he trying to come back?

AFTER dropping Chad off at Fred's, I went into the city.

How could I go home? Kujo, down the road, by the time we'd finished breakfast, had begun a yowling and barking so fierce that it sounded as if the Henslins had tied him to a post, then set a fire around him. Desperate, unrelenting. I could not stay home and listen to that. It had to end, eventually, I knew, but I knew it wouldn't end today. Too warm. Ninety degrees at 10:00 A.M. Kujo would be wild with the heat, and the scent. No, I would go into my office, I thought. I would shelve the books I'd left on the floor, on the chairs. I would check my mailbox. I would sit alone, in my office. I would try to think. It surprised me to think that I *could*. How was it, I marveled, that I could drive? That I could think? That I could look into the future at all and imagine that it would continue to exist? How was it that I had the sure sense that things could go on, and that nothing that had happened could have changed everything?

I had slept peacefully through the night.

I had eaten breakfast.

I had taken my son to work.

All the time, my lover's body, in my backyard.

If it did not seem real, could it be real?

THE COLLEGE parking lot was almost empty when I got there. In the summer there were always only a few classes in session—but the sun on the chrome of those few cars was so bright, I could barely see to park. It flashed in sharp fragments. Blazing. Blinding. Shrapnel, made of light.

My eyes watered.

After I'd parked, I passed a hand across them and saw black triangles and stripes where the sun on the chrome had embedded itself—and then I blinked, and then I stepped out, and then I saw it, parked four spaces away from my own car.

Bram's red Thunderbird.

I HAD to put a hand to the wall of the cafeteria when I saw him—

Wearing a black T-shirt.

Holding a Styrofoam cup.

Sitting at a table across from Amanda Stefanski, who was leaning forward, her eyes watery and bright, wearing that orange dress, laughing at something Bram was saying.

When they saw me watching them, my palm open on the wall (holding it up, my legs like water and air under me), they looked at one another, and Bram stood up, leaving his cup on the table, and Amanda Stefanski behind him. He stopped a few feet away from me. He said, "Sherry, are you okay?"

"No," I said.

He turned and nodded to Amanda, who looked away, and then he said to me, "Let's go to your office, Sherry. Let's not do this here."

In my office, I took a sip from a bottle of water that had been sitting on my desk, unopened, since I'd last been there, weeks before.

Aqua-Pura. A mountain on the label. A stream pouring whitely down the side.

But the water tasted warmer than room temperature. It tasted stale, like rain that had puddled in a parking lot—like water that had been drawn from a well that had long ago been abandoned to the animals, to the earth. I sat at my desk. Bram stood above me. "Look," he said. "Is this about Amanda?"

"No," I said.

Amanda?

"Because you're the one who called this off, babe. And you can bet after your fucking husband leveled a .22 at my face, I got the message loud and clear. I mean, I wanted you, I'll admit it, *bad*—but not bad enough to get myself killed."

That's the beauty of it, now it's over . . .

Jon hadn't killed him.

He'd *threatened* him.

No blood had to be shed over this, for this to be *over*.

And then, as if I were at home, on my own back porch, I heard it, plainly, again—the sound of Kujo howling, that dog straining at his leash, that wild yelping, and I said, "Bram. Garrett's missing, Bram. Did you—say something? Did you *do* something?"

Bram looked at me blankly. He cleared his throat. He said, "No."

"But you told me," I said, "that you'd threatened him, that if he—"

"No," Bram said. "I never said anything like that to Garrett."

"What?"

"I never said anything like that to Garrett," Bram said, as if I hadn't heard. "I mean, I told Garrett about me and you, but I never had to threaten Garrett. Garrett's no competition. He's just a kid. He's—"

"But why did you tell me—"

"I just wanted you to know that I *would*," Bram said.

Then, he shrugged.

He said, "I guess I wanted you to think I was a tough guy, babe. But that game's up now." He looked at his hands. "I guess you met my mother."

"Yes," I said.

"Yeah, well, what can I say?" He put his hand on the doorknob. He opened the door. Over his shoulder, he said, "I'm just a tough guy who lives with his mother. And I never threatened Garrett Thompson. Sorry to disappoint you. But now you know."

He stepped out into the hallway.

He closed the door behind him.

Kujo was back by the time I got home, his broken leash trailing him through the scrubbrush.

Ninety degrees. Now, it was summer, utterly. The lilacs were browned. A few still clung withered to the branches. Some had dropped to the lawn, still half in bloom, and to the driveway, making a crushed purple carpet there.

But they were over.

From the bedroom window where I sat I could hear a steady, humming, gray cloud of flies rising and falling in the scrubbrush. And, far above those, in a mercilessly blue and cloudless sky, four enormous buzzards circled, lazily, but descending—a slow, graceful choreography of flight and appetite.

From the bedroom window, I could see everything.

I could see for what seemed like miles.

I could see every blade of grass, as if each one were lit from within.

Every leaf, on every tree, shimmering brilliantly, individually, as if the very source of all life were burning whitely through every vein.

I could have counted them.

I could have named them.

I could have cataloged the differences between each one, the thousands of them. Every detail distinct. Each wing on each bee. Each wildflower, and each speck of dust settling on each petal. Each bristled hair on Kujo's back. The discrete waves and particles of sunlight—on the dead lilacs, on the grass of the backyard, on the scrubbrush, at this moment—distinct from every other moment—and the next, and the next, and the next, until it had all been accounted for, it had all been claimed—but, I knew, I couldn't stay long enough to do it. I could not simply observe it from a distance, write it all down. I had to leave the window, go out there, and be a part of it.

I TOOK a towel with me, held it over my nose and mouth—and still the sweetness was so powerful I had to step back, close my eyes (*breathe breathe breathe*) before I could step closer, before I could see.

Kujo had cleared away the dirt.

Kujo had finally done it.

He sat at the edge of it, wagging his tail at me.

See? See? See? that wagging seemed to say.

His dog eyes were wide and brown.

You didn't believe me, they seemed to say. *You tried to drag me away. But now you see.*

OH, YES, I saw it, then—

That bag of fruit Mrs. Henslin had brought to me. (*I'd left it on the porch.*) The rabbit under the florist's tires. (*The bouquet of red roses.*) The doe in the median. (*The blood on my bumper.*)

The body.

The ruinous rolling on and on of years.

Of decades.

The loosening of flesh. The spots and wrinkles that came with age. My father, tied to a chair, rotting away.

Also, the softness of the child's cheek. The rosebud of the mouth on a breast. The small boys on the living room rug with their miniature cars and trucks. The little motor sounds they made. The coffee table. The scratches on its legs. "*Garrett,*" I said.

He looked up at me with wide, surprised eyes—eyes full of earth, but Garrett's eyes.

"*Oh, Garrett,*" I said.

One arm flung over his chest, like an afterthought.

One knee bent, as if he were trying to stand.

Wearing the white button-down shirt he'd worn to dinner, gray with dirt.

And Kujo, silently standing at the edge, looking down, then looking up at me.

See?

IT SURPRISED me, then, to find myself knowing exactly what to do.

I'd learned what to do.

In the two decades of being a wife, a mother, it seemed that this is what I had been preparing for—exactly this. The years of housekeeping, as if in a dream, had taught me this. All the dusting and tidying up, all the years spent with my knees in the dirt beside the flower bed—the weeding, the pruning, the seeding, the mulching:

I had been destroying evidence and planting evidence half my life.

I knew exactly what to do.

I went to Chad's room, turned on his computer, dragged the whole hard drive to the trash, and emptied the trash.

I took the clothes he'd been wearing that night to Stiver's out of the laundry basket, to the living room, where, despite the heat—eighty-five degrees in the house, according to the thermostat—I made a fire in the woodstove and knelt in front of it, and fed Chad's clothes to it piece by piece.

They burned slowly but, after a while, they were nothing but ash.

Still, these were the incidental things, these were the worst-case scenario things. Just as you always hoped that the first aid kit in the linen closet would never be necessary, you kept a tourniquet in it just in case. Just as you hoped the guests wouldn't run their fingers along the bookshelf when they came to visit, you

ran a feather duster over it before they arrived. After these inci-
dentals, I called Jon at his office and asked him how many loads
of dirt we'd need to dig a hole the size of a man, to fill it with dirt,
and to plant a garden over it.

"A dump truck should do it," Jon said. "Why, hon?"

I told him to come home early, and I would show him why.

"I can't, Sherry. I've got—"

"You have to," I said. "Chad's in trouble." I hung up.

And then I called Fred's Landscaping and asked them to deliver the fill dirt late that afternoon.

The secretary, a gravel-voiced older woman I had never seen
in the flesh but to whom I'd spoken several times in the past
when I'd called to find out what time to pick Chad up, told me
they couldn't do it.

They could deliver it within an hour, she said, or they could
deliver it tomorrow—but they could not deliver the fill dirt at
five o'clock.

I inhaled. I put my free hand to my temple. I sighed. I cleared
my throat. I thought, how many such arguments had I had in my
life? How many little, bitter quarrels about such small things? (*We
can't issue your refund without a receipt. We can't reschedule that appointment.*) Now, it was as if on the phone with this woman every one
of those hundreds of disagreements had culminated in this
one—this climactic final battle over something inconsequential,
and all-important. I cleared my throat again, and she cleared hers.
I said, "Look, I have to have the fill dirt today, but I also need a
few hours to prepare the space where the fill dirt will be placed.
I need it to be delivered at five o'clock."

"No," she said, "I'm sorry, ma'am." Not sounding the least
bit sorry.

I said, "I'm Chad Seymour's mother."

"Oh," the woman said, and her voice softened then. She said, "Oh. Just a moment." In less than a minute she had picked up the receiver again to tell me they would do it.

Five o'clock.

She said, "You have, Mrs. Seymour, the loveliest son. Honestly, Chad is the most charming young man I have ever known."

"Thank you," I said.

FRED drove Chad home from the job they'd been doing at a golf course—setting mole traps, planting crab apple saplings.

When they pulled into the driveway, Jon and I were just, then, setting fire to the scrubbrush we'd gathered up from around the hole we'd dug. Jon was standing in the driveway, leaning against the hood of his Explorer, wiping his face with a towel. Two or three times that afternoon he'd had to stop the shoveling to throw up. Once, he'd sat down in the scrubbrush and wept into his hands. "Sherry," he'd said. "How could he have done it? No matter what he believed had happened—how could he? I could never—"

"Of course you couldn't have," I said. Did I sound accusatory, or defensive?

"Sherry," Jon said, looking up at me, surprised, "are you defending Chad? Are you disappointed that *I* didn't kill someone?"

I turned around to him with the shovel, and said, "We don't have time for this."

It was ninety-five degrees.

The flies were biting at our bodies, which were drenched in sweat.

The sound of them was disorienting, so loud it was as if they were a single, enormous machine, not a thousand smaller machines. It seemed that they'd never clear away, that their frustration was infinite, that they would go on swarming and biting us forever—but, after a while, they grew more subdued, and then dispersed, and eventually even the buzzards—confused? disappointed?—disappeared over the horizon.

As we burned the scrubbrush, despite the temperature, I stood close to the bonfire and watched the dry leaves and stalks light up and disintegrate so fast it was as if they had never existed. That scrubbrush made a swishing sound as it combusted, vanished, as if being blown away, rather than burned. I watched closely, trying to witness the moment at which it was gone forever—trying to see if there *was* such a moment, and if it could actually be witnessed.

The heat was stunning, and I let it move in on me until I could feel it in my blood.

I crouched over it, staring into it.

Fred came up behind me then and said, "That was a lot of fill dirt. A lot of work. You trying to cover up something here? Got a body back here?"

I looked up. Fred was looking at the place where we'd spread the fill dirt and cleared the scrubbrush. He was wearing a sleeveless undershirt and khaki shorts. I could see the crushed veins on his arms and legs pulsing just under the flesh, as if there were blue butterflies drowning inside him.

"No," I said. "I was just tired of the mess."

"I don't blame you," Fred said. "This is better. You could really do something with this now."

He suggested bushes.

Flowering bushes, ornamental trees—some deciduous, a few evergreens. Juniper. Boxwood. Berberis. Cassinia. "It could be a little topiary garden," Fred said. "If you're the kind of lady who likes to shape a thing herself, and doesn't mind the work."

"I don't," I said.

"You could train some ivy on a frame—a rabbit, or a deer. We could clear more of this scrubbrush. You could have yourself a museum."

We talked about it for a long time, just the two of us.

Chad was inside. As soon as they'd stopped in the driveway, he'd gotten out of Fred's truck and gone directly into the house, slipping in fast without saying anything at all to me or to Jon, but not letting the door slam behind him, either. Jon was still behind us, leaning up against his Explorer, staring at the sky, watching the smoke rise from the fire.

But Fred stood with me right at the edge of that fire. I could see the heat, its wavering shine, in his face, and the fluttering of those veins on his arms and legs.

I looked at his chest, at that scar.

He would, I understood, have no more problems with his heart.

They'd taken it out of him when they'd opened his chest. They'd planted it. A new man had grown. Now, he would live forever.

CHAD said, "I didn't mean to kill him."

I said, "I know."

"How do you *know*, Mom? How do you know *anything*?"

"I know you," I said.

"No, you don't," he said. He was sitting at his computer. He'd begun to cry. The blank light from it turned his face in the dark bedroom to an underwater blue. The tears on his cheeks were liquid silver. "You don't know me," he said.

"What happened?" I asked.

"We got in a fight at the bar," Chad said. "We were drunk, and we got in a fight about you, and I told him I knew what was going on, that I'd figured it out already in California, that something was going on, that he was *fucking my mother,* that I knew it, and he just kept denying it, he kept saying there was nothing between you. I said I'd *seen* it. I told him I knew. He'd come to the fucking *house.* He was kissing you on the steps of the fucking porch. And what kind of an idiot did he think I was? What did he think I thought was going on—with him over here all the time, whispering to you in the kitchen? He said there was some other guy, tried to blame it on that teacher again, and then I just lost it, and the fight ended up outside, and I slammed his head against the car, and then he finally admitted it—" Chad began to cry more loudly. "And then when he was on the ground, and I—"

"Stop crying," I said.

My own eyes were so dry, it was as if I'd never shed a tear in my life. They were so dry, I couldn't shut them. I couldn't blink them. I said, "We have to think clearly, Chad. We can't waste time crying."

Chad put a hand to his mouth as if to hold it in. The tears were still on his cheeks, but he stopped crying.

I asked, "Did anyone see you?"

"Yeah, people saw," Chad said. "Sure, people saw us, but nobody stuck around. Nobody saw the end of it."

"Where's his car?"

"I drove it over to the gravel pit," Chad said. "After I brought him here, after I—and then I walked back home."

"Have you told anyone?" I nodded at the computer. "Did you write to Ophelia?"

"Yes," he said.

I shook my head. I put my hand on his cheek. He looked up at me. He was a child.

I could see it.

In the blue haze of the computer, he was the child I'd always feared would drown at the bottom of the public pool. He didn't know how to swim. If I didn't keep my eyes on him every second, what might happen? He would have no idea what to do — out of breath in the deep end, trying to reach the edge, the rope, the stairs. He would sink to the bottom. I would find him there. In that wavering blue light, he looked, now, like a man — but he was that child.

In the afternoon, Chad and Fred and two other men in the landscaping crew came out, cleared the rest of the scrubbrush, and planted the beginnings of my topiary garden.

I watched them from the bedroom window.

Twice, Chad turned away from the work, and looked toward the house, then turned back when he saw me watching from the window.

The day after that, he was gone.

I gave him my car.

"You can never come back here," I said. "Anything could happen. You have to stay away. I can't know where you are, in case anyone comes looking for you — because, someday, they will come looking."

"I know," Chad said, and he started to cry again.

I could not, myself, cry.

Many years would have to pass before I could, again, breathe, or dream, or cry.

In September, my father died. He was buried beside my mother. Standing above their graves, I wondered, absurdly, if she was surprised after all these years to find him returned to her. They told me he asked for Robbie over and over at the end.

Sue and Mack split up.

Mack got custody of the twins and took them to Canada to be closer to his parents. I learned of it through other members of the English department. Sue and I, after that last afternoon in the hallway, never spoke directly to one another again. Twice, I left messages for her, but she never called me back. Once, I tried to stop her in the parking lot; I called out, "Sue!" and she didn't even pretend not to have heard me. She turned, looked directly at me, turned back around, and continued to walk to her car.

Now, I almost never see her. Occasionally, a gray shadow passes my office, or flits out of a bathroom stall in the women's room before I've really realized who it is, but I've gotten used to the ghost of our friendship, in this form—glimpsing it once or twice a week out of the corner of my eye, like the hundreds of other ghosts of my past, recognizing it for what it was, and letting it go.

Bram married Amanda Stefanski.

("She's perfect," he told me, passing me in the hallway. "She's sweet. But that damn dog, that Pretty, that fucker hates my guts.")

Now and then we stop to speak, but if Amanda comes upon us, she gives Bram, and then me, a cold look—a warning.

Robert Z moved to New York City to teach poetry to inner-city kids, but Beth continued to speculate about Amanda, and Bram, and Robert Z (*Do you think he married her for money? How could she have given up Robert, for him?*) until the day she died—a small plane with Beth in it breaking into brilliant pieces over Lake Michigan.

And, the topiary garden.

Here it is, in all its splendor.

A swan. A swirled cone. A rabbit. A deer. A perfect pyramid.

Jon takes photographs. He posts them on a Web site for to-piarists. It could be, I tell Fred when he stops by to see the garden, a full-time job.

"That's how it is with anything you love," Fred says. "It takes everything you've got. It rips the time right out of your hands. It requires your whole heart."

The Henslins come down to see it, too, and shake their heads.

All that work, for nothing.

ACKNOWLEDGMENTS

I would like to thank Bill Abernethy, Lisa Bankoff, Ann Patty, Sloane Miller, Tina Dubois Wexler, and Carrie Wilson for helping me write and rewrite this novel—and for the many other kinds of support, friendship, brilliant advice, and assistance they so generously gave to me.